This book is dedicated to all birth-mothers who, for whatever reason, made the choice to give their child to another. Many still suffer silently in their own secret grief.

Out Of The Blue

Priscilla Z. Loba

AmErica House
Baltimore

First printing

ISBN: 1-58851-466-8
PUBLISHED BY AMERICA HOUSE BOOK PUBLISHERS
www.publishamerica.com
Baltimore

Printed in the United States of America

ACKNOWLEDGEMENTS

I gratefully thank the Creator of Life and the sentient beings who believed in me, encouraged me to write and helped with the creation and production of this book. I thankfully acknowledge - Ken Shapiro, Karen Carr, Karen Francis, Nancy Lieberman, Patricia Tilton, Jo and Dick Ripley, Richard Berry, Les Gals (Marion Herschberger, Christine Dull, Wanda Derksen, Michelle Uhl), Deanna Mellinger, Suzette McIntyre, Hal Bennett and Susan Sparrow, Joyce Kennedy, my professional colleagues, my cat-companion Gretchen, my faithful fetishes raven and coyote and... my son Andrew.

"...yea though I walk through the valley of the shadow of death, I will fear no evil, for Thou art with me..."

On the journey through the darkness in our souls, anything we have the courage to see can be transformed...

Blue eyed her cat sleepily. Mussels had wedged his long, gray body between the mattress and footboard of her four-poster, second-hand bed. His muscles twitched involuntarily. Cat dreams, Blue thought.

Mussels was her best friend, confidant and bed partner – and the only male she trusted. He opened one green eye and stretched luxuriously. Blue nudged him with her big toe. "Muss, you let me oversleep this morning." The slender cat responded with a toothy yawn.

Blue's size five feet gingerly touched the drab, olive-green carpet that blanketed the bedroom floor. Something about making contact with the floor jolted her memory. A dark, heavy feeling swept over her. "Oh god... Carlos," she said. She sat on the edge of the bed, unable to move. Muss shifted his gaze in her direction, eyes full of inquiry.

Sunday morning. Padding into the bathroom, she caught a glimpse of herself in the mirror. Her favorite faded pink nightshirt, the one with the holes in it, hung loosely off one shoulder. "Oh, you poor thing," she said, the curls of her dark brown hair matted against her cheekbone, "what hurricane spit you out?" Shuffling to the kitchen, still half asleep, Blue stirred Sanka into hot tap water. The muddy coffee circled restlessly in the chipped ceramic mug.

Her mind drifted to last night and the restaurant where she worked as a waitress. It had been a busy, noisy dinner crowd, with lots of rare steak and liquor orders. Carlos, her boyfriend, had come in late and closed the bar as he often did, drinking straight shots of bourbon between Harvey Wallbangers. She could feel his eyes following her, waiting for her to screw up... to catch her innocently flirting with a customer or for someone to make a pass at her. *Anything* that could happen would be her fault and she'd have hell to pay later. It made her so nervous, there were times she couldn't concentrate.

Blue remembered the day she met Carlos at the Topeka music festival a year ago – the summer of 1973. She had just dropped a hit of blotter acid. So when she saw him, he was larger than life – godlike. And she lusted. Shamelessly. He was the most gorgeous man she had ever seen in her twenty-four years. He had thick, black, curly hair and a full mustache. She remembered his faded, tight jeans and bright yellow and green tie-dyed tee shirt. He was psychedelic, she recalled. I couldn't take my eyes off him.

Carlos noticed Blue as well. Petite, with dark, curly hair, olive skin and an exotic look about her – he lusted too. By that night, they were entwined on a blanket, making out and between kisses, flattering each other with compliments. The two spent every day after that, mostly in bed, in love and inseparable.

After three months, they moved in together. Then the honeymoon shrieked to a halt. "*Damn* you!" Blue remembered screaming at Carlos after he'd slammed her against a wall in a drunken rage. "You're a drunk! And it's killing me and it's killing our relationship!"

"My *drinking* is not the problem," he had shouted back. "Your slutty behavior's the problem! I see how you look at other men. For all I know, you're *fucking* your goddamn customers!"

The two of them would argue long into the night. Then arguments escalated into fights. The fights turned physical. Their romance died and the vultures picked the bones clean. "I can't take this anymore," Blue told him. "Move out of my house before we kill each other!" Surprisingly, he packed up and left without a word.

We had another screaming match last night in the parking lot, she thought sadly. Carlos was drunk – again. He raised his fist like he was going to slug me, and he came damn close, she thought. I just can't seem to get away from this guy. I just let him *slink* around in my life like some kind of rabid animal.

I can still hear him. "If you're so high and mighty, how come you got yourself pregnant with a bastard child?" Carlos bellowed for the whole world to hear. "And you weren't even woman enough to keep him!" he accused. "Your preacher-daddy would roll over in his grave if he knew his little college girl refused to keep her kid because she wanted to whore around!"

"I just thank my lucky stars *you* weren't the father!" she'd shot back. "'Cause you're nothin' but a boozer! Getting drunk and bashing women around is sport to you! You're a loser – a no good *drunken* loser!"

The tan wall phone rang next to her ear. Startled, Blue reached for

10

it, and then changed her mind. I've gotta get out of here, she thought. She gulped the last of her coffee, rescued her blue jeans from the floor, slipped into a pair of loafers and grabbed a light jacket. As she backed the car down the driveway, his words were still ringing in her ears.

"Bastard child! Slut!" The vicious slurs wouldn't go away. "Shut up!" she screamed, hitting the brakes. "Stop it!" A pain punctured her heart and a cascade of tears refused to be contained.

It was too late. Self-hatred had taken hold. "Carlos, you're wrong... you're *so* wrong. I'm not a slut. *They* get paid. I let men use me for *free*!" she yelled. "I've been a *bad seed* all my life!" she exclaimed. "I hate myself – and I hate you, Carlos," she shouted, banging her head against the steering wheel. The pain felt good.

She drove Saffron, her 1968 Volkswagen, mindlessly – tears streaming down her face. "I should just floor this baby and hit a tree!" Suddenly, a jackrabbit darted in front of the car. She slammed on the brakes to keep from hitting it but it was too late. Blue scrambled out of the car. The rabbit lay to one side of the wheel. It was dead. Its body was crushed and blood ran from the side of its mouth. "Oh jesus, see what you've done now!" she said, with remorse. Gently, she laid the brown-furred rabbit in the grass. "I'm so sorry. I wish it had been me," she sobbed.

She got back in the car and pulled out onto the road. Making a left on Sweet Acres, she drove toward the bridge that covers the Litchasimmie River. This bridge should do the job, she thought. It had started to rain. Thunderclouds rumbled and lightening snaked its way across the Kansas sky. She rolled down the car window. "It's a perfect day to die," she yelled. Only the passing wheat fields heard.

The river's swift current gathered leaves and branches in a liquid dance, raindrops leaving momentary imprints on the surface. Blue had never learned to swim. She was afraid of water. When she was a little girl, her dad had taken her in a rowboat on the Potomac River. She remembered peering into the black, chilly depths.

Mesmerized, she had wondered what it would be like to topple over the side of the boat into the swirling darkness. And like a magnet – pulling her down – she bent over – then her father pulled her back, nearly capsizing the boat. Her inquisitiveness had almost killed her that day. And like a bad dream haunting her, Blue's curiosity with darkness had become the shadow in her soul.

How ironic, Blue thought, as she sat in the car. Fourteen years ago, when I was ten, my father baptized me in a river like this one. He was so proud to be bringing me to Jesus that he cried. I thought nothing could ever come between us, but it did.

"What happened to my little girl? Where did I go wrong?" he asked before he died, she remembered sadly. She had tried to tell him he'd done *nothing* wrong. Told him he'd been a good father. But I don't think he heard me, she thought.

Blue opened the car door and dashed into the rain. It pelted her as she approached the bridge. Rain and tears mingled, salty and wet, on her face. It was an immersion, a christening before the sacrifice. Blue quickened her steps as the Litchasimmie came into view.

The metal railing was cold and unyielding. Blue held on tight, her knuckles whitened. The wind danced with the tiny whitecaps carried by the waves. Oh my god! she thought. I'm scared... oh Jesus... close your eyes... just do it! The water called to her. She leaned over the railing, feet off the ground and, at the same time, held on for dear life.

Demons of self-loathing clamored to be heard. Dark compelling voices screamed, *"You're no good... you've always known that... you stupid bitch! You have nothing to live for. Let go... just fall. Dying'll be easy. No one will miss you."*

Look, Blue, just pretend you're falling over the side of a boat, she coached. As she released her grip to fall, she lost her balance and started to pitch forward. But the wind picked up – God's breath – straightening her – holding her – for an eternity – 'til she grabbed the railing.

In the Creator's eye, there was a young girl about to end her life, *not* alone, but with a majestic angel on either side. And it was the angels' love that brought Blue to her senses. As her feet returned to earth, her legs gave way and she crumbled. Lying on her back on the bridge's warm, wet concrete, she looked up at the darkened sky.

A hawk circled overhead. What's a hawk doing soaring in the rain, she wondered. Is it *crazy*? The magnificent creature suddenly swooped down toward her, and then abruptly changed directions – as if to gently chastise her. In absolute awe at the force of the bird's energy, she blurted out, "maybe there's hope for me."

Blue got up and walked away from the bridge. She trudged for hours in the pouring rain. It was a baptism, this time one of her own choosing. She felt cleansed... and soaked to the bone. The storm subsided and the sky became its azure self again. She searched the skies for the hawk, to no avail. But his energy – and their connection – stayed with her as she climbed into Saffron and headed home.

Am I losing my mind? She began to wonder as she drove. How could I come so close to ending my life? Blue pulled the car off the road... to stop the shaking. Closing her eyes, she could still see the bridge and the raging river below. Her eyes flew open. "I've gotta talk to someone," she said aloud.

The ceiling fan made a comforting whirring sound. "And what were you feeling standing on that bridge, Blue?" an interested voice asked. This woman has the kindest face I've ever seen, Blue thought. The clock on the wall ticked loud seconds as the young girl thought about her answer.

"My heart was pounding," she told the therapist. "I felt driven, but I was scared and lonely, real lonely. I felt numb – like I was standing next to myself, looking at my body about to jump. But the hawk brought me back."

Blue had never considered talking to a shrink before... not since her parents took her to a psychiatrist at thirteen. He couldn't find anything wrong with her and told them they didn't need to bring her back.

Now, eleven years later, Blue had shut her eyes and pointed to a name... any name, in the yellow pages. Her fingers found Dr. Love Mae Montgomery. I can't go wrong with a name like that, she thought. She called the number and made an appointment.

"Blue, do you want to live?" The challenging tone in Love Mae's voice brought her back.

"I... I don't know. Sometimes I do and sometimes I don't, I guess."

"I don't know your mother, but I'll bet that you're as ambivalent as she was," Love Mae predicted.

"What do you mean?" Blue felt confused. "What does almost jumping off a bridge have to do with my *mother*?"

"I'll *tell* you what. I suspect your mother had mixed feelings about being pregnant. She wasn't sure she wanted to *be* a mother." The doctor was looking at Blue with conviction.

"I *still* don't understand what that has to do with me now," Blue said defensively.

"Do you know, Blue, that babies in the womb can feel whether they are wanted or not? They know instinctively." Love Mae paused. "So, when a baby senses that it might not be wanted, it enters the world without a strong message about the will to live or even the right to be here."

Blue was beginning to understand. "That's why I could consider killing myself?" she asked.

Love Mae's gaze was penetrating. "Yes, Blue. That's why. Unless we have that will to live feeling from birth, we feel insecure about ourselves and our rightful place in the world." She continued. "I can see, just from talking to you today, that you believe your mother has rejected you. If you had a secure feeling about your mother's love, you wouldn't be sitting in this office with me."

Blue shifted uncomfortably in her chair. "I don't want to talk about this," she said, remembering the guilt she felt when she was told her mother almost died giving birth to her. "I just wanted somebody to tell me I wasn't crazy for almost jumping off a bridge – not that my mother didn't want me."

"You got more than you bargained for with me, didn't you? Love Mae told her.

"Yeah. I guess so. You seem to know more about me than I know about myself."

"Blue, I like you," the doctor said. "I believe you're here because almost killing yourself scared the *shit* – pardon my French – out of you and you want to understand why you almost jumped off that bridge." Love Mae's eyes were so warm, Blue wanted to cry. "There's a reason lurking behind the choices we make... and we'll get to yours. I'm very glad you came to see me, Blue," she added. The young girl was silent. "I want to quote you something a wise old woman once said, *'When you let go of everything you need, love is the only thing that's left.'*"

"That may be true – but not for me," she said, starting to cry. "How could there be love left when there was never any there to begin with! You just don't know what it's like," she said, tears spilling. Embarrassed by her outburst, she ran out of the office.

Once on the street, Blue wandered by shops and restaurants, hands jammed in her jacket pockets. There was a jukebox blasting a Jefferson Airplane song through the open door of a bar. *"Don't you want somebody to love... don't you need somebody to love."* Plastered would feel good, she thought, as she walked in.

"What can I get you, young lady?" the bartender asked.

"Give me a draft, please. Start a tab," she replied. She watched him fill the glass. I don't really want to get drunk, she realized. Not today. She spun off the barstool and headed for the door.

"Hey, what about..." she heard the bartender say. Blue looked across the street and spied a large Catholic Church. She jaywalked, climbed the steps and tried the heavy, wooden door. It was open. Hesitantly, she entered the sanctuary and sat in one of the padded pews. There, amidst religious icons and burning candles, she thought about the therapy session, cried for her dead father and wondered if her mother had ever wanted her.

Standing in the cafeteria line, Blue reached for the large piece of chocolate cake that beckoned – the one way in the back. The downtown Wichita cafeteria was her favorite lunch stop. And cake was lunch. Just cake. She savored each chocolaty morsel. She always ate chocolate cake when she was upset.

It had been almost two weeks since her suicide attempt. Thank god I haven't been thinking about jumping off any more bridges, she thought, between surgery bites. I owe that to Dr. Montgomery. But I just wish... I'd *really* like to figure out who I am.

Blue liked this old cafeteria, where the dark, wooden chairs were covered in pea green plastic and the waitresses wore crisp uniforms with bleached-white aprons. One wall was lined with mirrors, which made it easy to people-watch. But today her attention was on other things; like her coffee date with George.

He's late. Maybe he changed his mind, Blue thought. Meeting for coffee had been his idea. Why did I let him talk me into this, she wondered. She had met him in a local bookstore just days before. She was browsing in the psychology section, looking halfheartedly for a book on mothers' and daughters' relationships.

There was something about him, she remembered. I saw him and he literally took my breath away. Honest to god, I couldn't catch my breath. Then, when I turned around to leave, I ran headlong into his chest, she recalled. God, I was *mortified.*

"Want some company?" A male voice startled her out of her reverie.

"Oh, hi... you scared me. I didn't see you." Blue felt bashful all of a sudden.

George pulled out a chair and sat down. He lit a cigarette. "Mind if I smoke? You want one?" Blue pulled a cigarette out of his pack of Kools. She had started smoking again. It calmed her nerves.

"Do you meet all your men that way – head to chest?" he teased her.

"No!" Blue said in her defense.

"Hey, I'm not complaining. It worked for me." George grinned, showing his dimple.

Blue relaxed. "Want a bite? Of my cake that is."

"I like your sense of humor, Blue Spencer," he said, smiling broadly. "No cake, but I'll have some of your coffee." He poured himself a cup from the brown plastic carafe on the table.

"Go ahead," Blue replied. "I've had enough. Coffee on top of these pills I'm taking is making me pretty shaky."

"What kind of pills – if you don't mind my asking."

"Oh, something my doctor gave me. He said it was for fatigue." Blue replied. "I've been so tired lately. All I want to do is sleep."

"Don't take offense, but it sounds like you've got the blues," George commented.

Blue stiffened at his diagnosis. "Oh no, my doctor just thinks I'm under a lot of stress with my job and all..." She fell silent, wanting to say more but deciding against it. "They're these little black capsules and they make me real hyper. Instead of sleeping, I do things like clean my apartment at three o'clock in the morning."

"Pretty clear to me your doctor gave you black beauties, amphetamines – you know, speed. You can do more than clean your apartment on those things. You could clean the *White House* and then sit down and write the fuckin' Constitution of the United States."

Blue couldn't help laughing. She liked George. He had a casual way about him that put her at ease. "A woman writing the Constitution!" she quipped. "Now that would change the face of government forever!" They both laughed.

George looked at his watch. "Bummer. I gotta split. I'm supposed to jam with some musicians over on Water Street. I'll give you a call." Before Blue could even say good-bye, he was out the door. He turned and waved, a cigarette dangling for its life from his lips.

The party was already in full swing that night when Carlos and Blue arrived. Here we are, the happy couple making another phony appearance together, she thought. Old habits die hard. They parked behind a car with a bumper sticker that read, "America – Love it or Leave it."

"I'd just as soon leave it," Carlos said with a sneer. "I'm sick of bustin' my butt for the Man." He'd been fired that day for drinking on the job and was in a black mood. "They won't have me to kick around anymore," he snarled at Blue as they got out of the car.

"Yeah, you and Dick Nixon," Blue retorted, losing her patience. Carlos had stopped at her apartment after work, drunk. He had guzzled beer and whined all afternoon about losing his job. Blue seethed with anger when it came to his drinking. She was often his punching bag when he got drunk and was getting tired of it. I'm gonna *dump* this loser, she thought angrily. He's battered me with his gutter talk and hit me one too many times!

The door flung open. "Hi, you two!" The hostess, Barbara, was a voluptuous woman with a mane of dyed-blonde hair piled on top of her head. Her leather mini-skirt was just inches short of her crotch and her boots were not far behind. "Drugs, sex and rock and roll – forever!" she said, laughing. "Come on in. We started without you." She took Carlos by the arm, leading him away from Blue. "How about a beer, you handsome brute!" she flirted. "If you want to trip out, the drug den's upstairs. We got pot, mescaline, peyote, hash, blotter acid – *anything* you want."

Blue scanned the crowd. Barbara and Carlos were occupied in the kitchen, so Blue slipped upstairs. The room was crowded. *"Hey Jude, don't be afraid... take a sad song and make it bet-ta."* *Beatles* tunes were at maximum sound from the stereo in the corner. An array of people lounged in assorted positions. A smoky mixture of marijuana, incense and tobacco filled the air. Orange lava lamps and candles were the only light. It took a minute for her eyes to adjust.

"If you're gonna smoke, then you gotta take a toke." Blue was alarmed by the familiar voice. A hand thrust a joint in front of her. It was George. She started to shake. Carlos downstairs; George upstairs. Oh my god, she thought.

"I didn't see you downstairs," she said, still trembling.

"That's because I'm up here," he quipped. "I'm not able to be in two places at once yet, but I'm workin' on it," he teased. George paused – inspecting her face. "You look like you've just seen a ghost."

"Oh... no, no. I was just surprised to see you," Blue said quickly, trying to hide her shock.

"Well, you looked *un*pleasantly surprised. You here with somebody?" he asked.

"Nope," Blue lied.

"A woman alone," George wisecracked, using a roach clip to take the last hit off a very short joint. "Now that's an opportunity," he said, checking Blue's reaction.

But Blue was distracted. She was desperate to figure out a way out of her dilemma. I could tell him I'm going to the ladies' room, she thought, then go downstairs and tell Carlos I'm not feeling well and need to go home. And if he refuses to take me, I'll call a cab.

"I *said*, now that's an opportunity," George murmured, leaning toward her ear. His breathy whisper interrupted Blue's thoughts and sent delicious shivers down her spine. She turned toward the sound. Instantly he sought her lips and kissed her full on the mouth. His lips were large and strong... and hungry. His hot breath, the way he devoured her with his mouth, the reefer, drinking on an empty stomach – it all made her dizzy. And Blue Spencer passed out.

All she could see was an orifice – forming words and making sounds. Her eyes began to focus. Is this the mouth I just kissed? she wondered. It was asking questions. "Do you know what year this is? Who's the president of the United States?"

"Gerald Ford. 1974," she answered. "Oh, my head. It hurts. Why is my head hurting?" Blue complained, fully conscious. Now the mouth had a face... a woman's face.

"You passed out – and hit your head on a table on the way down. Do you remember anything?" The woman's long, soft gray hair and silver earrings dangled just above Blue's nose.

"No, the last thing I remember was kissing him," she told her, pointing to George. "Then I lost consciousness."

"That must have been quite a kiss," the woman said wryly.

"I'm a bodacious kisser, but I've never kissed a woman and had her pass out on me," George said, laughing at his own joke. Blue could see him out of the corner of her eye.

"You know," the woman chided George, "this girl could have a concussion. That's *not* funny."

Blue jumped to his defense, wanting to avoid bringing attention to what happened. "Oh, my headache's going away. I'll be fine," she said bravely. "I'm going to the restroom. I feel a little queasy."

"Here, let me help you up," the woman offered. "I'll go with you."

"Thank you," Blue replied weakly.

She locked the bathroom door and was alone. I've gotta leave *now*, she thought. She looked in the mirror. "Oh my god, I look like death," she said, shocked by her appearance. She splashed water on her face, drying it with a towel. Just as Blue sat on the edge of the bathtub to steady herself, there was a knock.

"Hey, you okay in there?" It sounded like the woman with the gray hair.

"I'm fine," Blue said, trying to sound composed. "Really."

She waited several minutes, and then opened the door. Glancing down the hallway she was surprised to see Carlos, leaning against the wall. A beer in one hand, he stroked the thigh of a woman Blue didn't recognize. As drunk as he is by now, *he* probably doesn't recognize her either, Blue thought. They were kissing, his hand groping for new, fleshier territory. She watched as the woman's hand traveled down toward the crotch of his jeans like a dowsing rod. Their behavior should have disgusted Blue, but instead the sight of such brazen lusting aroused her. It was like watching a pornographic movie. A voice invaded her voyeuristic moment.

"This is your opportunity," the inner voice was saying. *"Now you have all the justification you'll ever need to dump him. Do it, Blue. Do it!"*

I can't, she argued. He might get angry.

"Take the chance anyway," the voice insisted.

She took a deep breath, walked up to them and tapped the woman on the shoulder. "Do you know you're kissing my old man?"

"Who's the bitch?" the woman said to Carlos.

"The *bitch* is this idiot's old lady!" Blue snapped angrily.

Carlos glared at her. "Can't you see I'm busy?" he said with irritation. "This woman's giving me a rush I could only dream of with you!"

"It's over, Carlos," Blue said, glaring at him. "I'm done with you!" she told him, not caring who heard. "I've taken your abuse long enough! Don't bother stopping by tonight – or ever!" Her simmering fury erupted like a volcano. She turned, ran down the stairs and out the door.

Blue started walking. A stranger offered her a ride. She declined the offer. In your dreams, she thought, hurrying on. She found a pay phone and called for a cab. In ten minutes she was in the back seat on her way home. "Excuse me for asking," the cab driver said, after a few minutes, " but why is such a pretty girl like you so upset. Man trouble?" he intruded.

"I'd rather not talk about it," Blue retorted, ignoring his compliment.

"Well, I can understand that... but sometimes, it helps to talk about things. The guy must've been a real jerk," he persisted, undaunted by her curt answer.

"*All* the men I end up with are jerks. Every single one of them," she brooded.

"Hey. You're a beautiful young lady. Kinda remind me of my Donna. She's my daughter," he told her. "Got two young kids and a jerk for a husband. I keep tellin' her she deserves better, but she won't listen," he said, shaking his head. "Ya gotta believe that you deserve more than a jerk or that's all you'll ever have. They're a dime a dozen."

"What are you, a psychologist moonlighting as a cab driver?" she quipped. "I saw my shrink already... but after what happened tonight, I think I'd better go back."

"Nothin' wrong with that," he offered. The cab slowed down. "This your place?" the cabby asked.

"No, it's a little further. That's it, the one with the cat sitting in the window."

The cab came to a stop. The driver turned around. "This ride's on me, little lady," he said. "You can pay me by calling your shrink tomorrow. We got a deal?" He smiled at Blue like a benevolent father.

"Deal," Blue said, touched by his offer. She wanted to throw her arms around the kind stranger, but didn't. "Thanks for the advice – and the free ride," she said, giving him one of her million-dollar smiles. "I hope your daughter knows how lucky she is to have you for a father."

The cabby shrugged and smiled. "Take care of yourself," he reminded her.

By nine o'clock the next morning, a substantial pile of men's shirts, pants, shoes, belts and underwear dotted Blue's front lawn. They were not boxed or bagged. Nor were they neatly folded. They were strewn. Everywhere. And it was raining.

Blue knew Carlos had spent the night with the woman he was fondling at the party. "He'll be furious," she said, "just furious. He loves his fancy wardrobe... with his Italian shoes and Pierre Cardin shirts!" She surveyed the soggy menagerie. "A few hours in the rain and none of it will be so fancy anymore, Carlos!" she announced with satisfaction.

Blue felt righteous outrage. "I'm *not* that creep's hostage anymore," she told Muss, who had watched the entire goings-on from the living room window. "My cab driver buddy was right. I deserve better!"

"C'mon Muss. We're going to take a little ride. I don't want to leave you here. Carlos never liked you and I don't want you hurt. We're going to Mom's."

"Meow..." Muss complained as Blue lifted him off the bed where he had been sleeping comfortably. Against his will, she put him in the front seat of the car and shut the door. Once Saffron was in gear, Mussels was always an anxious passenger. *She's got me in this metal death machine again. All I can see is everything whizzing by. It makes me dizzy... oh no, I gotta relieve myself. If I pee in here, she'll yell at me for sure. Does she expect me to hold it like a dog?*

"Muss, please stop crying. You're a real drag when you're like this," Blue pleaded. Mussels ignored her and kept meowing.

Today was Sunday; the day Ruby would be home alone, watching Billy Graham on television. Ever since Blue's father died, her mother followed Reverend Graham's ministry every Sunday. It took the place of sitting in a church pew, as she had done for thirty years, listening to her husband preach the Sunday morning sermon.

Whenever Blue suggested to her mother that she might be lonely and meeting people would help, her mom would get angry. "If *you* spent less time chasing after men and more time on your knees praying like I do, you'd be a daughter I could be proud of!" she would retort.

Blue's face would burn with shame.

Thinking about it almost caused Blue to miss the turn onto her mother's street in the nearby town of Haysville. There it was, the little aqua-colored frame house with the multi-colored spring flower wreath on the front door. It was her mother's sanctuary, a shelter from the world.

"Why do I come here?" she asked herself. She pulled into the driveway, feeling the dread that always made her chest tighten just seconds before seeing her mother. It's always judgment day with her, Blue thought. Ruby's critical looks were searing and her comments cutting – about her daughter's appearance and the way she was living her life. And she never failed to mention both.

The door opened, revealing a petite woman with dark, slightly graying hair. "Hi, mom," Blue said, trying to sound cheery. Her words tumbled over themselves, trying to keep Ruby from launching her attack. "You look so pretty today. Is that a new dress you have on? I've never seen that one before." Blue was only delaying the inevitable. And it came.

"Well, you must need *something* or you wouldn't be here," her mother said sarcastically. "You know, if you didn't wear so much make-up, you could save a whale of a lot of money. But I suppose you need it to attract all those men."

Her words pierced like daggers as Blue stood waiting to come in. She and her mother were so different. At times it had made her wonder if she had been adopted. Blue was pretty, followed the styles of the day and displayed her femininity freely. Her mother was a plain woman, wore practical clothes and liked to recall stories of herself as a tomboy. The truth was, Blue was more like her grandmother; who had been a voguish dresser and appreciated the attention of men. She often questioned if her mother ever recognized their similarities.

"Oh gee zooey, mom. I left Muss in the car," she said. Cats were one thing she and her mother *did* have in common. Ruby was a cat lover and had three of her own.

"Well, you'd better bring him in. He'll get lonely out there all by himself," her mother insisted. Ruby Spencer's affection for Mussels was a once-removed way for Blue to get her mother's love. "I'll have to put my babies away so Muss can have the run of the house," she said brightly.

My mother loves my cat more than she loves me, Blue bemoaned silently as she brought Mussels into the house.

"Oh Muss, you're my sweet baby, my little angel," Ruby cooed, picking up the sleek, gray cat. "But you're so skinny!" she exclaimed. "I'm sure your mother never feeds you. She'd probably treat her own child the same way... if she ever decided to raise one," she taunted. "Well, if you lived with me, young man, you'd never go hungry."

Her hateful comments were making Blue angry. Ruby sat down on the couch. "I don't know why your mother doesn't take care of you. I guess it's because all she thinks of is herself," she said, kissing Muss on the nose. "She's too busy running all over creation, looking for some *man* to lay under. You could be dead and stiff as a board and *she'd* never know it!"

Ruby had plunged the knife too far this time. *"THAT'S ENOUGH, MOM!"* she screamed. Muss jumped off of Ruby's lap, scrambling to safety. Blue leaped out of her chair and lunged at Ruby. "Shut up! Do you hear me?" Before she could stop herself, she had her hands around her mother's neck. It felt small and fragile. "Can't you ever just *shut up about me?"* she shrieked.

Her mother was starting to lose consciousness as the pressure of her first-born's fingers cut off her windpipe. Her eyes began to roll back in her head. "I hate you! I hate you! I hate you," Blue kept saying over and over.

Blue's arms suddenly fell limply at her sides. Her knees buckled and her body sank onto the spotlessly clean Berber carpet of her mother's living room floor. She could hear her mother moaning and gasping for breath. "Oh my god," Blue repeated. "Oh my god..."

Blue drove herself to a pay phone. She put in her dime and dialed, fingers shaking. *Rrring... rrring... "Please* pick up the phone."

"Dr. Montgomery's office. May I help you?" Beatrice the receptionist inquired politely.

"Is the doctor in?" Blue asked breathlessly.

"Yes, but she's with a patient," was the reply.

"I need to talk to her – *now*," Blue said tearfully.

"She just took someone into her office. I can have her call you between patients."

"I can't wait that long!" Blue's voice became shrill. "I'm calling from a pay phone. Please, I've *got* to talk to her!"

"I'm sorry..."

"I just tried to kill my mother!" she blurted, interrupting the receptionist.

The other end of the line was silent. "Hold on. I'll buzz her," she said.

"Hello." Dr. Montgomery's voice came on the line.

"Hello Dr. Montgomery. This is Blue Spencer. I..."

"Blue, call me Love Mae," she interrupted. "Now what's wrong?"

"Love Mae, I'm sorry to bother you, but I had to talk to somebody. I was at my mother's house... and I got real angry and... and started choking her..."

"Blue, slow down. Take a deep breath. Just tell me what happened," the doctor instructed her.

"Well, I was feeling lonely, so I went to visit my mother. She kept insulting me... like about how much make-up I wear, how I chase after men, how I'm not a good mother to Muss. She went on and on. I just couldn't tune her out this time, Dr. Montgomery. Before I could stop myself, I lunged at her. All of a sudden my hands were around her throat. It's like it wasn't me anymore... I was just so angry. For all I know, she might be *dead* right now!" Blue said hysterically. "Oh, Love Mae, what am I going to do...?" Her voice broke as deep sobs took over.

The doctor was silent for a moment. "Blue, listen carefully," she said firmly. "Give me your mother's name and phone number."

"Her name is Ruby Spencer and she lives in Haysville on Birch Avenue. Her number is 576-8876."

"Okay. I'm going to phone her and see what I can find out. Then I'll call you. Don't worry," Love Mae said calmly. "Just sit tight for now. When you've composed yourself, you'll want to tell her how sorry you are."

"I know. I *am* sorry. Is she going to have me arrested for assault?" Blue asked.

"I don't know the answer to that, my dear. We'll cross that bridge when we come to it. I want you to set up an appointment to see me this week. I'm going to transfer you to Beatrice now – okay?"

"Okay. Thank you. Thank you so much." Blue was blowing her nose when the receptionist answered.

"The doctor has an appointment available tomorrow at 4:00," she said crisply. "Would you like to come in then?"

"Yes, please," the frightened girl said urgently. "Thank you."

"You're welcome. See you tomorrow at 4:00."

Blue started walking. She stopped at the Catholic church she frequented when she was troubled. She opened the heavy door. The sanctuary of Saint Albert's had a slightly musty odor and was empty and dark, except for hundreds of brightly burning votive candles that created a beautiful, soft glow.

She sat down in her favorite pew, the one directly in front of the statue of Mary. Blue wasn't Catholic and often felt she was trespassing. But talking to Mary was comforting. Sometimes she even answered her, as if her voice was in Blue's head.

Desperate for guidance, she began talking to the statue. "Oh, Mary, why did I try to kill my mother? How could I have *done* such a terrible thing?" In the silence that followed, a muffled cry distracted Blue. It was coming from behind one of the alabaster columns in the sanctuary. She heard it again. She looked up at the mother of Jesus. "I suppose this is what you brought me in here for today," she said.

"Yes, dear one," a serene voice answered.

As she walked toward the sound, she stubbed her big toe on the end of the pew and practically fell headlong onto the hard, marble floor. She saw what looked like a bundle of clothing in a pile on the floor by the base of the column. As she moved closer, the profile of a woman emerged. She was crying softly.

Blue touched her shoulder lightly. "Are you okay? Can I help you?" she asked.

Startled, the woman jumped at Blue's touch. "Nobody can help me," she said, her voice forlorn.

Blue crouched beside the woman. The scent of blood, saliva and perspiration assaulted her nostrils. "What in the world has happened to you?" Blue could see dried blood on the woman's face and hands. She had a deep gash by her right ear. "Oh gosh, you're badly hurt," Blue exclaimed. "Let me take you to a hospital."

"No!" the woman told her. "They'll want me to press charges. He'll *kill* me if I cross him! He's a junkie and I never know what he's going to do."

"Who's going to kill you?" Blue asked.

"The man I've been living with. He's always high on something and lately he's been talking about Charley Manson being his idol. He really scares me," she said tremulously. "I came here because it was the only safe place to go. I've been coming to this church whenever I can to pray the Mass. The priest here knows me." The woman's voice faded. She was curled up in a ball, like an infant in a womb. Blue felt compassion, seeing her this way... so vulnerable and helpless.

"What did he *do* to you?" she asked gently, reaching out to pull the hair away from the woman's eyes.

"He... he beat me so hard I blacked out," she replied. "When I came to, he was raping me. I don't know how I did it, but I got away from him and ran into the kitchen. God must've been helping me. Then he came after me. That's when I bit him... he grabbed a kitchen knife and cut my face.

He called me horrible names and told me if he couldn't have me, nobody would because he was going to carve up my face. I kicked him hard, in the balls, and he let go of me. Then I ran out of the house. Oh, Mary, mother of God, help me," she moaned. "I've been trying to leave him and I think he's gotten wind of it... oh god, what's going to happen to me?" The woman's wrenching sobs tugged at Blue's heart.

Blue looked up to see a man in a flowing white robe approaching them. In the darkness, she could tell only that he was bearded with brown hair. Gee zooey, she thought. It's Jesus Christ! I'm having a vision!

When Blue saw the toes of his tan and brown, soft-sole saddle shoes, she realized then it was only the Parish Priest, not Jesus. "Thank god," she murmured.

The priest knelt down beside the two of them. He recognized the woman on the floor. "Laura, it's John, the priest. I'm here to help you." He extended his hand to her. She took it and squeezed it hard.

Blue introduced herself to him. "My name's Blue, sir. I need help too, but this woman needs it more. Her boyfriend beat her up and then raped her. I offered to take her to the hospital, but she said no. What can we do?" she asked.

"Laura, are you sure you won't go to the hospital?" John inquired. "You've been seriously injured and need medical care."

"No – please. I don't want anyone to know what happened. He'll kill me if he finds me. Maybe I'd just better leave here." She stood up awkwardly, like a fawn trying to get up for the first time. Her legs gave way. John and Blue grabbed her before she fell and gently guided her to a pew.

"Laura, I can't just let you wander out onto the street in this condition," the priest said firmly. "I'm going to take you to a woman's shelter just down the street. They know me there. When a woman comes to them who's been beaten or raped, they won't contact the authorities without her permission. They'll protect your need for anonymity. And they have access to medics who will take care of your injuries and counselors to talk to."

"Please," Blue implored. "Listen to this guy... I mean, the priest. You've got to trust *somebody*."

Laura looked at John and said, pain in her voice; "I've *never* had a man in my life that I could trust, including my father, who didn't take the opportunity to beat me whenever he felt like it. Men have always betrayed me..."

The priest looked at her tenderly. The heavy, gold cross around his neck reflected the candlelight. "Well, Laura, I have one thing going for me," he said. "I'm a man of the cloth, and my promise to God is to serve others. You'll just have to take my word for it."

Laura was silent. She allowed the two of them to help her up.

Together they put her in the priest's car and drove to the shelter. It was only after she was registered and taken care of that Blue could breathe a sigh of relief. As the priest drove her back to her car, Blue realized how much she identified with Laura. "That might've been *me* lying on the floor with a bloody gash on my face," she said to the priest. That could have been me, she thought.

Blue was five minutes late for her appointment with Dr. Montgomery. As she walked into the office, a man brushed by her without speaking, slamming the door on his way out. The doctor watched him leave, shaking her head and smiling. She looked at Blue. "Next?" she said with a laugh. She had a great laugh, throaty and full. She was pretty too, sharply dressed and very feminine – with graying hair, artificial lashes that complimented her blue eyes and pearly white teeth.

"Hi, doc. Sorry I'm late," Blue said, avoiding her gaze.

"I bet you were debating about whether you wanted to see me again or not," Love Mae said.

"How'd you know?" Blue was surprised.

"Oh, I have that problem quite often," she replied. "People don't know what to feel about me, like the guy who just left. I have this habit of calling things the way I see them," she chuckled. She closed the door behind them. Her cozy office felt like a womb, safe and warm. It was beautifully decorated, with mauve and cream-colored couches and lots of pillows. On the floor, a soft, white sheepskin rug completed the effect.

"Thank you for taking care of the… the thing that happened with my mother. I don't think I could've done it myself," Blue said.

"Well, I'm glad for the both of you that she was all right," she replied. "How did calling her to apologize turn out?"

"It didn't," Blue said flatly. "When I called, she told me she didn't want to talk to someone who almost killed her. Then she hung up on me. I called her back, but she wouldn't answer her phone. She hates me now."

"Hate's a strong word, Blue. I think she's just hurt and confused."

"Confused? About what?" Blue asked.

"About having a daughter who is angry enough to want to strangle her. She's wondering what she's ever done to you for you to feel such murderous rage. I think she believes she's failed as a mother."

"Why?" Blue asked.

"Because, in her eyes, you've disappointed her as a daughter," Love

Mae continued. "And she can't accept that because *who* you are is a reflection on her."

Blue started to cry. The first tear came, then the second – silently foretelling the words to follow. "All I've *ever* wanted is to be loved," she said sadly. "By her. By anyone. I know my dad loved me, but he never came to my defense when mom said mean things to me."

"Did you ever think your mother might've been jealous of you?" Love Mae offered.

"No," Blue replied. "All I knew was that she said things to put me down. She'd tell me I looked like a streetwalker and that I was boy crazy. Then she and dad would argue about me and she'd accuse him of being too soft on me," Blue said, her voice tinged with hurt. "To keep the peace, dad would agree with her and I would get blamed for *everything*. I felt beat up, except the words hurt more than any belt could've."

"And that's why you've always believed you were, excuse my language, a piece of shit. You think you're worthless and deserve bad treatment from people," Love Mae told her.

"I've even gone *looking* for bad treatment," Blue added. Love Mae handed her a tissue. "When my baby was born, Love Mae, they didn't come to the hospital. They didn't even *call* to find out how I was. Neither one of them *ever* offered to take me and the baby home. I was alone... so alone that I gave him away."

Blue wiped her tears and blew her nose. "I'll always blame *them* for that," she said angrily. "If they'd been there for me, I *know* I wouldn't have given my baby up. Dammit, I wasn't strong enough to be a mother to my own son. That's pathetic!" Blue looked at Love Mae, tears running down her cheeks. "Why didn't they come and get me, Dr. Montgomery? I was just a kid. Why didn't they?" She asked, convulsing into sobs.

"They couldn't Blue," Love Mae said gently. "Because *they* weren't strong enough either. Having a baby didn't bring your family closer together. It alienated you. Strong, loving families pull together in painful times. Your family wasn't strong, so enfolding you and your baby in their bosom *wasn't* an option." She paused to give Blue a chance to reflect. "Do you know where your son is now, Blue?" she asked.

"No."

"Have you ever thought about trying to find him?" she queried.

"Yes, I think about it all the time. But I signed a legal paper that keeps me from ever showing up in the town where he lives. I would just be disrupting his life if I went looking for him." Blue's voice was despondent.

"Blue, I'd like to tell you something personal about myself," Love Mae interrupted.

"Okay."

"I had a son. He's dead now. He died of cancer when he was twenty. The hell of it is that I'll never be able to kiss him or touch him again." Love Mae's blue eyes teared. "Don't let your shame about having an 'illegitimate' child be a noose around your neck. Finding your son will be the most important thing you will ever do in your life. And if you really want to find him, you will. It'll be something you'll never regret."

"Sometimes, all I want is to forget it ever happened," Blue countered. "I just want to go on with my life. But goddammit, every time I see a baby or hear one crying, I want to crawl out of my skin. I can't stand it!"

"Stand what, Blue?" Love Mae questioned.

"That somebody else has one and I don't! I can't stand it that I gave away my own flesh and blood! I can't stand... I can't stand... the fucking pain!" She began hitting her legs with her fists, sobbing loudly. Love Mae got up out of her chair, grabbed Blue's hands and took her into her arms. Together they rocked back and forth and the young girl cried as if she would never stop. But she did.

It was Blue's twenty-fifth birthday – October's child. The day came and went without a card, a present, or a phone call. It was ten p.m. and she had been drinking most of the day. Finishing a liter of cheap wine, she held the green bottle over her mouth and waited for the last cranberry red drop to fall. It splattered on her tongue. "Don't know how I would have gotten through the day without you," she said to the empty container.

"You know what, Muss? I'm a cheap drunk. Anybody want a cheap drunk?" she offered the four walls. "My daddy's dead and my mother won't talk to me. Carlos is screwin' anything with a skirt!" Feeling no pain, she continued her dismal monologue. "The only friend I have doesn't even know it's my birthday... guess I could'a told her. And where the hell is my therapist when I need her? George hasn't called me for days..." She stopped. Wait a minute, she thought. "George... I know where George is. He's playin' at a bar downtown tonight. And Blue Spencer is gonna show up, my friend," she announced to her four-legged companion.

Muss sat on the bedroom dresser surveying the room from his lofty perch, watching a ritual he had seen many times. *She's putting this crap all over her face; green on her eyelids, black junk around her eyes... stuff that makes her eyelashes stick together. Now she's smearing red all over her mouth... looks like she's bleeding. She's putting on some lacy thing with strings hanging down, (those are fun to play with). She's slipping her legs into some stretchy, black, see-through things that hook onto the strings. Now she's dancing around to music in front of the mirror while some guy on the record player with a terrible voice is singing she's "just like a woman."*

"Muss, I know what you're thinking," Blue informed her cat. "That I'm gonna go out, get a man, bring him home, and you'll be relegated to the basement." Muss looked at her blankly. "You must understand," she told him. "I like to look sexy, but nobody can touch. So don't worry. You're still my number one guy," she told the cat as she pulled her favorite mini-skirt over her hips.

She buttoned the ruffled, cream-colored blouse, the one that accentuated her modest cleavage. The brown leather boots that came up to her knees, clung tightly to her well-shaped calves. "Should I wear a hat tonight?" she asked Muss. "My beret, perhaps," she decided, without waiting for an answer.

Blue's depression was lifting. She was on a mission. "I don't know what it is about that man, Muss. He's just so mysterious and sexy and... and intoxicating." She pursed her lips and moved her hips rhythmically to the music. "Ooh baby, you'd better be hot tonight," she told her reflected image. "Because you may have lots of competition and you've gotta make him notice *you*!"

A last once-over in the mirror and Blue was satisfied. "Perfect!" she exclaimed. Muss found a spot to curl up in and was pretending to sleep when Blue waltzed out the door into the velvet night. The autumn air was chilly. Blue's mini-skirt and light jacket wouldn't ordinarily be enough to keep a person warm – but after drinking a quart of wine, a chill wasn't even remotely possible. She walked, a little unsteadily, to her car and started it up. Saffron complied reluctantly, like a horse with an unwanted rider.

Fall was a season of melancholy for Blue. Her son had been born in the fall, the son she had given away. It marked another year of not watching him grow up. A poem came to mind she had written – something about autumn leaves falling to their death... an aching reminder that giving up her son was a death, too.

Blue stopped herself. "Tonight there will be no depressing thoughts," she told herself. "Only the magic of sweet seduction." I can just imagine it, she fantasized... *I walk into the club. George doesn't notice me right away. I order a beer and stand where I know he'll see me. And I look hot – really sexy. Our eyes meet and I can tell he wants me. He's lusting, but I play it cool. Stay out of his reach, just enough to make him want me more. Finally he can't stand it any longer. He throws down his guitar, jumps off the stage, picks me up and takes me into the back room. We kiss passionately, as we tear each other's clothes off. I'm totally at his mercy...*

Blinding lights startled Blue. Lost in her fantasy, she had driven Saffron over the centerline in the road and was headed toward an oncoming car. She swerved sharply to avoid an accident. "Oh, christ! I could have been killed," she said. She was still trembling as she pulled into a parking space in front of the Purple Onion. "Just calm down, Blue," she instructed.

The popular Wichita club was crowded. People were standing around outside. The band must be taking a break, she thought. Her eye caught a statuesque brunette, leaning up against a parked car, smoking a cigarette. She wore black hot pants, a lacy top, black stockings and boots. And she was gorgeous.

A man, only a few inches taller, was talking to her. He flicked his cigarette into the street, bent over and kissed her full on the mouth. When he turned to go into the bar, Blue recognized him. "Damn! It's George. And there's my competition," she said, eyeballing the woman.

She walked into the dark, smoky establishment. The band's break was over. They were playing a Joe Cocker tune and the lead singer looked strangely like the flailing Joe himself. And there was George – in his glory. A lock of black hair hanging over his left eye, he was playing his guitar like a lover caressing his beloved. Blue's heart skipped a beat. I want this man and I'm gonna have him, she thought. I don't care *who* the hell he's been kissing. She headed to the ladies' room for a quick touch-up.

There she was. Standing squarely in front of the mirror, it was the tall, gorgeous brunette George had kissed. Absorbed in rearranging her hair and replenishing her lipstick, she hardly noticed the diminutive woman behind her. As Blue brushed on a second coat of mascara, she eyed her, thinking. She's not so gorgeous. Her front tooth is chipped and she has an ugly mole on her temple. *How dare she kiss the man I want!* she fumed.

She moved toward the sink as if she were going to wash her hands. The bathroom floor was wet. Blue pretended to slip. She kept herself from falling by grabbing the woman's arm. As she pulled her arm down, the lipstick the woman had been applying made a long red mark across her cheek and down her chin. A wide, bright, red mark. A hard-to-remove mark. "Oh, I'm so sorry, but I think I've hurt my knee," Blue said, grimacing.

The woman looked at Blue – her angry eyes flashing "What's *wrong* with you, bitch?" A stricken expression took shape as she began dabbing the red mark with a wet paper towel. But it was only getting worse. As the lipstick smeared, the entire lower portion of her face was turning red.

"Nobody calls *me* a bitch!" she yelled, remembering her mother's name-calling. Seizing a handful of the woman's hair, she gave it a hard yank. "Here, let me arrange your 'do' for you," she said venomously. As they struggled, the bathroom door opened, then closed quickly.

The woman, at least seven inches taller than Blue, grabbed her arms and pinned her. She sank to the floor, unable to move. But she still had her mouth. She bit the woman soundly on the shoulder. "Ah–h!" she cried, releasing her hold. Just as Blue began tugging on the woman's hot pants, she felt a strong grip on her arm. In the next second, someone lifted her up.

"A customer just told me there were two broads fighting in my bathroom. I didn't believe her – but I do now! For your information girls, I don't allow bathroom brawls in my club! You either stop it, or you're both out of here on your *butts*!" It was the owner of the club and he was mad. Blue tried to jerk her arm free of his grasp, but he wouldn't let go. "Now, tell each other you're sorry," he ordered them.

"She's sorry, all right," said the woman. "She's the sorriest bitch I've ever met!"

"Is that the *only* word you know in the English language?" Blue countered.

"Okay. I'm gonna to count to ten," he said, sounding a lot like a father. "One... two... three..."

"Sor-ry," Blue said in a voice laden with sarcasm.

"Well, I'm *not* sorry," the woman yelled. "Because you ruined my night! Just don't ever let me catch you on the street, because I'll kick your *ass*, cunt!"

"Okay. That's enough! You're out of here," the owner told the indelicate brunette. "You ought' a clean up your language, lady," he added, as he strong-armed her out of the bathroom. He pointed at Blue on the way out. "And if I hear anything else out of *you*, you're gone too!" he told her.

The woman swore at him as he escorted her out of the club. Blue collapsed into one of the bathroom stalls. She felt faint. She looked at her trembling hands. There were several bloody scratches on them. I don't believe I just did that, she thought. I didn't think I had it in me.

After a few minutes, Blue ventured out to inspect the damage. Her hair was mussed, her lipstick smeared and her sexy cream-colored top had a small tear in the sleeve. One of her black mesh stockings sported a quarter-sized hole in it. "You look a little rough around the edges," she said to the mirror, "but at least there's no threesome anymore!" Only the bathroom walls heard her claim of victory.

The band was on break again. Blue looked around for George. She spotted him at the bar, walked over and tapped him lightly on the shoulder. Her heart was pounding. He turned around on the barstool, beer in hand. "Hey!" he exclaimed. "How long have *you* been here?"

"Oh, only a few minutes," she lied coolly. "Some woman was being escorted out as I was coming in. Did you see her?"

"Nah, I didn't *see* anything, but I heard there was a fight between two chicks in the ladies' restroom. I would've paid money to have seen that," he said with a laugh.

"I guess we both missed the excitement," Blue quipped, flashing her white teeth.

"So babe, we'll just have to make our own," George said, planting a kiss squarely on her lips. "Can you dig that?"

Blue just smiled.

She awoke from the dream with a start – crying. It was the one Blue always had – the dream about giving up her son… *She's in a living room. The people who want to adopt him are there too. She's handing him over to them. They take him from her arms. But instead of letting him go, she holds on tighter. They pull him away. She pulls him back. Somehow he slips out of everyone's grasp and falls through a hole in the floor and disappears. Her screams wake her up.*

Mussels pushed his cat-face against Blue's cheekbone, purring loudly. *This usually works*, he thought. He notched up his purr-volume a decibel. *She'll stop crying and realize it's just a big waste of time and feeding me isn't.*

"Oh, Mussie, you big sweetheart. You know when I'm sad, don't you. You always rub your big ole' head against me when I'm upset." He rubbed her face again and licked the salty wetness of a tear.

"I was a terrible mother," she told Muss. "I crammed cereal down that baby's throat when he wouldn't eat for me. I got mad one time and stuck him with a diaper pin." She laid belly up on the bed, recriminations floating through her mind like filmy poltergeists.

How could I do such unforgivable things?" she asked, guilt lodged in her throat like a stone. But Blue was a child taking care of a child, with nobody there to help her. "Oh my baby, please forgive me," she sobbed into her pink satin pillow. "Will you ever know me? Will you even *want* to know me?"

Love Mae's prophetic words interrupted her sobbing. *"Finding your son will be the most important thing you'll ever do."*

Kneeling by the side of her bed like she'd done as a little girl, she prayed. "God, I don't know if you exist," she said, through her tears. "But if you do, please help me find my son."

Blue crawled back into bed. She seldom talked to God, so praying felt strange. *My father always prayed out loud*, she recalled. *The worst times were when we'd be in a restaurant and everybody could hear him going on and on. Nothing was more embarrassing…*

As a child, her minister-father expected his daughter to be in church. Her mother would often wake up on Sunday morning with a migraine.

In spite of the pain, she would put a smile on her face and drag Blue to church. "After all, we *are* the example," she would say. Blue had always wondered if her mother ever resented traipsing to church with a splitting headache.

She left her parents and their religion. I felt like church property as a kid, she reflected. I didn't even own my own soul. Hypocrisy was everywhere, and I was the butt of it. I remember how Mrs. Krum used to talk about me behind my back, all the while being nice to my face. None of it made sense to me. The day I realized how sanctimonious and hypocritical "God's people" could be, that's when I decided I didn't want any part of it, she remembered.

I wanted my freedom – ran right out of the frying pan and into the fire. Enter Theodore, she thought wryly. God, I was so crazy in love with him. What an arrogant ass he was! But his IQ was off the charts and that bedazzled me, she recalled. He was right down my alley – handsome, charming, a poet, an agnostic and eventually the man responsible for my swollen belly.

By this time, Blue had smoked half a pack of cigarettes. Reviewing her life required it. It quieted the pain. Blowing smoke into the stale bedroom air, Blue lifted her head off the pillow to gaze at the clock. "Hmm... This means I'm about an hour late for work," she said, the hands of the clock pointing to eleven. The mattress made a creaking sound as she eased out of bed. Maybe today will be my last at that godforsaken hole.

She punched in her time card an hour and a half late. "Hey Blue, the boss has been lookin' for you," Rita, one of the waitresses whispered. "And he's pissed."

"I don't *give* a damn. I'm sick of rude customers and skimpy tips," she retorted, pulling her hair back and tying on an apron.

The next eight hours were excruciatingly slow. "Sir, would you care for some dessert?" she politely asked her last patron of the evening, a regular at the restaurant.

"Sure, honey. What are my choices – besides you?" Her customer, fat and balding, had been getting progressively drunk throughout the evening. His comment was Blue's last straw. Irritation flew out of her mouth like a blunt-nose bullet.

"You know, buddy," she said. "I oughta' pour this coffee all over your bald head, but I'd get in trouble for that. However, accidents *do* happen," Blue threatened as she tipped the glass pot and spilled hot coffee all over the table. The brown liquid spread quickly and was heading toward the man's lap.

"Aw – *shit!*" He jumped up to avoid the scalding libation. "You... you stupid broad! I ought'a have you arrested!" The man's face was beet red.

Blue ignored him. She walked toward the kitchen carrying her tray of dishes and the infamous coffeepot when her boss appeared out of nowhere. "What did you *do* out there?" he asked.

"I just poured coffee all over your customer's table – and if I could've I would've poured it all over *him*!" Blue said without hesitation.

"Why in the *hell* did you do that?"

"Because I'm sick of customers who are drunk and insulting!" she shot back.

"You're *supposed* to take insults! You're a waitress!"

"Not anymore I'm not! I quit!" Blue was still holding the tray of dishes.

"You can't quit! I'm *firing* you!" Her boss yelled.

"As of this very second?" Blue asked.

"Yes, this very second!"

"Fine! Then *you* can take care of these!" Blue dropped the tray of dishes on the floor with a loud crash, barely missing his foot. Bits of broken plates skittered across the greasy floor and leftover food splattered everywhere.

"Get out of my restaurant and don't ever come back!" her boss yelled, the veins in his neck popping. "You've cost yourself some money tonight, young lady! Those broken plates will be comin' out of your last paycheck!" Blue walked away as he was speaking to her. She opened her locker, tore off her apron and grabbed her coat.

"You don't have to worry about me ever showing up here again! I'll *never* be back and I'm gonna tell everybody I know not to come here either!" she yelled, heading for the employee's exit.

"Blue," the cook said, pulling her aside. "It's about time *somebody* told that bastard off! I've always wanted to, but I'm glad it was you because you read him the *riot* act, honey! Take care of yourself," he told her. "We'll miss you around here."

"Thanks, Woody. I'll miss you guys too. Tell everybody good-bye for me," she said as she pushed the heavy restaurant door open and walked to her car.

Examining her reflection in the rear-view mirror, Blue felt larger than life. Smiling, she exclaimed, "I don't have to take crap from him or anybody else! I'm *through* taking crap! For the first time in my life, I had the balls to stand up for *me*!" She drove Saffron home on wings.

The next morning reality hit. 'Shit, I've lost my job!' was her awakening thought. *Now* what am I going to do? I have no money, other than the little bit I have left from my dad's life insurance policy. And that's not gonna last much longer...

Depression began creeping around Blue like a dampening fog. She felt stuck, like being in a pool of glue, unable to move. It was all too much – a mother who wouldn't talk to her, nightmares that left her crying, perpetual loneliness and her job a thing of the past. She canceled her therapist appointment, stopped eating, refused to answer the phone and locked herself in her apartment. She camped out in bed with Muss. Covering her head with a pillow, she tried to drown out the voices of persistent demons that fed, like Dracula, on her vulnerability, despondency and self-hatred.

The phone rang late Thursday night. She answered sleepily. It was George. "Hey, Blue." She could hear music and people talking in the background. "You hibernating? I haven't seen you since that night at the club."

"Hi, George," she said, her pulse quickening. "I quit my job last week. So, I'm bummed. I'm just stayin' in these days."

"I can hardly hear you. There's too much noise here." George was shouting into the phone. "Listen, you've got the blues, girl. I've got a cure for that."

"Yeah? What."

" I'll give you a clue. It starts with a long ride in the countryside, with the top down on the Galaxy. How does that sound?"

Blue paused. "Well, I like the countryside, and convertibles. When?"

41

"How about Saturday around noon?"

"Okay," she told him, her mood taking a definite upswing.

"I gotta hang up. It's too noisy to talk. Be cool, kiddo." There was a click.

"Bye, Geo..." Blue hung up, her sentence unfinished. "He *called* me." She said reverently.

Saturday came – beautifully. The Kansas sky was cloudless, the sun benevolently warm. George wheeled his Ford Galaxy into Blue's driveway. Her heart skipped beats. There he is, she thought, peering through the curtain. He looks so confident. Enviously, she believed confidence was something only men had; not women, and certainly not her.

There was a knock at the door. George stepped in without waiting for her to answer. "Hi," he said impishly. "You ready, good-lookin'?"

"Yes!" she said emphatically. "This is the first time I've been out of the house in days," she told him as they walked toward the car.

"Welcome to the outside world," he quipped, opening his car door. Blue got in on her side. She felt reckless and excited, shifting in her seat. She was drawn to George's charisma and magnetic personality, but at the same time, she felt apprehensive. There was a kind of undeniable darkness about him...

In minutes, they were out of the city limits. With the top down on his red convertible, Blue's dark hair flew wildly in the warm wind. It made her feel free and sexy. "I love this feeling," she yelled. The noise of the wind and the car radio made it hard to talk in a normal tone.

"What feeling?" George yelled back.

"Freedom!" she shouted. "I love it!"

George pushed in the car lighter. It popped out and he lit a Kool. He took periodic drags but soon lost the ash in the wind. He let the cigarette go. "Doctor said I shouldn't be smokin' anyway," he said. "Ever since I came back from Nam I've been suckin' down three packs of those cancer sticks a day."

"Is that what the war did to you?" Blue questioned.

"That and a whole lot more," he shouted.

"I don't believe in killing," Blue yelled. "The aftermath of that war will keep destroying the people of Vietnam and their land for a long time."

"You got *that* right... destruction for decades to come," George shouted back.

Blue had known George almost six weeks, meeting him a few months after moving to Wichita – not too long before she booted Carlos out of her life. Prior to knowing either one of them, it had been a hard year for her – young and pregnant. The baby's father, Theodore, had disappeared from her life. Nine months later alone and scared, she delivered a seven-pound baby – only to give him up three weeks later.

Out of nowhere, Naomi and Robert called her from Oklahoma. Perfect strangers to Blue, the two of them heard she was going to give up her baby and they wanted to adopt. Naomi asked if she would live with them until she delivered. Blue accepted.

After twenty-four hours of excruciating labor, she gave birth. Lying in her hospital bed, she held her son's tiny body in her arms. Powerful instincts took over and she changed her mind, deciding to keep him. But in only a few weeks, needing her own mother and overwhelmed with *being* a mother, Blue called Naomi in tears and asked her to come and get him...

"Hey, little bitty, pretty one. Are you on this planet?" George's voice brought her reeling back.

"Oh, sorry. I was just thinking about some people I used to know," she shouted above the noise.

The car slowed as he turned into a driveway. The tires spit gravel and thick dust left an opaque cloud. "Where are we?" Blue inquired.

"This is my buddy's place," he replied. "He's a guy I dropped out of the sky with in Nam. You don't mind, do you?"

"Hey, that's cool," she said casually, concealing her disappointment. The truth was, she wanted to be alone with George.

He looked over and gave her a wink. "You're okay, Blue."

A muscular, stocky man burst through the back porch screen door. "Hey, Georgie-boy, my man – slow down. You drive your car like that broken-down piece-of-shit you commandeered in Nam. It's a good thing I'm quick on my feet... jeezus!" he said, jumping out of the way. He stopped abruptly when he saw Blue. "I don't believe I've had the pleasure. You gonna introduce me to your woman, George?" he asked, continuing to stare at Blue. I bet you've been keepin' *her* a secret."

"I keep *all* my women a secret, Den. If I didn't, you'd have 'em for sure! Blue, meet Denny. Denny – Blue."

Denny walked around to her side of the car. "Blue, nice to meet ya.

She's a *fox*, Garret." With a gallant gesture, he helped her out of the car and kissed her hand.

"That's why I keep all my beautiful women anonymous. You can see how the man operates," George teased, giving Blue a grin.

Blue gave Denny one of her million-dollar smiles. "Why, Denny," she cooed, "you must be the one remaining true gentleman on earth. I didn't know there were any left."

"Hey, I'm a dying breed," he volunteered, giving her a wink. "Well, come on in. We'll break out the beer," Denny said. "Hey, George. Got any reefer with you?"

"You know I'm always stocked." George threw him a good-sized bag of grass.

Several hours had passed. Blue stepped outside for some fresh air. The setting sun filled the sky with scarlet, pink and purple. She loved Kansas sunsets. The land was flat and the horizon's blazing colors could be seen without obstruction. It reminded her of a time, as a small girl; when she and her dad sat on a hill behind their Virginia home and watched God paint the sky as the sun went down.

She missed her dad. He had died so suddenly a few years ago. But you never really *knew* dad, she thought. He was like a slippery fish. As soon as you thought you had him in your hands, he'd slide right out... always using the church to keep his distance.

Blue and her parents had been close when she was young and able to be influenced. But when adolescence arrived, she became someone neither one of them understood. That's when they turned against me, she thought. From then on I was the scapegoat, the willful girl they couldn't handle, and it was never the same.

Blue pushed the memories away, only to notice, in dismay, the sunset's disappearance. "What's the good of havin' a woman if she's running off all the time to watch a sunset?" She heard a deep, throaty voice behind her. A hand lifted the skirt of her gauze dress and squeezed the soft flesh under her panties.

George's touch was possessive. It alarmed and excited her... like the passionate kiss they'd shared at the party. She let out a gasp as she turned around to face him. "You know how to surprise a woman, don't you," she said breathlessly, looking up at him. But his look startled her. His eyes seemed vacant, almost hard. "It's a little chilly," she said with a shudder. "Can we go in?"

"You bet we can, *sweethaart*," he said, imitating a Humphrey Bogart accent. He grabbed her by the waist and pulled her towards him. "It's too breezy to get naked out *here*," he said huskily.

Blue was remembering the very first time she noticed George, before running into him at the bookstore. He was standing on the sidewalk in downtown Wichita, talking to a homeless man and sharing a smoke. She watched as he put a generous handful of money in the man's hand, giving him the peace sign as he walked away.

That impressed her. He acted down-to-earth and didn't seem to think himself better than anyone else. He looked good too, she remembered. He wore a tweed wool blazer, a little too short in the arms, and jeans that looked like he'd been born in them. They hugged his long legs right down to his shiny, brown leather boots.

A shock of thick, black hair hung carelessly over his forehead. He had beautiful, sexy hair, she remembered. Hair I wanted to grab a hold of. She recalled the moment their eyes met as she walked toward him. He had nodded, smiling at her to reveal a mouthful of perfect, white teeth with a little space between the two front ones and sensuous, full lips that embraced them all.

"You want a hit?" Denny asked, breaking her spell. He was leaning against the kitchen wall, completely stoned. He passed it to her. Blue inhaled the sweet smoke and held it. "You remember in Nam what old Cooper would say to us?" he asked George. "He'd say, 'girls, lock and load. Lock and load.' I wonder how many fuckin' times we heard Cooper say that. You always knew when you heard it you were headin' into a landing zone and it was time to kill or be killed."

George was sitting in the faded, yellow upholstered chair in the corner of the kitchen. Blue passed him the joint. He took a long hit, then several short ones. "We heard it so many times that I felt like fraggin' the bastard," he retorted. "What were those cigarettes, man... the ones we smoked over there?" he asked, talking as he held his breath.

"The ones with weed in'em?" Denny queried.

"Yeah," George said.

"Dien Bien Phu, man," Denny replied. "We called 'em bennies. God, they were potent..."

Seconds later, George was laughing so hard tears were rolling down his cheeks. "Hey asshole," he said, wiping them with the back of his hand. "Do you remember the night in Nam... during monsoon season, when we got so stoned we stripped down to our underwear and chased those pigs in the pouring rain? And you fell on your ass in the mud?" He continued, his shoulders shaking with laughter. "I tried to pull you up, but I was so ripped that *I* fell on my butt! We both laid there in the middle of the road laughing like fuckin' bedpan idiots."

"Yeah, I remember," Denny laughed. "It was *your* brilliant idea to chase those damn pigs. I swear I had one by the back leg before I went down. Jesus christ... the stuff we did, it's a wonder we came out of that war alive."

"No shit, man. There were too many ways to die in that hell hole." George's face was serious. "It was a fucking nightmare... and you just prayed you'd wake up the next morning and it would be all over and you could go home. Then when you got home man, everybody hated you," he laughed derisively. "No thank-you's, no pats on the back, no 'good job, soldier.' Just people staring at you in disgust. I even had a few spit on me! We fought that bloody war for what? For nothin' that's for fuckin' what!" George concluded angrily.

"Nobody won that war," Denny said. "Christ... I'll never forget that bent-over, old Vietnamese woman. She was carrying around two hundred pieces of American shrapnel in her body. She's probably still alive... a walking munitions."

Denny got quiet, his mind creating pictures – of disembodied arms, legs and torsos. Of faces half blown off. Buddies screaming in indescribable pain. The bloody images crowded his memory. "Fuck man, let's just shut the hell up! I can't take this!" His voice cracked as the pain slipped out. Blanching, he looked as if he would vomit.

Denny had been one of the first young men in Wichita to sign up for the war. Serving his country was what he had always dreamed of – just like his father had in World War II. Mom was crying, he remembered, and dad had tears in his eyes when he shook my hand. My dad was so proud the day I left for boot camp. He said, "Be a good soldier, son. We don't need medals, just do your best. Keep your nose clean and write us when you can."

George noticed Denny's faraway look, one he'd seen before. "Hey, man. You okay?" he asked. This wasn't the first time he felt afraid for Denny. He'd seen him strapped to a bed in a locked hospital ward so he wouldn't blow his brains out. He remembered their camping trip when Denny woke him up with blood-curdling screams. George understood. He had nightmares about the war too.

"C'mere babe," George told Blue, motioning her to come over and sit on the arm of his chair. "Denny's patriotism got him into trouble," he told her, in a confidential tone. "The idiot couldn't wait to rush off to Da Nang and be a marine. He *volunteered* for combat, so he could kill those jungle boogers. I guess he wanted his pop to be proud of him. He got to fight all right... jungle combat that would scare the shit out of anybody. And it was the Cong's jungle. That was the hell of it. Helicopters dropped you out of the sky in the middle of the night into an open field. Take your choice – land mine explosion, sniper fire, ambush. You were so terrified you pissed your pants."

Denny's voice sounded distant. "You know, George. After a while, I stopped countin'."

"Yeah, man. I know," George answered. "I stopped too. After dropping eight million tons of bombs in eight years on a country, you kinda lose count," he said sardonically. "We have fucking Nixon and Johnson to thank for that."

Denny continued, as if he hadn't heard his friend. "You wanna know *why* I stopped countin'?" His voice had a shrill, desperate tone. "Because, after awhile, every dead body just looked like every other dead body. They all looked the same, starin' up at me with those lifeless eyes... all those bodies... and the stench, man... the stench. *Jesus Christ*." His voice trailed off. The three of them fell silent and the hum of the refrigerator was the only sound.

Blue watched the gray hashish smoke curl lazily up toward the wooden rafters. She was dizzy and high. The war stories had been gruesome and depressing. On the stereo the Rolling Stones were telling the world that... *you can't always get what you waa-nt*. The story of *my* life... Blue thought.

I'd like to be back home under the covers with Muss. George doesn't even act like I'm here. Piqued, she walked into the kitchen and opened a beer. Thumbing absentmindedly through one of Denny's girlie magazines, her thoughts drifted to Carlos. He had his faults, but at least he didn't ignore me on our first date, she thought angrily.

"Denny, could I use your phone?" she asked.

"Sure darlin' – in the bedroom." Denny replied, without looking up. Blue guessed which room he meant. Once in the room's sour-smelling darkness, she flipped the light switch and sat on the edge of the bed. Looking around, she noticed a poster of Janis Joplin taped to the wall above the bed. On the nightstand was an assortment of Mad and Playboy magazines, several candy wrappers and a empty carton of chocolate milk. She dialed the number. Carlos answered.

"Carlos. It's Blue."

"Well, *you've* been a stranger. Where're you callin' from?"

"A friend's house," Blue answered.

"Hey baby, I miss you. Listen, that woman at the party was a stupid mistake," he explained. "I had one too many and she came on to me. You know how women are about Italians."

"That's no excuse, Carlos. You're drunk. I can always tell," Blue said.

"Oh, you can, huh? How can you tell, miss know-it-all?"

"Because it's the only time you're nice to me," she replied.

"I might be *real* nice and surprise you tonight," he told her.

"What do you mean?"

"I may show up on your doorstep to prove just *how* nice I can be. But if I do, you'd better be alone," he said.

"Don't threaten *me*, Carlos. If I remember correctly, your hands were all over that chick at the party. I told you it was over between us and I meant it!"

"You know, Blue, you forgot *one* thing when you gave me the boot!" he said angrily. "I still have a key to your apartment. You dig? And another thing," he continued. "After what you did to my clothes, I'm sendin' you a bill for the dry cleaning, bitch!" Blue heard the dial tone.

She slammed the receiver down. "He's *still* an ass," she said. "Always will be. Where in the *hell* did my good judgment go, calling him?" She lit a cigarette, exhaling angrily.

"Hey, you callin' an old boyfriend or what?" George yelled from the living room. "There are a couple of lonely, drug-crazed hippies out here needin' a woman!" he said. "We're *'one toke over the line, Sweet Jesus... one toke over the line,'* " George and Denny sang their off-key duet.

Blue appeared in the doorway of the bedroom. George was rolling a joint. "Jus' jivin'," he said, with a wink. "There's only *one* drug-crazed hippie out here who needs ya."

Blue looked at the two bleary-eyed men, shook her head and laughed. "Mercy, mercy... what am I gonna *do* with you boys," she teased. They were happily stoned and giggling like schoolboys. She wanted to lighten up, forget her conversation with Carlos. "Hey Denny, you got any munchies? This girl's starving," she said. Denny was so ripped, he could barely respond. He just laughed sillily and pointed toward the kitchen.

Blue opened the refrigerator and took inventory of the contents. She decided on a hunk of yellow cheese, a couple slices of bread, a jar of mustard, a jar of sweet pickles and a beer. The art of creating a sandwich when you're as high as I am is no easy task, she thought, laughing at herself. Licking the pickle juice that was running down her arm and swiping mustard with her tongue about to drip from the corner of the bread, she managed to plop into the beanbag chair by the stove.

Across from her was a huge poster of Jimi Hendrix taped to the wall. She gazed at the sixties rock-and-roll icon as she ate. Her mind drifted back in time. The food was bringing her down. She began thinking about the steady stream of men she'd been with over the last four years. How did I end up here, she wondered, looking around, with someone I barely know?

I guess it's because I just can't stand to be without a man, she thought. I can hear my dad saying, *"Whatever happened to you, Patti? Whatever happened to my little girl?"* Good question, daddy. If I knew and you were alive, I'd tell you, she thought bitterly.

Her parents named her Patti, after her dad's sister. By the time she turned thirteen, she hated her name. It sounded conventional and Christian. Besides that, she never liked her aunt. She promised herself that after she left home, she would choose a new name – like a rite of passage.

She kept her promise. Every bit of eight months pregnant, she walked into an Oklahoma courthouse and applied for a name change. In a few weeks, her name was officially Blue. For her, it was obvious. *"Love, love, my love is blue,"* was the song she sang over and over again during those nine months. It was the way she felt about love and her loneliness.

As she popped another beer, George sauntered cockily into the kitchen. "Hey, how about one of those for George? Denny, I think I've got a lush on my hands," he yelled. "You've been chuggin' those like lemonade on a hot summer day," he chided. "You tryin' to drink me under the table? I think I'd better take you home. It's way past your bedtime," he said, kissing her on the mouth.

His casual kiss turned into a passionate, probing one and Blue kissed him back. After several minutes of tonguing every inch of each other's mouths, they broke apart. "Every time you kiss me," she said breathlessly, "I get lightheaded and tingly all over. I feel faint. What is it about you, George?"

He left her question unanswered. "Let's go, baby," he said huskily.

"Okay," Blue replied weakly.

They peered into the living room. Denny was passed out on the chocolate brown, corduroy couch. He had been a weightlifter since Nam and the couch sagged in the middle, straining under his weight. George and Blue left him there and walked out to the car, arms around each other. The air was balmy, the stars brilliant and the moon so full they could have driven home without headlights.

The two were silent for a while as the Galaxy purred along. "So what *were* you doing in the bedroom?" George finally asked.

Blue took a deep breath. "If you want to know the truth, I got bored with your war stories and called a friend." Carlos *was* a friend at one time, she rationalized.

"A friend?" he inquired.

"Yeah, a *friend*," she replied.

"Blue, you're a mysterious lady – secretive. You never lay all your cards out on the table, do you?"

"I'm a Scorpio. What can I say?" Blue quipped.

"Now me," he continued. "What you see is what you get. I'm an out-in-front man. But you... you like to hide. You've got secrets that you don't tell anybody. And you're naive, kid. You trust the *wrong* people, especially when it comes to men."

Blue knew he was right. "You mean," she challenged him, "that *you* never keep just one card in your back pocket?"

"Nope. I learned the hard way that keepin' secrets was a cheap high and not worth the consequences."

"So, Mr. Garret, you gonna make an honest woman out of me?" she said sarcastically.

"Didn't you tell me you were a preacher's kid?" he asked.

"I think I mentioned it," Blue replied.

He chuckled. "Every preacher's kid I ever met didn't know who the hell they were. I may be a dope-smokin', fucked-up Vietnam vet, Blue, but I realized a long time ago who I was. I know people, Blue. I can sense what kind of heart they have. I've got street smarts. Not too many people can fool me.

"But you, princess," he continued his diatribe, "don't know the first thing about how people really live because you've been sheltered all your life. You don't know about the rough side. I hang around the people that nobody else gives a shit about. They're my kind of people – the underdogs of the world. Some of them are real diamonds in the rough." He looked at her and paused. "I can tell you dig me, Blue, but you don't have a clue about who I am. You..."

Blue interrupted him. "Has anybody ever told you how incredibly arrogant you are? You think you can put me in a box and spit me out as this or as that? You don't know me either and there's much more to me than meets the eye, *dude*!"

He looked at her and smiled. "You're real cute when you're angry."

"Don't patronize me!" Blue *was* angry. Stonily silent, neither one spoke.

They stopped at the corner of Main Street and Woodson. George made a right turn onto her street. As they rounded the corner her apartment came into view. There was Carlos, leaning against his car, arms folded. Oh my god, he *was* serious! she realized.

George pulled into the driveway and turned off the engine. Blue wanted to crawl under the seat and disappear into the floorboard. He gave her a hard stare. "So who's the guy? The 'friend' you called tonight?" he said sarcastically.

"Yeah, that's him," Blue answered.

"Getting to know you, getting to know all about you..." George started singing.

"Okay, you've made your point," Blue said quietly.

"Hey baby, daddy's home," Carlos announced. "You can tell your funky driver he can go now. Dismissed, asshole," he yelled at George.

"Shut-up Carlos," Blue shouted.

"Is that any way to talk to the man who's the best fuck you ever had?" he wisecracked for George's benefit. He threw his empty beer bottle on the ground like a gauntlet. "I hope you like hospital food, man, because that's where you're gonna be when I get through with you!"

George was out of the car before Carlos took his next breath. They hit the ground with a thud as punches flew. George pummeled Carlos in the face and stomach. Carlos gave George a serious uppercut to the jaw. The final blow sent Carlos's head flying backwards as George's fist found its home in his face. He fell to his knees and everything went starry and black.

George was on all fours. He noticed blood dripping from someplace on his face and wiped it on his shirtsleeve. His heavy smoking left him gasping for breath. He felt weak. Collapsing, he rolled over onto his back and passed out. That's when the flashback came...

His platoon was conducting a night bombing. He couldn't see what or who he was shooting. All he knew was that they were raiding a village. He could hear the villagers – screaming, crying and moaning. There were men, women and children – all of them wounded or dying... then horrible silence. Leaning on his gun for support, he slowly lowered himself to the ground. He sat on his haunches, sweat running in tributaries down his body. His ears were ringing and a cold sensation spread throughout his body. That's when he started shaking. Uncontrollably...

Sounds of sobbing brought him back – heartfelt sobbing. George lifted his head to see Blue sitting on the stoop of her apartment, crying her eyes out. There was no sign of Carlos. Looking at her, he felt a wave of shame about what he had done. He'd lost control and he knew it. He'd fought with a total stranger and made Blue cry. What the hell did I do that for? he thought. What the fuck's wrong with me?

"Well, Blue," he said lamely. "At least I didn't *start* the fight. This guy's *your* problem. If you can't keep your men straight, it's your own damn fault."

Silence greeted his rude remark. "Yeah, you're right," she said finally. "I made the mistake of thinking I could find a decent guy who would care about *me*. But you're just like all the rest of them. All you care about is George Garret."

The absolute quiet between them created a space for night sounds to emerge – crickets chirped, wind rustled the leaves. George was starting to feel pain from the fight. He sat up. "Oh, god..." he moaned. His whole body hurt. The moist ground had dampened the back of his shirt and his jeans were patterned with blood and dirt. He looked around at Blue. She was standing behind her screen door looking out. "Okay," he said. "I guess it's time for 'ole George to go. I'm sure you won't want to see *me* again."

Blue didn't answer. She just closed her door and turned out the porch light. Once inside, she fell against the wall – trembling. Her heart was pounding. Her legs gave way as her body slid slowly down to the carpet. Silent tears fell, making little splash marks on her dress.

Too tired to think, Blue succumbed to exhaustion and dropped onto the green striped couch. She felt relieved knowing George was gone. Hell of a way to cap off an evening, she thought. With a fight! Thank god this night is over.

The apartment was quiet. A floor lamp was on. Blue looked around the living room. "Well, I can see Carlos used his key to get in," she said. "And he left his mark. He's trashed the place. Must be payback time..."

Beer cans littered the floor and ashtrays brimmed with cigarette butts. A jumbo bag of Lay's potato chips, half-empty, graced the coffee table and an open container of bacon and green-onion chip dip was not far away. Too tired to clean it up, his mess was the last thing she saw before she fell asleep.

George opened his eyes. They felt like slits. "Ouch... damn." He flinched as he touched the cut over his right eye. He looked at the clock... almost noon. Another restless night. His sleep filled with nightmares, he often awoke in the middle of a dream screaming. His bed was soaked with sweat and it was always the same dream. *He's with his squadron in a huge rice field, bombs exploding all around them. Just before he's hit, he watches, horrified, as a grenade blows the torso of his buddy from his legs...*

I'm getting too old for this. I've been fighting all my life – ever since I was a kid. Maybe its time for me to stop, he thought, reaching for his Kools. Inhaling deeply, he let the smoke shoot out his nostrils. I'll call Blue. Tell her I'm sorry. He grabbed the phone and dialed her number. One ring and he lost his nerve. He hung up.

George thought about his father's dying words. *"Son, don't spend your life doin' what I did. Smokin' tobacco and drinking rot-gut whiskey will put you in an early grave."* I miss the bastard, he thought. He was one mean fucker... no meaner than ma, though. God, could she yell.

Dave's gone too. My only brother... fucking railroad accident cut *his* life short, he remembered. Ma's still around, but she's a bitter old woman. Shit... I've practically lost my whole family. So what the hell am *I* still doin' here, he wondered. He dropped his cigarette into the half-empty bottle of cola by the bed. It extinguished itself with a hiss.

Blue stepped out of the shower and glanced at the clock. "Oh god, I'm gonna be late," she said, dressing hurriedly. "I hope she's running behind today, because I am. Don't know what I would do without that woman, she thought, stuffing a blouse into her bell-bottom jeans. She ran out the door, jumped into Saffron and took off.

"I can't wait for this elevator," Blue told a stranger. Bolting toward the stairs of the fifteen-story building, she ran up six flights. She burst though the door of the doctor's office, panting and out of breath. "Is she still in session?" she asked Beatrice.

"Yes. She's running over again today," the receptionist replied.

"Thank god. Oh boy, am I out of shape," she confessed, collapsing into one of the waiting room chairs. "I just ran up six flights of stairs."

The office door opened and Love Mae's patient walked out. "Laura!" she exclaimed, a surprised look on her face. It was the woman she had helped in the church.

"Blue!" the woman responded happily. The two young women hugged like long lost friends. "How *are* you?"

"Well, I'm *here*," Blue said. "Doesn't that tell you anything?" Laura laughed at her dry humor. "I'm so glad to see you. How did you find Dr. Montgomery?"

"A counselor at the women's shelter told me about her," she replied.

"Don't you just love her?" Blue was enthusiastic.

"She's great!" Laura said, equally excited.

"Whatever happened to the man you were living with who beat you up?" Blue asked, lowering her voice.

"He's dead," she said matter-of-factly.

"What?" Blue's jaw dropped in astonishment.

"He was drinking and hit another car – head on. He was killed instantly."

"Oh my god."

"It's okay. I don't miss him," Laura said. "In fact, I'm glad he's gone. He made my life miserable."

"Oh, I'm so relieved you're all right," Blue said, throwing her arms around her.

"Me too," she said, returning the hug. "Go see your shrink now. She's waiting."

"Bye, Laura."

Love Mae ushered Blue into her office. "It's been a while, young lady," she said. "Have you been hiding?"

"Yeah... under the covers," Blue quipped as Love Mae closed the door behind her. "I quit my job and got depressed. So I stayed in bed for a week," she told her.

Dr. Montgomery was good for Blue. No matter what she told her, Love Mae never seemed to judge or criticize her. Instead, she taught her things her mother never had... about the pitfalls and how easy it is for a woman to make a man her source of self-worth. She tried to help Blue understand her relationships with men and how her lack of esteem for herself fueled the fire of the men who she let abuse her.

"There are men who hate women and they're like good hunting dogs," Love Mae said. "They can pick up the scent of their prey and circle her for the kill. They can 'smell' a woman who's a victim. That's why it's important for you, Blue, to stop acting like you *deserve* to be abused. You bring a lot on yourself when you do that." Love Mae's powerful words echoed in her head as she drove home.

Turning onto her street, she recognized the red convertible parked in front of her house. It's George... damn. What's he doing here? she wondered. He was sitting on her porch steps, a cigarette hanging carelessly from his fingers. At his feet was a half-empty fifth of Jack Daniels.

George didn't look up as Blue approached. "Did I ever tell you that my granddaddy used to make corn whiskey in his basement? I had my first taste of it when I was nine. It was kinda sweet and made me feel warm inside... I guess that's why I still drink it now. Reminds me of my grandpa," he told her, punctuating the end of his monologue with a swig.

"Sorry about the other night," he apologized, looking up at Blue. "I can be a real jerk. I knew what I was doing, fighting with Carlos. I just didn't wanna stop." He looked past her, remembering something. "My dad used to get angry like that. He'd take it out on me, but I never knew why. He'd backhand me and I'd go flying across the room like a piece of paper. When I got big enough to fight him back, he stopped. I guess he decided to quit before I could hurt him."

Blue could see George being hit by his father – violently, unexpectedly. "I bet you're pretty pissed at your father for hitting you like that," she said cautiously.

"Nah. Not anymore," he said, brushing it off. "He was a mean sonovabitch... and then he died. But he was my father."

"Then you've forgiven him?" Blue asked.

"Now you sound like your fancy doctor. Look, I came over to apologize, not to be analyzed. Okay?"

"Sure," Blue replied.

"Want a swallow?" he asked, handing over the bottle.

Blue took a mouthful of the whiskey. The liquid tasted sweet, warm and stinging as it traveled down her throat.

"Hey, let's smoke some reefer. Have some laughs," he said.

"I can't, George."

He pulled a joint out of his cigarette pack and lit up. "You know, Blue," he said, "the only time I feel happy is when I'm jammin'. I love playin' the blues because the blues come from way down deep in your soul. They're about bein' down on your luck, havin' hard times and lovin' your woman," he told her.

He took a deep drag and gazed at the sky. "I haven't loved a woman in a while," he said, after several minutes. "Not since Maria left me for some educated prick. I wanted to kill her for that – him too! God, what a woman... she was beautiful, Mexican and the only chick I've ever known that had a temper worse than mine."

"Look, George, you'd better go," Blue said abruptly, interrupting his sentiment. She was irritated listening to his whining about Maria. "I don't have time for this. I gotta go to bed." She went in the house, letting the screen door slam behind her.

She heard George's car door shut and his tires squeal as he pulled away. "I probably pissed him off, Muss," she told her napping cat. "But I don't care. I don't feel like playing nursemaid to a narcissist!"

George wasn't pissed, until he started thinking about it. "Wait a minute," he said. "Who the hell does she think she is, dismissing me! I'm spillin' my guts and she tells me she's gotta go to bed." He began thinking about Carlos. "I bet she's screwin' that Spic. Keepin' that poor fuck in her back pocket just in case!" He hit the steering wheel with his fist.

Five o'clock in the morning and George hadn't slept a wink. He had been obsessing about women and how they control and manipulate. How they say one thing to your face and do something different behind your back – like sleep with another man.

The sun was a thin crimson line on the horizon when George got into his car and headed back to Blue's apartment. He had convinced himself that Blue was betraying him, deciding she was just like Maria – dishonest, scheming and couldn't be trusted. And he was angry. Another woman double-crossing him... again. He could feel hot fury burning in his body.

Knuckles whitened on the steering wheel, George stared straight ahead, not noticing the world waking up. People were going to their jobs, drinking their coffee as they drove. Streetlights blinked off as natural light took over. Morning newspapers landed on front porches. But all he could think about was Blue. "She thinks she can play a fool's game with me. We'll see about that," he said with a sneer.

A tapping sound stirred Blue out of sleep. *Tap, tap, tap.* Insistent tapping. Startled, Blue awakened. I've been dreaming, she thought. Closing her eyes, she tried to remember the dream. Something about packs of wild dogs... and they were chasing me. I could hear their jaws snapping at my ankles. *Tap, tap, tap.* She sat up in bed, heart pounding. She listened, breathing shallowly. Muss was looking intently at the bedroom window.

"Blue. Wake up. It's George. Let me in." She could see his profile through the thin curtains.

"What are you doing here?" she asked.

"I've gotta see you. It's important," George said, with a pleading tone. She got out of bed and went to open the door, despite an inner cautionary voice. George shoved it open with such force that she fell backward onto the floor.

"God, George. What the hell's wrong with you?" she said, getting up. "If you'd just waited, I'd have..." The look on his face made her stomach knot with fear.

He pushed past her and began to pace. "I've been up all night. Something's been eating at me." Blue said nothing. He glowered at her. "You're acting just like Maria did before she dumped me – sweet to my face, but under that phony shit, makin' plans to kick my ass out! I know you, Blue. You women always have another man in the wings. You're not sure about me, so you're bangin' Carlos just in case we don't work out!"

George towered over the terrified young woman. His pupils were dilated and his eyes bloodshot. As he moved closer, she could smell alcohol on his breath. "George, you're scaring me," she said, folding her arms across her chest protectively. "I want you to leave now."

"No, baby... you don't get it. I don't *want* to leave. I've got questions and you're gonna give me answers." He continued moving toward her. Blue backed up, almost falling as she stumbled over one of Muss's cat toys.

"Why are you *doing* this to me? I haven't done anything to *you*," she said, her voice full of hurt and fear.

"Look, save the crocodile tears!" he said sarcastically. "I don't trust what you or any woman says. You're all liars. You act so saccharine... so sanctimonious. Then you lower the boom and us poor fucks never know what hit us!"

Poking his fingertips in her chest, he shoved her into the bedroom and onto the bed. He pushed her and she landed hard, knocking the wind out of her. "I don't know why I'm even *bothering* with you!" He backhanded her. It felt like she had been hit with a two by four. "You *hear* me, bitch?" he said, slapping her again.

For a brief second, George's hand became her mother's palm against her sixteen-year old face, delivering a stinging, jarring slap. He straddled her, pinning her shoulders to the bed. "So, are you fucking Carlos?" he demanded, glaring at her. Blue lay motionless, frozen under his weight and his rage. He slapped her again. Her cheek burned and tears came to her eyes. *"Answer* me!" he commanded.

"No! I'm not fucking Carlos!"

"Liar!" He backhanded her again.

The phone rang, startling them. "Who's that?" George asked.

"I don't know," Blue said in a weak, raspy voice. *Rrring... rrring.*

"Don't answer it," he said.

George unzipped his pants. "I have something for you," he said seductively... something you've wanted ever since you met me."

"George, please. I don't want it – not this way. Please," Blue pleaded.

"You can't always have things the way you want them in life, little girl. You never learned that, did you? Well, I'm here to teach you that you can't fuck with George Garret. Besides, you *know* you want it," he said sadistically. "So just lie back and enjoy the ride."

He unbuckled his belt and pulled it out, snapping it in front of her face. "I'm gonna use this on you," he threatened. "You know why? Because you've been a *bad* girl – and bad girls get spanked. Now turn over," he said, pushing her onto her stomach.

Blue lay face down on the bed, cringing. He grabbed her wrists and held them behind her, yanked up her pink nightgown, exposing her buttocks, and hit her hard with his belt. "Are you going to be a *good girl* for George?" he asked. "You gonna stop *fuckin' around?* Are you?" He hit her again, this time harder. Blue cried out. Just as he drew the belt back to hit her a third time, there was a knock at the door.

"Blue, are you in there?" a female voice inquired. "It's Laura. I called you a few minutes ago, but there was no answer." More knocking. "Anybody home?" she inquired insistently. Blue prayed he would release her. George softened.

"All right," he said brusquely. "You can go to the door, but you play it straight, girl. You understand? No innuendoes, no secret signals, no give-away looks. Got it? You convince her that everything is *just fine* before you send her away." Blue nodded numbly.

When she got to the door, Muss was meowing to go out. She pushed him away from the door with her foot. "No, Muss. Not now," she mumbled. She opened the door a crack just as Laura was turning to leave. "Hi," Blue said.

"Oh, hi! You *are* home! I got your address from the operator when I called information," she explained. "I thought I'd come by and we could go for breakfast somewhere." Blue didn't answer. "But I guess this isn't a good time, is it," Laura said, noticing her friend's pained expression.

"It's really not. I woke up with a splitting headache," Blue lied. "I took a couple Darvon and I'm feeling kinda groggy. I wouldn't be good company." Blue's mouth felt like chalk and she had broken into a sweat. Seeing the concern in her friend's eyes was bringing tears to her own.

"Blue, are you okay?" Laura asked. "Are you alone? Is there someone with you?" Blue kept quiet. "Why won't you let me in?" Her probing questions were making Blue nervous.

George had come into the room and was hiding behind the door. He gave Blue a sharp kick in the ankle. "Wrap it up," he whispered threateningly.

"Laura, I've got to go. I'm feeling dizzy," she said thinly. "I need to lie down." She started to shut the door.

Laura pushed the door open. "Let me help you, Blue," she said. "You look like you're about to faint."

George gave her another kick. Blue winced with pain. "No, really. I'll be *fine*," she told her friend. Laura saw the distress in her eyes and the two women shared a split second of knowing. "I have to go," Blue said and shut the door as Laura looked on.

"Get your ass back in the bedroom – now," George said in a deadly whisper. "But before you do, make sure your little friend is gone," he hissed. "I don't want anybody snooping around." Her heart sank as she looked through the Venetian blinds and saw Laura driving away.

George pushed Blue into the bedroom. He stripped down to his underwear. "Take off that nightgown," he said roughly. "And get on the bed." He noticed her hesitation. "If you *don't*, I'll rip it off you, bitch!"

Blue obeyed and climbed on the bed gingerly. "Spread your legs!" he ordered. She didn't move. He slapped her. "I told you to spread your legs, cunt!" he ordered, pulling them apart. He straddled her and Blue started pushing him away with her hands.

"George, please don't! Please! Pleeeeease..."she screamed. He ignored her begging and entered her. Oh god, he's raping me, Blue thought. Oh, god...

She heard George's voice. "*Now* who's fuckin' who? Her vagina was on fire with shards of pain as he thrust himself into her again and again. Her mind tore itself away from her body... to fields of red tulips. Blue watched in amazement as the flowers uprooted themselves in slow motion and swirled around her. Blooms encircling her... red, blood red... bloody red until she was encased in red petals. A sonorous voice reverberated and the tulips vanished, leaving her red-stained and naked in the field. Instantaneously, Blue plummeted back into her body and her suffering.

"You know, I could just *press* my *thumb* into your *neck* and *kill* you in a *second*," George was saying, punctuating intermittent words with a thrust of his angry cock.

Blue glanced at his tortured face, contorted with evil. I'll kill you first, she thought as their eyes fastened on each other. I'll destroy the darkness in you!

As if he'd heard her speak the words, George stopped. He let out a groan. She felt the heaviness of his body crushing her small frame. Lying underneath him, Blue felt leaden... non-existent... dead. She turned her head to the side as he removed himself from her. He pushed off of her and sat back on his haunches. "*Jeezus*..." he said, breathing hard. "I'm out'a shape."

He stood up and put on his pants. Lighting a cigarette, he started to pace, head down, like he was thinking. Minutes passed. "You're a lucky woman, Blue. I spared your life," he told her as he cleaned invisible dirt from under his fingernails. "Do you know that I carry two cyanide caps around with me that I've had since Nam? And did you realize I could take one of those right now and be dead in a matter of seconds?"

So do it, asshole! she wanted to say. Instead, Blue merely stared at the faded green-flowered wallpaper on the bedroom wall, her anger on hold for future expression. Unable to move, she felt catatonic and entombed in a body cast... peering out from behind eyeholes. She prayed George would leave her alone now... and that his talk of suicide would come to nothing.

George stopped pacing. He stared vacantly at Blue lying on the bed, cigarette smoke curling up over his eyes. "You want to go together?" he asked in a low voice. "We could do it – you and me. We could do it now..." He slid down the wall he'd been leaning against and sat on the floor.

Blue's vagina was throbbing. Her right eye felt swollen. There was pain radiating from her neck to her shoulder. She lay very still, like a deer freshly wounded. Tears ran silently out of the corners of her eyes, soaking her hair and the pillow that cradled her head. She desperately wanted to leave her body... not to die, just to go back to the fields of red tulips.

George's eyes were closed, his head resting against the wall. Old, rotting rage harbored since before the war was now spent. He had spewed it all over an innocent woman. Blue cried quietly – waiting for him to leave so she could nurse her wounds. It was over and the life of Blue Spencer was changed forever. Never again could she allow herself to be vulnerable to a man. From now on, sex equaled violence and the bedroom would be a battleground.

The next day Blue felt a paralyzing tiredness that dragged her down like the anchor of an ill-fated ship. Her body was numb. "Why did he do it?" was her only question. No answer came. But one was formulating that would surface like a worm; crawling up out of the ground on a rainy day... *the rape was her fault.* She had angered George by playing a serious game with the wrong man. I pushed him too far, she thought. I'm just a cock-tease... guess that means I deserved it.

That must be why I didn't grab Muss and run out the door when I had the chance, she concluded. I could've escaped with Laura and none of this would've happened. How could I be so spineless? Blue stared blankly out the window, enveloped in silent confusion.

It was 6:00 p.m. and she hadn't gotten up. Blue had been lapsing in and out of a restless sleep. She couldn't stomach her bed. The memory of what happened there was nauseating. She nested in the corner of her green-striped, too-soft couch where she stayed for days. Food held little interest. She felt comatose. Every noise startled her.

The weeks that followed were like a surrealistic dream. Venturing into the outside world, Blue felt damaged – like bruised fruit. She wanted to hide. She *did* hide, looking out from behind green-leafed bushes. She questioned her strange behavior. But nothing and nowhere felt safe – only the spaces behind shrubbery. Sitting there on her haunches, like a rain forest native, she wanted to be invisible.

But she wasn't. Some passersby stared. Others looked away. But no one stopped to inquire about her well being. Such is the way of the world – shamefully short of good Samaritans. Blue continued sleeping and living invisibly until one day she stopped.

That's when she took George back in her life... to fill the void of loneliness sitting in her heart since childhood. He didn't offer an apology for the rape and she didn't ask for one. The two of them simply took up where they left off, as if nothing had happened. It's the way Blue wanted it. It's the way it was.

"Do you want your potatoes fried or baked?" Blue yelled from the kitchen to the living room.

"Can't you remember *anything*? You know I hate your baked potatoes. They're always hard as rocks!" George yelled back from behind his *Rolling Stone* magazine. "Fry 'em."

"Fry them yourself, smart-ass," Blue muttered under her breath. She lopped off a generous hunk of butter and watched it dance across the hot skillet. She could almost hear it screaming as it skittered and bubbled. "You want the skins on them?" Blue hoped he would say yes. She hated peeling potatoes.

No answer from behind the magazine. Whenever George is absorbed in something, you could rope a calf right under his nose and he wouldn't pay any attention, she thought. So, he'll get 'em as they come – fully clothed. Blue emptied the plastic bowl filled with unpeeled potato slices into the skillet. The sizzle got a reaction. "Hey, don't scorch those babies. Didn't your mother teach you how to cook?" George asked, concerned about his grub.

Blue picked up the heavy iron skillet with both hands and slammed it on the burner, splashing butter and potatoes all over the stovetop. "Can't you *ever* say anything nice to me?" she complained. "You know, I don't have to cook you *anything*!" She felt tears brimming. Silence. George ambled into the kitchen.

"You're too sensitive, Blue... probably because you could never do anything right for your mother. I guess that's why I love ya," George said, deciding to be sweet. Blue's anger melted. Putting his arms around her waist, he let one of his hands slip down to linger on her right cheek.

Blue reached around, moved his hand away and looked up at him. "Can't you ever be loving without groping me somewhere?" she asked. "You know, George, we've been livin' together for six months – but it feels like six years." She pulled away from him. "Most of the time you treat me like an old shoe, just kicking me across the floor whenever you feel like it. You say something nice to me and think somehow that makes everything okay and you can do whatever you want with my body."

"Oh, come on baby. Lighten up!" he told her. "You must be on the rag today."

"Just blow me off, George, like always..." Suddenly, the odor of potatoes just short of burned filled their nostrils. "Oh, damn! Now look what you made me do," Blue accused, rescuing the burning spuds.

"Hey, don't worry about it," he said, surveying his near-blackened dinner. "We'll drown those suckers in catsup and never know the difference," George placated, trying not to piss her off any further.

They sat down at Blue's garage sale purchase – the wooden kitchen table that she painted bright green. She had lavishly coated each of the four chairs a primary color. It made for kaleidoscopic eating, she thought. George, in his characteristic way, shoveled his dinner and Blue picked at hers. What appetite she *did* have had taken its leave soon after they moved in together.

Between bites, George griped about his job. "Did you ever work someplace and hate it?" he asked Blue.

"Yeah – that dump of a restaurant with all the drunks," she answered.

"I fuckin' *hate* my job. Do you know that I was in line for a supervisor position a month ago and they gave it to someone else less qualified?"

"No," Blue said. "You never told me that."

"Well, they did. They always do. I know why too. People are jealous of me."

Blue paused, fork in mid-air. "What do you mean jealous?" she asked. "*Who's* jealous of you?"

"Three or four guys who work the line with me. They hate me because I get a lot of female attention. I can't help it that the women there like me," he whined.

"That's nothing new. Chicks come on to you wherever you are," Blue said tightly. He was always flirting with women, making her feel insecure.

"Yeah, well, it works to my advantage when I'm playin' a club. It's just a part of being a performer. But it sure rubs those assholes the wrong way at the factory. Wouldn't make any difference what those dicks thought of me if they weren't buddies with the boss.

But I'll *never* get a break because they're always sucking up to him and he knows they don't like me. So I'm stuck at that job, makin' shit for money with no possibility of movin' up in the company. I'm not doin' it much longer, Blue," he issued. "I might just have to find another way to get bread." He threw his napkin on the plate.

Blue laughed nervously. "Oh George."

"You think I'm kidding, don't you," he said.

"Well, aren't you, G.G.?" Blue asked lightly.

He didn't answer. He just looked at her, eyes cold and hard. She shuddered involuntarily. He lit a cigarette as Blue started to get up. "Are you makin' fun of me, girl?" he questioned.

"No, G.G.," Blue replied anxiously.

"Sit back down here." His voice was stern. She perched her body cautiously on the edge of the chair. "I know you think I'm a loser. You always have. But let me tell you something..."

"You're wrong, Georgie. I think you're the greatest guy in..." Blue fibbed, attempting to coax him out of his anger.

"Shut up! Don't lie to me, bitch! You know how I hate that!" He picked up his glass of water and threw it in her face.

Blue sat in the red-painted chair, water dripping from her chin, stunned. All she could do was look down at her lap. It felt like he had just slapped her – again.

"I'll show you and the rest of the world that I'm *not* a loser. And if my excuse for a father was still alive, I'd show him too!" George pushed back his chair, toppling it over. He put his cigarette out on the tabletop, leaving an ugly, black mark and walked out the back door.

Blue looked at the cigarette burn, wet her finger and tried to rub it away. It refused to disappear. Another mar – another memory, she thought, gazing at it dispassionately. Realizing her face was still wet; she dried it with her napkin. She started stacking the dishes, running water to wash them – then stopped. "I'm not doing this," she said to the dishwater. "Especially for an jerk like him!"

She dried her hands, picked up Muss and carried him to the bedroom with her. She curled up in a tight little ball in the middle of the bed. George was always hurting her, humiliating her – taking his anger at the world out on her. Like a young child, she wept until she fell asleep.

Blue hadn't seen her therapist since the rape, too ashamed to tell Love Mae what happened. In fact, she hadn't told anyone. The rape was an open, seeping wound, lodged mercilessly in her memory. Escaping from her subconscious at night, it took distorted form in her dreams.

She would wake up sweating, her mouth open in a silent scream. Stomach pains plagued her. She avoided going to bed, in anticipation of frightening apparitions. When she succumbed to sleep, it was with the light on. Too weary to fight with herself any longer, she called Dr. Montgomery's office for an appointment.

Love Mae ushered Blue in. "I've been very worried about you," she said without hesitation. "I had a dream recently that something awful happened to you and I trust my dreams. So, tell me what's happened."

Blue looked her dead in the eye and said, "I was raped."

"Oh... my dear girl," she said immediately. "I'm so sorry." Love Mae's voice was heavy with feeling. "It was George, wasn't it?"

"How did you know?" Blue was surprised.

"I just had a feeling that he was going to hurt you, darlin'," she said, reaching over to stroke Blue's hair. "I know his type and I know how vulnerable you are. It was a rape waiting to happen." She reached for Blue's hand. "Can you tell me about it?"

Blue nodded and reported the story, without emotion. When she finished, Love Mae just looked at her for a moment, her eyes shooting sparks of anger. "Blue, I'm mad as *hell* he did that to you! He terrified you, violated you – and then threatened to kill you! You can press charges and put his ass in jail!"

"No, I can't," Blue said meekly. "I still love him."

Love Mae swallowed hard. Every fiber in her body was taut. She wanted Blue to take charge of her life, but trying to force it was not the answer. "Honey, I want you to know something. I was raped too, when I was about your age. It was someone in my family that I knew. I didn't press charges, but I wish I had. So, believe me I understand how rape feels," she said firmly. "Have you told anyone else?"

"No," Blue said. "No one. You're the first person." She felt like a little girl. She didn't want to think about putting George in jail. All she wanted to do was climb in Love Mae's lap and bury her head in her soft, coral blouse.

"Blue, let me tell you about rape," Love Mae said. "It's *not* just a violation of the body, it also defiles the soul."

"What do you mean?" Blue asked, alarmed by her words.

"Every trauma, especially one like yours, forms a layer over your soul," she said, matter-of-factly. "It's a protective reaction to an injury, but at the same time, creates a barrier between you and your soul – like part of your soul is unavailable to you, at least, until it has had a chance to heal."

Blue's eyes filled with tears. "You mean, I don't have a soul anymore?"

"No, Blue. You always have a soul, but it's been wounded." Love Mae got up from her chair and sat down next to her on the couch. "Come here, darlin'. I can see right now that you need a mother." She pulled her close and held her like a baby. Blue could hear her heart beating. "There, there. I know the tears are coming, so cry... just let it all out. We'll heal your soul together."

The dam broke. Blue had been numb about the rape for so long that bursting into tears came as a surprise. She cried loud deep, heart-stopping sobs – long held-in wails. She cried about everything that had ever hurt her. There was so much – a father who'd never really been there, giving away her baby, living like an orphan, a mother who rejected her, Carlos battering her, George brutally raping her, a lifetime of loneliness.

There seemed to be no end to the tears. But eventually, Blue opened her eyes and pulled away. Love Mae was looking down at her lovingly. Blue noticed the big tearstain on Love Mae's blouse. "Don't worry. It'll come out," Love Mae told her. "This one's a veteran. Been cleaned lots of times."

She sat up and blew her nose. The hair around her face was damp from tears. Her eyes were red and swollen. "First time you've cried about the rape?" Love Mae asked.

"Yes." Blue's voice was barely audible.

"We're not going to do anything more today. You're doing the best you can, but you're exhausted. Go home, draw a hot bath and take a good, long soak. Be very, *very good* to yourself. When you feel a little stronger, I want you to write yourself a love letter – as a way to express tenderness and concern for yourself. Come back again this week and

71

bring the letter with you. Okay?" Love Mae's voice was firm, but gentle. "You're in post traumatic stress syndrome and we may have to talk about prescribing you a little medication to get you through this."

Blue nodded and hugged her therapist like she would never let her go. "You're my angel mother," she murmured.

"Everybody needs at least one of those along the way," Love Mae said softly. "Now go home and start that bath water." She gave Blue a kiss on the top of her head.

Blue felt light, like a weight had been lifted. It was the first time she had felt any semblance of happiness in six months. Crying her eyes out had been cleansing, *especially* in the arms of someone who cared.

Blue came home to an empty house. Thank god, she thought. I couldn't *stand* the thought of seeing George right now. She went right to bed and was sleeping when the phone rang. "Hello?" she said. The voice on the other end was unfamiliar.

"Is this Blue Spencer?"

"Yes," she replied tentatively.

"This is the Wichita City Hospital calling you. Your mother, Ruby Spencer, was rushed here about a half-hour ago. We understand you are her only next of kin."

"Yes, I am. What's wrong with her?" Blue's voice filled with alarm.

"She's in serious condition and we think you should come as soon as possible. Just go to the emergency room and tell them who you are."

"Okay. Thank you." Blue hung up and scrambled to pull on her jeans. "Oh my god," she said. "There's something terribly wrong with my mother!" She made it to the hospital in short order, parked in the visitor's parking lot and charged through the entrance doors.

"I'm Blue Spencer," she said breathlessly to the receptionist. The hospital just called me about my mother, Ruby. Can I see her?" The woman was staring at Blue's feet. Looking down, she realized she still had her fuzzy, bunny slippers on and a nightgown tucked carelessly into her jeans. Oh, shit, she thought. She looked at her and shrugged helplessly.

Amused, the receptionist smiled and told her that her mother was in room 105, just down the hall and to the left. "You can go right on in," she told her.

Blue practically sprinted the distance down the hall, the bunny slippers making soft, padding sounds. When she got to the room, there were two doctors and several nurses standing around a hospital bed. Shocked by what she saw, she froze. There was blood everywhere – on the bed, the walls, the floor. She let out an ear-splitting scream.

Heads turned toward the noise. "Who are *you*?" one of the nurses asked.

"I'm her daughter," was all she could manage. Her knees started to buckle.

The nurse quickly took Blue's arm and sat her in a chair. "Your mother's heart has exploded in her chest."

"What!" Blue felt like someone kicked her in the stomach. "Can you save her? *Please*, can you save her?" she shrieked. The nurse quickly escorted her out of the room and tried to calm her.

"When that happens, there's nothing we can do," the nurse explained. "It's like the heart had an attack that was too big for it. She died just seconds before you got here. I'm so sorry." She paused. "You look too young to lose your mother. Where's your father, honey?"

"He's dead too," Blue sobbed. "I don't have *anybody*."

"Oh you poor girl," the nurse said, putting her arm around Blue. "You're all alone. That's just not fair." As they stood in the hallway, the gurney that held her mother was wheeled out of the room and through a set of double doors.

"Where are you taking her?" Blue called to them. But there was no answer, just the sound of the doors swinging back and forth. Blue broke away from the nurse and started running after them. "Wait! Come back!" she yelled. *"I want my mother! Mommy! Mommy!"*

Blue's eyes flew open. Her heart was pounding. Oh my god, it was just a dream, she realized... an awful dream. She grabbed Muss for comfort and squeezed him until he meowed in protest. She heard George downstairs, opening the refrigerator door, and then uncapping a beer. Reaching for the phone, she dialed Ruby's number, just to make sure she was okay. As soon as her mother answered, Blue hung up. Thank god she's alive, she thought.

George slumped in the blue painted chair in the kitchen, resting his arm, beer in hand, on the green tabletop. He was tired. His shift had been short a couple of people, so he had to do double the work. But his mind was racing. He twirled the half-empty Coors bottle with his fingers. There's gotta be a way I can get out of this motherfucking job, he thought. All I want is to make a name for myself in the music business – a *big* name! Now what do you have to do to get there, George baby?

"I've got it!" he said, hitting the table with his fist. "A heist!" He jumped out of the chair and began pacing around the kitchen. "Enough money to be able to leave here, get to Nashville and hire me the most expensive studio and recording artists in that town!"

"You're outta sight, Garret," he whispered, afraid he'd awaken Blue. He downed the rest of his beer and lit another cigarette. There's a lot of bread in the boss's safe, he remembered. I know because I heard him giving the total cash sales for the quarter to the accountant... and it was sizable! If I can find a way to get the combination and a key to his office, I can break into that sucker! He schemed.

But I need a partner. "Denny!" he said, reaching for the phone to call him. He picked up the receiver, and then put it down. "Do you really want to do this?" he asked himself. "Damn straight!" he answered

Blue sat on the bed with the phone to her ear. "I'm sorry, Miss Spencer, but we cannot legally release the information you're requesting. If you will remember, you signed a legal document that prohibits you from inquiries about your son, his welfare *or* his whereabouts," the attorney said sharply.

"Yes, I remember signing a document, but that was almost five years ago," she argued. "I'm not trying to get *custody* of my son. I just want to find out where his parents live. Can't you help me?" Blue said with frustration.

"I'm sorry, Miss Spencer," the attorney repeated. "I'm not at liberty to assist you in any way. Don't call me again about this." There was a click, then a dial tone.

Blue hung up the receiver, her heart dropping to the soles of her brown suede, platform shoes. "That guy doesn't have a compassionate bone in his body," she said dejectedly. George, in the next room, heard what she said.

"Who are you talkin' about?" he questioned. He came and stood in the bedroom doorway, his six-foot frame filling the space.

"I just called the attorney who handled my adoption case. Not only did he refuse to give me the new address of my son's parents, he told me never to call him again." Blue was close to tears. She slowly took off her shoes and let them drop, one at a time, to the floor.

George could see how deeply disappointed she was. "He sounds like a real prick," he commented. "Hey, I'm not playin' anywhere this week-end. I'll take off on Friday and get those records from that tight-ass lawyer. You know me, Spence... just an old hippie. I'll use any opportunity to take on the establishment."

Blue couldn't believe what she was hearing. She looked up at George, "Really, G.G. You'd do that for me?"

"Yep. Consider it done." He gave her one of his winks, the ones that always made her melt.

"Come here, Georgie," she said, holding out her arms. "You deserve a big, sloppy kiss for that." He walked over to the bed and she pulled him down. He fell on top of her and they rolled over, kissing. Blue could feel a warm, tingly flush spreading over her body. They kissed, openmouthed, their tongues seeking each other like hungry eels. George quickly fingered her. Blue began breathing hard and arching her body toward him.

"Ooh baby, you want it, don't you," he said confidently. "You want the best there is." He began taking off her clothes. "Oh girl... you've got those sexy lace panties on," he murmured, tugging at them with his teeth. Taking them slowly down her legs, he pulled them off her feet and went from toe to toe, sucking each one hungrily, like an appetizing morsel.

"Oh, Georgie, do me. Do me good," she said demandingly.

George slowly moved his tongue up her body, starting at her ankles, then to her calves and thighs. He bit gently at the soft mound of hair between her legs He stuck his tongue playfully in and out of her belly button, kissed her breasts and nibbled on her dark brown nipples. "You're not ready for me yet, little girl," he said, teasing her. "You need a spanking first."

"I *am* ready, daddy," she said, acting like his little girl. "I don't need a spanking. I've been good," she protested.

"Oh, I don't think so. I saw you giving some guy a look at the club the other night. I know how you are, you little tease. Now, come on," he told her. "You *know* you have to get spanked for that." He started to turn her over.

Blue wouldn't budge. "No... no spanking. Just have me, George. Have me *now*," Blue insisted, her body craving penetration.

"All right baby, I'll let it go for now. But next time you're gonna pay double," he asserted. Within seconds was inside her, his cock hard and insistent. "Oh, yes... yes," she moaned. "Hurt me G. G. – I want you to hurt me."

George accommodated, but it wasn't enough. "Do me *real* hard," she ordered. He pushed himself into her with such force that she yelled in pain. She let him continue, biting her lip to quiet herself. He climaxed with a guttural sound and rolled off her, reaching toward the nightstand for his Kools. He pulled one out of the pack, lit it and took a deep drag. Blue watched him make little circles of smoke... a ritual indicating his contentment.

But Blue wasn't content. She was frustrated. Ever since the rape, she'd get aroused and want him – but then, when he entered her, something inside just clicked off. It was like turning off a light switch. Mystified by it, she wondered if her body was saying deep down, "I won't... I won't give in."

This was her secret, one she protectively guarded. It was the only way Blue could feel powerful – to shut down and deny George her orgasm. Too occupied with his own climax, however, George never even noticed she was holding anything back. She wasn't hurting him... only herself.

He finished his cigarette, putting it out in the orange, ceramic ashtray by the bed. He turned toward Blue and idly fingered her hair. "Was it good for you, baby?" he asked.

She looked at him through half closed eyelids and lied. "Of course it was, G.G. You're the best." She leaned over and kissed him on the forehead, the bittersweet aftertaste of a lie on her lips.

She curled up beside him. Most of the time he's a selfish lover, she thought, so why do I tell him he's the best? Why won't I be honest... tell him how lonely and empty I feel inside. She felt his body relax. He was asleep and snoring. When it comes to sex with him, she mused sadly, I always feel alone. He never holds me or talks tenderly to me. Carefully moving his arm from around her waist, she quietly slipped out of bed.

Welcome to Ponca City – Population 26,000, the sign read. The sun outlined the horizon as George pulled in. There were few cars on the street. In the distance, he could see a sprawling oil refinery – Conoco Oil Company. He passed by The Ponca Bowl. It was already open. He turned into the parking lot of the Quo Vadis Motel. I'll crash here for a few hours, he thought. He checked into his room, hit the bed and was asleep in minutes.

The voices next door woke him. It was a man and a woman arguing. The man's voice boomed, "You bitch, don't *ever* talk to me that way in public again or I'll smack you seven ways from Sunday!"

The woman pleaded with him. "Aw, Harry, I didn't mean anything by it. It was just a joke. Everybody thought it was funny!"

"Yeah, that's the problem," he retorted. "You had everybody laughin' at me and I don't like being laughed at! You get a couple of brews in you, and it's hard tellin' what's gonna come out of your mouth! So keep it closed from now on, or I'll slap it shut!" George heard the motel door slam and then the sound of a woman crying.

Sounds like the woman's got a mouth on 'er, he thought. Her weeping had little effect on George, except to prompt him to check the time. It was 7:30 p.m. "I guess it's show time," he said, yawning. "I'd better eat something first and wait until dark to do my business." He checked the address of the attorney's office – 605 E. Third Street. He pulled on his jeans and a faded tee shirt with the "Make Peace not War" slogan on the back and walked out the door, heading for downtown Ponca City.

He had no trouble finding the office – *Markus H. Shapiro, Attorney-at-Law* was inscribed on the front door. He circled it, looking for all possible entryways. The office appeared to be an old, renovated brick house. Looks like Markus is workin' late tonight, he thought, noticing a male figure through the front window.

Across the street was the Bum Steer Tavern. He walked in, ordered a shredded ham sandwich, had a few beers, and played darts to pass the time while keeping an eye out for the attorney. He had just emptied his fifth glass of beer when he spotted Markus leaving the building.

It was almost 10:00 p.m. Streetlights blinked on. George's targeted entrance was the back door, partially hidden by several large bushes. He left money for the check, got in the car and took off. Making a left at the stoplight, he drove down an alley to the back door of the office.

There was a single light bulb burning above the door. He threw a good-sized rock at it, hitting it dead center. The glass shattered delicately, flying in all directions. He put on his gloves and used a crowbar to pry the old wooden door open. It surrendered with a groan.

As he walked into the office, he could smell the scent of leather, books and the pale odor of cigar smoke, as if the attorney had just lit one as he was leaving. His pulse was racing. He headed first for the large picture window and closed the blind. Pulling a flashlight from his back pocket, he began looking through file cabinets, under "S" for Spencer. There were Spencers, but no Blue Spencer. "Damn!" he said.

His eye caught a file cabinet in an adjacent room. In the beam of his flashlight, he read, *"Cases Three Years and Older."* He pulled open the unlocked drawer and found what he came for. There was Blue's file and in it everything she needed – the name of her son's adopted parents, their old address in Oklahoma City and their current one in Ponca City. He scribbled the information on a piece on paper, returned the file, shut the drawer and started to leave.

Just as he was walking toward the back door, he heard a noise. He crouched, barely breathing. The noise was coming from outside the building, in the back. "Shit!" he whispered, listening intently. That's all I need – to be arrested for breaking and entering, he thought. As the sounds became clearer, he realized it was just a couple of drunks having a brawl.

He heard someone swearing loudly, then a bottle breaking. The voices began to fade. He opened the door a crack. No one there. He made a break for the car, started it up and drove down the alley. The drunks, blinded by his headlights, held up their respective paper-bagged bottles in salute.

Blue had been waiting for George to come back ever since he left. She was nervous, smoking incessantly as she paced. Muss sat, sphinx-like, watching her walk back and forth. When she stood still long enough, he would rub against her leg and meow loudly, in an effort to distract her in the direction of his dinner dish. To no avail. "Don't bother me now, Muss," she would say, giving him a shove with her foot.

Just as the cat gave up and made a bed of the beanbag chair in the corner, George walked in. "Hey, doll. Your man's home from the hunt – and I got the kill."

Blue stopped pacing, her hands instinctively covering her heart. "How did you get it?" she asked, eyes wide. Did he just hand the information over to you?"

George sat down on the couch, propping his feet on the coffee table. "I was so smooth," he said with certainty. "You would've been proud. I walked into his office a stranger and we left as pals. Even had a couple of beers together." George was enjoying his lie.

"No! You're kidding," Blue said, impressed. "What convinced him to give you the information?"

"I sweet talked him. Played to his ego. Then I offered him money under the table. That was all it took. People can be bought, Blue," he told her matter-of-factly.

"Gosh... I didn't think..."

"Don't you worry your pretty little head about it. It's a done deal," George said, handing Blue the information.

She sat down beside him on the couch and read the hastily scribbled note. "Thanks..."she said gratefully.

"No problem. Anything for ma' woman," he said, putting his arm around her. "Phone number's right there. You gonna use it?"

"I haven't even thought about *that* yet. I'll just be devastated if I ask to visit him and they say I can't," Blue said, tears in her eyes.

"Hey, look at me baby," George said, taking her chin in his hand. "If they give you a problem, you just let me know..."

"Nope," she said without hesitating. "I want to do this myself."

"Okay, kid." He leaned over and kissed her on the top of the head. "Power to the people, baby."

Blue smiled at his encouragement. "Want me to fix you something to eat?" she asked.

"Nah. Not hungry." He reached in his shirt pocket for his car keys. "I gotta go take care of a little business. Don't wait up for me," he said as he walked out the door.

"But you just got home," Blue complained. "And it's three in the morning." Her words fell on deaf ears. He was gone.

Typical George, she thought. I should be used to it by now. But Blue had other things to think about. She now had what she needed to call Naomi and Robert. So there was a real possibility she could see her son. Sleepless, she laid on the couch and stared at the ceiling, thinking about what it would be like to see her son for the first time since she held him almost five years ago. Clinging to her image of their reunion and clutching the information George had given her, she fell asleep.

Denny opened the door. George's persistent pounding had awakened him. "Man, don't you believe in sleep?" he said testily.

"Hey butthole, you won't be sayin' that after you find out why I'm here," George told him. "Let me in, Den."

"Okay, but you'd better be here for a damn good reason," Denny said, opening the door.

"Is one-hundred thousand reason enough?" George asked with a grin.

"One-hundred thousand what?"

"A hundred thousand car radiators, dummy," he said sarcastically. "One-hundred thousand *dollars*, man!" George's voice was full of excitement. "Ever had that much bread in your hands at one time?"

"Okay, Garret. You got my attention," Denny muttered, waking up. "What the hell illegal scheme have you cooked up? How are we supposed to get our hands on all that dough?"

"Easy, Den. We're gonna rob the company where I work. I'm gonna find a way to get the combination to the boss's safe and we'll be home free. I've thought the whole thing out and it's perfect! You in it with me, buddy?" George waited expectantly for his friend's answer.

"Shit, man. I've never done anything like that before. What if we get caught?" Denny sounded worried.

"We *won't* get caught. I know that place inside and out. The only person we have to watch for is the security guard and I know when he goes out of the building to take his break. "It'll be a bitchin' heist! C'mon Den."

Denny was silent for a moment. "Oh, all right," he said reluctantly. "I'm about to lose my house to the bank, so I could sure as hell use the damn cash! But if this thing goes down bad," he added, "you're gettin' a cap in your knees."

"Okay. It's a deal. You can plug me wherever you want," George said impatiently. "You won't be sorry," he promised. "Now, here's what I've come up with so far..."

Blue woke with a start. She had yielded to the old, soft couch – the nagging pain in the middle of her back a reminder she hadn't made it to bed. Muss was curled up in the hollow of her neck. She rubbed her eyes. Today's the day I make the call, she thought. She argued with herself. Why should I call him? It'll just mess up his life. Then Love Mae's words surfaced. *"Finding your son will be the most important thing you will ever do."*

Blue padded upstairs and into the bedroom. The bed was still made. George hadn't been home all night. Her eyes shifted to the phone on the nightstand. "I've gotta do this now – before I lose my nerve," she said. "I wish Love Mae was here to hold my hand." She sat down on the floor, cross-legged, put the phone in her lap, and shakily dialed Naomi and Robert's number. She prayed for it to be busy. It wasn't.

"Hello, this is Naomi Matthews," the voice on the other end said politely. Blue fully intended on speaking, but nothing came out. "Hello?" the voice questioned.

Blue forced the words out. "Hello Naomi. This is Blue... Blue Spencer."

The voice was silent. For hours it seemed. Then Naomi spoke. "Well, Blue. I'm surprised to hear from you, but I've been expecting your call."

"You have?"

"Yes. It's about Jonas, isn't it," she said with quiet resignation.

"Jonas? Is that his name?" Blue asked.

"Yes, Blue. We named him after my father."

Blue could hear a child's laughter in the background. "Is that him laughing?" she asked. Her heart was in her throat. It was her son's voice, her own flesh and blood.

"Yes, that's him. Would you like to say hello?" Naomi asked kindly.

"Oh yes... oh no... I mean... I can't," Blue said, her voice trembling.

"Yes, you can. I'll put him on." Blue heard her instructing Jonas to say hello.

A child's voice came on the line. "Hel-wo?" he said brightly.

"Uh... oh, hello," Blue stammered. "Jonas? How are you?"

"I'm fine," was the answer.

"My name's Blue, Jonas. How old are you?" she continued, desperately hoping questions would keep him on the phone.

"I'm almost five," he said proudly.

Blue felt a lump forming in her throat. Resisting tears she said, "You're a big boy, aren't you?"

"Uh-huh. Are you my mommy's friend?" he asked.

Before Blue could answer, Naomi was telling Jonas to say good-bye. "Bye," he said.

"Good-bye, Jonas. Maybe I'll see you someday." Blue's heart was warmed and aching at the same time. "Oh, thank you, Naomi. Thank you for letting me talk to him," she said gratefully.

"You're welcome, Blue."

"Can I come visit him?" Blue blurted the question she was both longing and fearing to ask. "Just for a few days? I won't bother you. I'll stay in a motel..."

"As far as I'm concerned, Blue, it's all right for you to visit," she said. "But I'll have to talk it over with Robert first. Give me your phone number and we'll call you back in a couple of days. Okay?"

"Okay," Blue said anxiously. She was feeling a paralyzing fear that when they hung up, she would never hear from Naomi again. Then she remembered her prayer, asking God to help her find her son. Hope sifted through her heart like sand through an hourglass.

It was over. The terrifying phone call. Blue pitched herself on the bed and let out a celebrative whoop. Her fingers hurt from gripping the phone and her underarms were wet with perspiration. "Whoopie! I did it!" she yelled. "I really did it! George will be so proud."

But George wasn't proud. He was too distracted to pay any attention to Blue *or* her good news. All he could think of was the heist looming on the horizon. Soon as I can secure the combination to the safe, I'll be thousands of dollars richer, he thought as he cleaned up his work area. All I have to do now is pretend to be interested in that barn-ugly female accountant on the second floor, the one who has access to the boss's safe. I hear she's never been married and is starved for male attention. I'll give her what she wants and she'll give me my ticket out of here.

"Well, I'm gone," George told a co-worker. "See ya tomorrow." But instead of leaving, he bounded up the stairs to the floor where the white-collar offices were located. He peeked around the corner of the accountant's door. "Hi, Miss Hudson... Olivette Hudson?" he asked, grinning boyishly.

Olivette Hudson looked through her out-of-fashion glasses to see who was speaking. "What can I do for you Mr. uh...?" she stammered.

"Mr. Garret – but you can call me George," he said in his friendliest voice. "May I step in?"

"Oh, I apologize," she said blushing. "Please take a seat, if you can find one. Here, let me move that pile of papers so you can sit down." Her office was a jumble of towering stacks of paper, plants that had met a dry death and assorted coffee mugs in need of a wash. There was a filing cabinet in one corner, on top of which was a large framed photograph of a young woman who looked suspiciously like her.

As she picked up the chair's bundle of papers, her hip accidentally brushed George's thigh as he stood, waiting to sit down. "Oh, excuse me," she said, her face turning bright red. Flustered, she backed into her chair and sat down awkwardly, still clutching the papers tightly.

George came to her rescue. "That's gotta be you up there," he said, referring to the framed photograph. "You're a knock-out, Miss Hudson."

"Oh, well... yes, that *is* me," she replied, delighted with his compliment. "I usually take terrible pictures, but that one turned out pretty good." She cleared her throat, trying to regain her professional demeanor. "Now, what can I do for you, Mr. uh, George?"

"This is gonna sound like a weird request, Miss Hudson, but I could use your help."

"Help? What kind of help?" she asked.

"Well, I'm thinking about starting a very small business on the side – a one man operation. But I realized the other day that I don't remember how to keep the books, you know, the accounting part of a business. I wondered if you could refresh my memory. I hear you're very knowledgeable," George said with a sincere tone.

"Well, I've never taught anyone how to do what I do," she replied.

"I'd gladly be your first student, Miss Hudson." George knew he was out of character, humbling himself to a woman. But this was important. If she says yes, he thought, my chances at getting that combination from her will increase a thousand percent.

"Well, it's not standard policy, but I guess I could," she told him haltingly. "But it would have to be right at 5:00, before I go home. I couldn't take time away from my work to teach you," she said, her eyes bulging at him from behind her bifocals.

"I'll be here whenever it's convenient for you, ma'am," he said politely.

"Well, Monday I have a late meeting, but Tuesday would be fine. Make it around 5:15," she told him.

"I'll *be* here, Miss Hudson," George said, giving her a wink. Olivette flushed. As he left the office he could feel her eyes following the contours of his tight jeans. She digs me, he thought, descending the stairs. I'm in like Flynn. Wait till I tell Den.

George had been scarce around the house lately. I'm a fool, depending on him, Blue concluded, as she gathered up dirty clothes for a trip to the Laundromat. He can treat me however he wants and I have to take it... because he's paying the bills. She remembered how Love Mae told her she was trapped being with George. Laura had said the same thing. "But I love him," she had disputed her friend.

"When someone loves you, they don't treat you the way George does," she had said to Blue. "I oughta know."

She pushed Laura's words out of her mind. "I don't have time to think about this now," she said. The truth was, she didn't *want* to think about it. Afternoon sun spilled in the front window and onto the white, plastic laundry basket that was full to overflowing. Blue was carrying it toward the front door when she heard the phone ring. She dropped the basket, spilling bras, panties, George's underwear and socks everywhere. Taking two stair steps at a time, she made it to the bedroom by the third ring. "Hello?" she said breathlessly.

"Blue?" a female voice answered. "This is Naomi."

"Oh, hi," Blue said, trying to sound calm and collected.

"Robert and I have talked and we've decided to let you come and visit Jonas for a few days."

"Oh, Naomi, thank-you, thank-you! When can I come?" she asked excitedly.

"Well, I know this is short notice, but Robert and I are taking a few days off from work next week. Could you come then?"

"Oh, gosh. I'm taking my car in to be fixed next week. But yes... yes, I can come. I'll just take the bus," Blue said, without a second thought. "I'll begin making arrangements right away."

"Could you be here by Tuesday? You could stay until Saturday if you'd like."

"Yes, I can be there by then. If I leave early in the morning, I think the bus will get me into Ponca City by noon."

"We'll pick you up at the bus station," she offered. "Just let us know before you come when your bus will arrive..."

As soon as she put the receiver down, Blue was a woman in motion. "Geez Louise, there's so much I have to do before I leave," she said to Muss. She picked up the cat, tossing him in the air. "Wheeee... oh Mussie, I'm so happy! I'm going to see my son!"

Muss did not share her joy. Translated, his meow said, *"put me down or that tuna you just gave me is coming up!"* Being hurled through space was not his idea of a favorite after-lunch activity.

"Ouch!" she exclaimed, as the only suitcase Blue owned fell on her head from it's perch on the closet shelf. "I've only got three days to get ready and... oh, shit... I forgot the laundry! George will have my head if I don't get his underwear and socks washed." She dashed down the stairs and was busy recovering the spilled clothes, dispassionately lying where they fell, when George walked in.

"Hey, Spence, tornado come through here?" he said, with no offer

86

to help pick up the scattered clothes.

"No," Blue said, not looking up. "I just dropped them when the phone rang. Naomi Matthews called me and..."

George interrupted her. "I'm gonna be out late tonight, jammin' with the band for our gig on Saturday," he informed her, leafing through the mail. "Where's dinner?"

Blue felt a flash of anger. "You're asking the *wrong* person the *wrong* question at the *wrong* time!"

George looked up from the mail. "You're in a *stellar* mood. Jaws tight about something, Spence?" Blue kept quiet. "I thought we had an agreement; I call the shots, you carry them out. Now... where's dinner?"

"There *is* no dinner!" she retorted. "Can't you see I'm busy doing *your* laundry that's all over the floor? But do you lift a finger to even help me pick it up? No! So, why should I fix you dinner?"

"Jesus christ, Blue – get off my back! Wouldn't you call paying the bills helping you? If you want somebody to lick your ass, call up Carlos. *He* can be your fuckin' sycophant! I don't need this! I'm *gone*!" George said, storming out the front door before she could reply.

Blue plopped down beside the laundry basket, bra in hand. "Doesn't take anything for him to go off!" she said angrily. "I know he doesn't *love* me... so why do I stay? Thank god I never told him about the few thousand dollars I still have from my dad, she thought, reaching in her shirt pocket for a cigarette. Love Mae was right when she said I'm like a trapped animal being with George, Blue realized. He treated me nice at first, then got pissed off and raped me. By that time, I was his possession... somebody he could order around. "Dammit!" she said angrily, exhaling a long silent stream of smoke.

"Girl, if you know what's good for you, you'll refuse to let anyone *ever* own you again!" she lectured, pacing the floor and smoking. "And for *god's* sake, watch out for steel traps the next time, so you don't have to chew off your leg to get free!"

Absentmindedly, Blue gathered the remaining clothes. Voices of self-loathing began approaching as faint whispers, but she intervened. "Don't make a bad moment an eternity, Blue," she admonished. "Just get yourself to Ponca City. Everything else can wait, including the damn laundry!"

A loud clap of thunder startled Blue awake. She looked over at George, who hadn't stirred with the noise. Pouring rain was bringing Tuesday morning to the Kansas sky. She bolted out of bed, afraid she'd overslept. The clock said 6:30 a.m. The bus didn't leave until 7:50. Her suitcase was packed. All she needed to do was grab lunch and call a cab. She showered, dressed, gathered her things and tiptoed down the stairs.

Breakfast was the remainder of a half-eaten meatball sandwich George left in the refrigerator. She crammed oversized bites of the cold sub into her mouth. "You make sure G.G. feeds you," she told Muss. "He promised he would." She picked up her furry friend and gave him a big, wet kiss, leaving a greasy spot on his head. "Good-bye, George," she said, closing the front door behind her. The cab she had called was waiting patiently. The driver put her suitcase in the trunk and opened the door for her. She stepped in gingerly. "Greyhound bus station please," she said.

The blue and gray bus sat idling, exhaust fumes adding an acrid smell to the morning air. Blue was standing in line to pick up her bus ticket, when a dirty, disheveled old woman approached her. She was carrying a large, woven net bag over one shoulder, stuffed with the necessities of her life. Beside her was an equally dirty, scruffy dog on a frayed rope, yapping protectively at anyone within a few inches of his mistress. "Honey, you look like a nice girl," she said through chipped, tobacco-stained teeth. "Could you spare some change?" She thrust a grimy, open palm in front of Blue's nose. An unsavory body odor filled the space between the two women. Taught to be polite to strangers in need, Blue started digging through her purse for quarters. "Whatever you have will be much appreciated," the woman continued, as if reciting an often-repeated line.

Blue found four quarters lying at the bottom of her oversized purse and dropped them carefully into the woman's hand. "Thank you, miss. God bless ya," she said. Blue watched her as she shuffled off toward a snack machine. "C'mon Freckles, it's breakfast."

"Do you want a ticket or do you just wanna watch that old woman

88

and her mutt?" the ticket agent asked in an unfriendly tone.

"Oh, I'm sorry," Blue said, embarrassed. "I wasn't paying attention. Yes, I want to buy a round trip ticket to Ponca City."

"That'll be $23.95. The bus leaves at 7:50 sharp. He's on time this morning," the agent said without looking up.

Blue paid for her ticket and boarded the bus. She took a window seat and settled in for the long four-hour ride. As she was sliding her purse under the seat, she heard a male voice say, "Is this seat taken?" She looked up into the face of a person with gorgeous dark eyes and two coal black hair-braids resting on his chest... and a brilliant smile.

He was the most beautiful man she'd ever seen. "No... no," she stammered, irresistibly attracted and feeling shy. He sat down, holding his travel bag as if its contents were priceless. A black hat with a single feather and a colorful, beaded band sat on top of his bag. Blue noticed his hands, long-fingered and brown, were adorned with turquoise and silver rings. He sat quietly, looking straight ahead. Blue's mind was racing. What would a romantic evening be like with *him*, she wondered.

The bus backed jerkily out of its parking space, jarring her out of her fantasy. "What's your name?" he asked, turning toward her.

"My name's Blue," she answered. "Blue Spencer. What's yours?"

"Soaring Hawk," he replied. "That's my Cherokee Indian name. My American name is Richard."

Suddenly the hawk flew across her mind, the one she encountered that day on the bridge. The memory brought a chill, covering her arms with goose bumps. She felt drawn to this man but hardly knew how to talk to someone who treated her so respectfully. "Where did you get those rings you're wearing?" she asked hesitantly.

"I made them," he answered. "One of the ways I support my wife and children and my tribe is by making jewelry. My father taught me the craft before he abandoned his body and joined Great Spirit. I'll pass it on to my sons when I'm old."

He's married... has a family, Blue realized. Her fantasy about leaving George and marrying Soaring Hawk faded quickly, the one where... *they are both dressed in white fringed buckskin at their wedding ceremony. Around her neck is the beaded wolf necklace he's made for her. He's wearing a headdress of hawk feathers. There's a great bonfire. People are dancing and laughing. He carries her lithe body on his broad, strong shoulders – his bride, his Indian princess. She's happier than she could ever imagine. He puts her down gently and they melt into a passionate kiss...*

"Oklahoma state line coming up." The bus driver's announcement ripped through her daydream. "We're stopping for a restroom and food break." The bus slowed and turned into the parking lot of a small restaurant and gas station.

"So, how many children do you have?" Blue asked politely, her heart heavy.

"I have five little ones and one on the way," he said proudly.

"Oh, gosh. You'll have to make a lot of jewelry..."

His laughter interrupted her. "You forget. I have to *work* for a living, you know, a regular job." Everyone had gotten off the bus and they were the only two left. He turned toward her, eyes serious. "Blue, there's something special about you," he told her. "I believe you have much of Great Spirit inside, but you're afraid to share the sacred pipe with it."

"What do you mean?" Blue questioned, taken aback by the personal nature of his comment.

"The meaning is for *you* to discover," he said. "All I will tell you is, don't let your fears cast a shadow over your bright spirit. They will only dim your Light." He paused for a moment. "I'm going to call you Bright Spirit, Blue Spencer – so you won't forget who you really are."

Blue's face must have revealed her happiness, because Soaring Hawk smiled broadly. "Your spirit dances," he continued. "I can see it in your eyes. But your spirit has been wounded, like a bird who can fly, but not without great difficulty."

Blue was embarrassed. This man could see into her soul. "No one's ever given me a name like that before. I like it... Bright Spirit," she pronounced her new name reverently. Several passengers climbed back into the bus as the driver announced their departure. Blue looked out the window, smiling with secret delight.

Ponca City – 25 miles, the road sign read. Soaring Hawk had strategically placed his black hat over his face and was sleeping. In a matter of minutes, she thought, I'll see my son for the first time since I gave birth to him. She played and replayed the scene in her mind.

90

Questions buzzed in her head. Will he look like me? Will that birthmark on his left temple still be there?

The bus turned into the station. Blue wanted to hide under her seat. I can't do this, she thought. I just know I can't. Soaring Hawk awakened. He stretched his legs and turned to her, taking her hand in his strong, warm clasp. "I could feel your fear as I slept," he said. "Just remember that whatever path you are walking today, Great Spirit is walking with you."

Blue looked at him with gratitude. "Oh, thank you." She was about to say more, when something pulled her to look in the direction of the window. There they were – Naomi, Robert and Jonas. The minute she saw Jonas, tears spilled over her lashes and ran down her cheeks. She couldn't take her eyes off the beautiful little boy.

The bus aisle was crammed with passengers waiting to get out. As Blue got in line, she looked up to see a bearded man scowling at the two of them. It was the man who had been staring at her since Soaring Hawk took his seat beside her. "What the hell is a pretty white girl like you talkin' to a dirty Injun for?" he said loudly. She could smell alcohol on his breath. "Don't you know they never take a bath? C'mere sweetheart, talk to a *real* man," he said, as he reached out and pulled her to him.

"Women should be treated with respect, brother," a voice said over her shoulder. "Let go of her arm – now!" Soaring Hawk's voice could be heard throughout the bus. The authority in his voice was unmistakable and no one spoke.

Still holding on to Blue's arm, the man challenged him. "I'd love to take a punch at a slimy ass like you. You make me sick! We should'a gotten rid of ever' last one of you when we had the chance!"

"What you say about my people doesn't matter because I know you're ignorant, but if you don't let go of her arm, you'll wish you'd never met me." Soaring Hawk's eyes were blacker than the night sky. The man would not release Blue's arm. Suddenly, a gurgling sound could be heard as he was lifted off his feet by Soaring Hawk's hand at his throat.

She ducked out of the way of the two of them and headed toward the front of the bus. She paused at the door to look back at her friend. Soaring Hawk had let go of the man and was moving toward the front of the bus. The man slouched in the seat rubbing his neck protectively, looking like a child who'd been punished. No one was offering to help him.

"Keep a cool head, Bright Spirit," her newfound friend reminded her. "And remember – no matter how things look around you, trust Great Spirit."

"I will, Soaring Hawk. Thank you. Bye," Blue replied.

She stepped off the bus and came face to face with her son standing beside his mother, a woman with an ample bosom, full hips and rounded cheeks. For a split second, seeing her with Jonas left Blue teary-eyed and speechless. Robert offered her a handshake. She shook it numbly. Naomi reached out to hug her.

Then the unexpected happened. Jonas stepped away from his mother and extended his arms up toward Blue. She hesitated, as if questioning her right to respond. She looked at Naomi for permission. She nodded and Blue lifted him into her arms.

It was all too much. Blue broke into a sweat and her knees went weak. She collapsed onto the pavement, taking Jonas with her. When she came to, there were hands everywhere – checking her pulse, wiping her forehead, and loosening her belt. Jonas and Robert were gone. Naomi was bending over her. "You fainted, Blue. Just lie still for a few minutes."

"Oh my god, where's Jonas? Is he okay? Did I hurt him?" she asked, grabbing Naomi's arm.

"Jonas is fine. He just has a tiny scrape on his arm. The two of you didn't have far to fall. Robert's is looking after him." Naomi's voice was comforting.

"I'm so sorry," Blue exclaimed. "I have low blood sugar and if I go too long without eating, I can faint. I packed a lunch, but I was too excited to eat it."

"Well, we'll get you something. Let me help you up," Naomi said.

"Thank-you," Blue said, getting to her feet. She had been so exhilarated about the prospect of seeing Jonas, but now all she felt was fear. Perceived or real, it was rearing its unsightly head, convincing Blue to bolt and not look back. Like a gargantuan bird, Soaring Hawk's words unexpectedly swooped into her mind. *"No matter how things look around you, trust Great Spirit."* She took a deep breath.

Today was it – the *coup de Gras*. George had finished four accounting lessons with Olivette, who by now was completely enamored with him; today's would be the last. With flowers in hand, he was going to ask her out. And she would say yes. He was sure of it.

Finishing his shift, George cleaned up in the restroom. He combed his hair and splashed on Brut aftershave. You're a handsome devil, he thought, smiling at himself in the mirror. He walked down the street to a nearby florist shop and made his purchase of two-dozen white daisies. Pleased with his choice of blooms, he sauntered confidently up the stairs to Olivette's office.

Reviewing his plan, he imagined... *I'll walk casually into her office, give her the flowers along with my most dazzling smile... ma used to tell me I could charm the musk right out of a muskrat with my pearly whites. She'll accept the posies with a blush. I'll be an attentive student. Shower her with compliments. Then I'll ask her if I can take her out for a drink – to thank her for all her help.*

Wearing his most dimpled smile, he looked into her office. No Olivette. Shit! he thought. He laid the daisies on a chair and walked to a neighboring office. He stuck his head in the door. "Hey, where's Olivette today?" he asked the attractive young girl.

"Oh, she didn't come in this morning. She took the day off. And Miss Hudson *never* does that," the young secretary said, flashing a flirtatious smile. "Oh, are you Mr. Garret?" she asked, suddenly remembering Olivette's message. He nodded. "I'm so sorry. I was supposed to tell you that Miss Hudson wouldn't be in today."

"That's cool," George said casually. "I'll just catch her later. Thanks," he replied, giving the young girl a once-over. She smiled, eyeing him seductively.

He went back to Olivette's office and picked up the bouquet. Then it hit him. If I can find out where she lives, he thought, I'll just show up on her doorstep. He tried opening her desk drawer. It was locked. He rifled through papers in piles on her desk. Nothing. He spotted a magazine on top of her file cabinet. He turned it over and there it was

– a label with her home address on it.

I know exactly where that street is, he thought. This was a much better idea – making a special trip to give her flowers. It would make Olivette think he really appreciated her. "George my man, you're a wizard!" he uttered, under his breath. She's got the combination to the safe, he thought. She's told me where she keeps it. And if I play my cards right, I'll get it... easy.

During one of their lessons, George had used his charm to get Olivette to talk. Predictably, she let it slip that she carried the combination to the company safe around in a locket she wore all the time. Inside the locket was a tiny piece of paper with the numbers that opened the safe.

"Hey, where ya goin' in such a hurry?" a co-worker called out as George practically sprinted out of the building.

"Home. To my woman. She said she's got a surprise waitin' for me," George lied as he hurried out. "Keep the faith, man." But Blue was the last person on his mind. All he could think about was Olivette and the locket around her neck.

It was 5:30 p.m. "It's too early to drop in on her. The bitch is so ugly, I gotta wait until dark," he said, laughing at his own joke. He bought liquor at a state store, and then stopped at a beer joint on Wichita Avenue to wait. Sipping his Coors, he fantasized... *I'll tell her how beautiful and sweet she is. Treat her like a queen... tell her I can't understand why someone hasn't snatched her up already.* George was taking pleasure in his scheme.

Then... god, I hope she drinks, he thought. He continued his fantasy. *I'll get her drunk and start kissing her. She won't be able to resist me. I'll make a game of it.* He tipped his glass for the last drop of beer. *We'll take our clothes off. Then I'll tell her she has to take everything off, including the locket. She'll be so turned on that she'll do anything I ask. I'll fuck 'er until she begs me to stop,* he continued. *I'll hold her, whisper sweet nothings, pretend to be interested in her. Tell her what a great lover she was. Then I'll leave, give some excuse about why I have to go – and the locket will go with me. When I see her at work, I'll return it. Just tell her I walked out with it by mistake. She's so naive, she'll believe me.*

He turned down her street. The brick, ranch-style house at the end of the block was hers. He pulled into the driveway. With flowers and liquor in hand, he rang the doorbell. He heard a woman's voice ask, "Who is it?"

"It's George... George Garret," he replied. "I stopped by to see my favorite teacher."

There was no answer for several moments. Then he heard one, two, three locks unlock. Olivette Hudson opened the door with a slight frown on her face. "How did you find out where I lived?" she asked.

"Uh... well, I just happened to see your address on the back of a magazine in your office. I... I came to give you these," he said, handing her the daisies. Her frown transformed into a toothy smile. "I'm diggin' standing out here talking to you," George said sweetly. "But do you think I could come in?"

"Oh, dear. I've done it again," she replied, a flush reddening her face. "Please, come in. And thank you for the beautiful flowers. I can't remember the last time... I'll go put them in a vase," she said, walking into the kitchen.

"It's just a little appreciation for all your help, Miss Hudson," George said.

"Oh, please, call me Olivette," she told him.

"I brought you another surprise," George cooed, following behind.

"Oh, Mr. Garret, you shouldn't have."

"Please Olivette, call me George." Standing beside her, he pulled a bottle of tequila and a package of margarita mix out of a paper bag. "Did you know that I'm known all over the state of Kansas for my exceptional margaritas? But I only make them for people who are very special to me. Like you," he said, with a wink.

Olivette, captivated by his compliment, let the glass vase filled with flowers slip out of her hands. It made a clanking sound as it hit the side of the white, ceramic sink. "Here, let me help you," George offered, picking up the vase and putting it on the counter. "This one," he said, pulling out a single bloom and snapping it off its stem, "is the one that goes in your hair." He playfully put it behind her ear. "Go look at yourself... in the mirror," he instructed.

She gazed, entranced, into the mirror that hung on her dining room wall. What she saw was a younger version of herself – blushing, eyes bright. George was making her feel that way. What *he* saw was a fortyish woman, with frizzy, overly permed hair, a mouth barely covering a set of protruding front teeth, and a nose that would look far better on a man. I'm going to have to get sloshed just to be able to do this, he thought.

"You know, I have a beautiful sister," Olivette said abruptly. "Her name's Rochelle. Younger than me. Growing up, people would tell my parents how pretty she was," she told him, dabbing at a blemish on her chin. "Then they'd look at me and tell them what a smart little girl I must be. I was an ugly duckling next to her," she informed him, arranging stray hairs. "I still am." Her voice was tinged with sadness. "Boys were always asking Rochelle out. But not me... I never had one single date. I was too homely for them... the boys, I mean."

George was touched by her honesty. "Hey, I can understand what you're saying, Olivette. My brother was better lookin' than me when we were kids – smarter too. I felt like a real geek next to him. But none of that matters now. He's dead," George said flatly.

"Oh, I'm sorry," she offered. "It must have been terrible to lose your brother."

"Yeah, it was. He was killed in a railroad accident... decapitated. I saw the whole thing. But I don't want to think about stuff like that right now," George said, coming up behind her, lifting her hair and kissing the back of her neck. Her skin was malodorous. "Let's not talk about things that are downers," he said, trying to ignore the way her body smelled. "I'll make you forget you ever *had* a sister."

"Mr. Garret!" she said, feigning disapproval. "I don't think we should be doing this. We have a *professional* relationship. And besides, I hardly know you."

"You're right, Olivette," he said, acting chagrined. "I don't know what came over me. As you were talking, I was looking at your beautiful neck... and I... I just couldn't resist," he told her apologetically.

"Hey, I know what you need," he suggested, turning her around by the shoulders. He could feel her hunger for a man's touch. "Let's chill – have a drink and some laughs. Forget the heavy stuff. You got any limes?" he asked.

"I think one or two maybe," she said, peering into the refrigerator's crisper.

"That'll do. Lead me to your blender. You sit down," he said, pulling a kitchen chair out for her, "and let old George be your personal bartender for the night." With a flourish, he started mixing the margaritas, adding a generous amount of tequila. At high speed, the blender frothed the light green liquid, grinding ice into tiny pieces. "Salt?" She nodded yes. "Then I'm ready to pour, madam," he said gallantly.

They sat on the couch, sipping. "I'm not a drinker, but I could become one," she giggled, feeling the effects already. This is the best margarita I've ever had."

"I told you I was the best. The next one will be even better," he said smoothly.

"Really?" she asked, sounding like a teen-ager.

"Uh-huh," he replied. He leaned over and kissed her neck, traveling toward her ear with his mouth. Jeezus, what am I getting myself into? he wondered.

"Ah... oh," she gasped as his tongue thrust its way into her ear. "Please, George. I don't think you'd better..."

"I'm sorry... damn. I'll stop. But you're just so *irresistible*," he whispered huskily. "It's hard to keep myself under control around you, Miss Hudson," he sweet-talked her.

"No one's ever accused me of being too irresistible, Mr. Garret," she told him. "I'd like to believe you but..."

"You stay put," he interrupted her, "and I'll make us another round." George gave her a peck on the cheek and got up to make more drinks. "These had better be doubles or I'm gonna lose my cookies," he mumbled to himself, pouring the tequila into the blender.

"Did you say something about *cookies*, George?" Olivette inquired. It was becoming clear she was on her way to serious intoxication.

"I was just saying that I bet you make the best damn cookies in the world," he called out from the kitchen.

"How'd you know that? I make great peanut butter cookies... it was my grandmother's recipe." She was silent for a moment, and then changed the subject. "You know, George, you're the first man who has *ever* made me feel even remotely attractive. I bet you have women all over you," she said, her words noticeably slurred.

"The only woman I want all over me is *you*," he said, handing her another drink.

"You know you don't mean that," Olivette took the drink with a sad smile. She didn't sip this one. She gulped it. "I shouldn't be doing this, you know. I'm respected in this community. I go to church every Sunday. If Pastor Cleveland saw me now, he'd be very, very shocked." She got up unsteadily and walked toward the stereo. "But Pastor isn't here so dance with me, George," she instructed him.

"No, sweetheart," he said, grabbing her arm and pulling her onto his lap. "You know what I want to do right now?"

"What, you studly man," she asked sloppily.

"I want to play a real cool game," he answered, setting up his next move. "The object of the game is to see who can get their clothes off first," he explained as he slowly unbuttoned his shirt. "And I bet I beat you." He lifted her off his lap and laid her down on the couch.

Olivette was so drunk by now that everything he suggested was peachy with her. George began kissing her neck and breasts. Through her thin dress and bra, he could feel her chest. Her tits feel like hard, little lemons with nipples, he thought, nibbling one of them with his teeth. "You ready to play our little game?" he asked her seductively.

"Oh, yes... yes," she said, seeking his mouth hungrily.

Kissing this woman is like kissing a goat, he concluded, as he bussed her full on the mouth. Skip the foreplay, man – just get it over with, he thought. Fuck her and get out the door.

His shirt was off. "Now it's your turn, Miss Hudson," he told her in a singsong voice. "Take off that dress," he instructed, helping lift it over her head. "Now, I'm next." He stood up, unzipping his jeans and watched her eyes travel down his body as he pulled the tight denims off his long legs.

"Ohhh... Mr. Garret," she said with reverence, as he revealed his jockeys and the generous bulge behind them.

"Your turn, teach," he kidded her. "Off with the bra and panties." He reached around and unhooked her brassiere, releasing her small breasts, and then slid the white, cotton underwear down her cellulite-ridden legs.

"Oh, George, you're seeing me in my birthday suit," she said, childlike. "I've never let anyone..."

"Let me be the first, then, my love. With your gorgeous body, guys would be givin' their eyeteeth to be in my place right now," he lied.

"You're just saying that because you feel sorry for me," Olivette said petulantly. "Oh, what the heck. Lies work. Get me another drink, Georgie. And take off that underwear, so I can see what you've got," she ordered.

Fuck man, he thought. This is bitchin'. I've got her right where I want her. "Whatever your heart desires, doll face. But you better be sure you're ready for this," he teased, referring to his privates. Not waiting for an answer, he went to the kitchen and began pouring straight tequila into two glasses. She won't know what hit her with this, he thought. "Here I come," he said, slipping off his boots, socks and underwear. There was no answer.

George walked into the living room – a buck-naked Adonis. Olivette was lying on the couch, nude and spread eagle. Passed out. Her smallish breasts were flattened on her chest, nipples flaccid. Her right leg was sprawled halfway off the couch, creating a clear view of her private parts. Her belly protruded from her torso. Her head was turned to one side, mouth open. And she was snoring.

George stood over her for a minute, trying to keep from laughing. "Olivette?" he called. No answer. She was out cold. "There really is a God," he quipped. "I don't have to fuck this woman now." I can simply open the locket, he thought, copy the numbers and close it back up. She'll never know.

He knelt down and very carefully opened the heart-shaped locket. Inside it was a folded piece of paper. He took it out and wrote down the combination on his arm. Olivette stirred, snorting and turning her head to face him. Oh, jeezus, don't open your eyes, he panicked, putting the paper back in the locket. As he closed the metal heart, it made a distinct clicking sound.

She roused. "George?"

"I'm right here, baby. You're just taking a little nap."

"I feel funny... so dizzy." She fell back into unconsciousness.

He got up and gathered his clothes. George had a handsome body – long legs attached to a muscled pair of cheeks. "Where are my damn cigarettes?" He said, looking around the room.

"George?" her plaintive voice interrupted his search. "Where are you?"

Terror struck. "Here. I'm here," he said, coming over to the couch.

"Kiss my titties, George. They've never been kissed until you..."

Obeying, he leaned over and placed his mouth on her nipples, sucking them until they became firm, like little sentinels. He looked up at her to see if she was conscious, his mouth still servicing her breasts. She moaned once, became still and started snoring again.

This is my chance. I'm bookin', he thought, moving quickly. I got what I came for. Dressed, except for his boots, he tiptoed toward his exit. Pausing at the door, he looked back at Olivette's naked body. He must have had a twinge of conscience, because he covered her up with a nearby afghan. Carefully unlocking the door, he let himself out, jumped in his car and started the engine.

If the music thing in Nashville is a bust, this could be my back-up career, he thought, as he drove away. "George the gigolo," he remarked proudly. "Damn, I'm good!"

When he arrived home, the house was dark. It was 11:30… not too late to call Denny, George thought, turning on the light in the kitchen. He reached for the wall phone. After four rings, a voice answered sleepily, "hullo?"

"Den. Hey bro, it's George. Got news that'll wake anybody up, even you. I've got the combination to the safe right here in my hand. It's easy street from here on out."

"Do you share all your news flashes in the middle of the fuckin' night? What time is it anyway?" Denny asked, unhappy about being awakened.

"Hey, it's time to get rich, Den. What's a little lost sleep when we're gonna be rollin' in bread!" George said excitedly.

"So I take it Miss Hudson produced," he said in the middle of a yawn.

"Did she ever. It was perfect. The old girl made it so easy. By the time I got ready to make my move for the locket, she was passed out cold."

"No shit, man? What the hell did you do to her, knock her out?" Denny asked.

"Hell no. I didn't do anything. All it took was three of my famous margaritas and she was an inanimate object," George said, laughing. "I didn't even have to *take* the locket. Just copied the numbers off the piece of paper inside it. Then I split. She was snoring when I left."

"George, you're somethin'", Denny said. "Nobody else could pull that off but you. I'm impressed, man."

"Listen," George said. "*Anybody* could do it with Olivette. That's the hungriest woman I've ever met. I felt sorry for her. I should' a fucked her. I don't think she's ever had a man."

"Hey, you're gonna have a hard enough time shakin' her off *without* fuckin' her. As far as she's concerned, she's got a new boyfriend,"

Denny said. "Mark my words."

"No way. Olivette and me are history," George retorted.

"Hey, man. I'll bet you a hundred dollars that girl's not finished with you yet," Denny warned.

"I'm not worried," George boasted. "I'm quittin' that shit-eatin' job, takin' the money and goin' to L.A. or Nashville... where the action is."

"When we doin' the deed?" Denny asked.

"In about a week. When the boss's on vacation. But, hey, in the meantime, we gotta get together and go over our plans again, down to the very last detail. Blue's in Oklahoma, so why don't you come over tomorrow night and we'll put our heads together."

"Sounds good. Now, will you let me go back to bed?" Denny implored.

"Sure man," George replied. "Sweet dreams – or better yet, have a wet dream."

"Yeah, right," Denny replied. "I haven't had a sweet dream *or* a wet dream since Nam. See ya tomorrow."

Blue had been with Jonas for three glorious days. "Oh Jonas, you goose," she laughed. They were on the floor in his bedroom, playing. She was helping him make a pair of dog-ears and a tail out of brown construction paper. "You're the most fun," she told him, cutting out an ear. "I'm taking you home with me."

Blue stopped short, realizing what she had just said. Spontaneously; from her heart. Being with her son for less than a week was fueling the fire of her imagination. Like storm clouds silently forming, Blue fashioned a fantasy – she and Jonas against the world... just the two of them. It was only natural they should be together.

With a howl, the little boy ran toward Blue and fell into her arms, knocking her backwards. "Oh Jonas, you're a heavy one," she said laughing, letting herself fall so that he was lying on her chest. The two of them were still – Jonas with his head resting close to her face and Blue with her arms around him.

Savoring every second, she remembered an earlier time almost five years ago, when she held her newborn son in her arms. "Jonas," she said softly. He looked at her. "You were *never, ever* a mistake. You were just a surprise." Not understanding what she was telling him, Jonas, still playing dog, just barked.

Naomi's voice broke the spell. "Jo-nas. It's time to take your medicine, like a big boy. You know, the syrup you love?" Neither Jonas nor Blue stirred. "Jo-nas?" she repeated. Jonas was an asthmatic child and had been taking medication for his condition since he was a year old. It was by no means a cure. He would have it all his life.

"You'd better go take your syrup, my little goose," Blue said as Jonas lingered in her embrace. Naomi opened the bedroom door and saw the two of them in each other's arms. A look of surprise passed over her face. She quickly covered her feelings with a smile.

"Hey, little man. Playtime's over," she told him with an air of authority. Jonas scrambled out of Blue's lap and obediently followed his mother. Blue sat there, feeling the hollow vacancy that replaced Jonas's little body... and the aching emptiness in her heart.

Tomorrow she would be leaving with no idea of when or if she would see her son again. Oh, mom, she thought. If only you had cared enough to come to the hospital to get us and take us home. He wouldn't be living with strangers, he'd be *mine*. Tears spilled onto her cheeks.

Blue spent a restless night, tangled in the bedcovers and her recurring dream – the one about giving Jonas to Naomi and Robert. She awoke, sweaty and crying. It was 3:15 a.m. The house was still with sleep. She got out of bed and went to the bathroom. Without thinking, she walked down the hallway to Jonas's room and opened the door carefully, tiptoeing to his bed. The moon was full and its light surrounded Jonas with a numinous aura.

He was lying on his back, head turned slightly to one side. Tendrils of dark hair, dampened from sleep, clung to his temple. Blue couldn't help reaching over to lightly stroke his cheeks. He was breathing softly. She knelt down on the floor beside his bed. She gazed at her son for a long time before she climbed in beside him. And in the light of an Oklahoma moon, the two of them slept and dreamed until morning.

The journey home was lonely. Blue sat very still, as if frozen in her seat. This time there was no Soaring Hawk. It was just as well. She wanted to be alone with her thoughts. Images of minutes ago flooded her... saying good-bye to Naomi and Robert. Leaving Jonas. The pain was so deep her heart hurt.

Arms that had fiercely embraced her son, now ached with emptiness. She could still see his little hand waving to her as the bus pulled away. Resting her body against the window, Blue curled up in a ball, legs drawn up against her chest, head down – and wept.

Four hours passed. Passengers talked and laughed. The bus made its usual rest stops. People got on and off to stretch and relieve themselves. Blue, in bellbottom jeans, a lavender tee shirt and denim-jacket, didn't move. She laid on the seat in a fetal position, pretending to sleep. Through tear-swollen eyes, she stared vacantly at the orange and red fabric of her seat and the littered floor beneath her.

The bus made its final stop. Blue was home. More than likely George'll be gone, she thought. There won't be anyone to talk to... about how I'm feeling or what it was like to be with Jonas. I can't pick up the phone and call mom, she realized sadly. Ruby didn't want to hear about her grandson or even admit Blue had ever birthed a child.

She caught a cab and rode home in a funk. Typically friendly with cabbies, today she didn't say a word. Why did I go there, like some baby sitter? she wondered. To watch *them* raise him? I can't have him... can't even borrow him. You went there, idiot, she thought, because you like punishing yourself... wanting what you can't have.

It was times like this that Blue allowed her inner demons their wild dance. Harsh, judgmental voices in her head sang a song of shame passed from generation to generation in her family. The demons distracted her from the pain of loss. Their litany beckoned – fuck a stranger, get drunk, drop some bad acid, have a fight with George, hurt yourself. One brand of pain to replace the other... anything to fill the void left by Jonas.

Mussels was the first and only one to greet her at the door. "Hello Muss, you big charmonsky," she said, nuzzling him. "I missed you.

I guess *you're* my baby... the son I never raised." She put him down and climbed the stairs to the bedroom. The suitcase fell where it was dropped. With little strength to fight her demons, Blue retreated under the bedcovers and there she slept the rest of the day.

It was Jonas's face that appeared when she woke up... his smile, that little birthmark on his temple, hazel eyes peering out from underneath long, dark lashes. Images of the two of them together raced through her mind like flashcards. Too distraught to linger with any one scene, Blue made the images go quickly, like an old silent movie where the actors moved fast and jerky.

What stopped them was a sudden pounce from Muss onto Blue's big toe protruding though a hole in the bedcover. Blue yelled as his razor-sharp teeth penetrated her soft flesh. "Ow, Muss! You're mad at me for goin' away, aren't you?"

In the stillness that followed, a door opened and shut downstairs. Men's voices, one obviously George's and the other his friend Denny's. "Blue?" George yelled. "You here?"

Why should I answer him, she thought. If he really cared about whether I'm here or not, he'd come looking for me. George ran up the stairs and into the bedroom, to Blue's surprise.

"Hey Spence," he greeted her. "When'd you get back? And what are you doin' in *bed*, woman?" He perched on the edge of the mattress, leaned over and gave her a kiss on the mouth. He smelled like pot. "Hmm... like kissin' a dead fish," he said flatly. "What's wrong with you?"

"I don't know where to begin, G.G.," Blue said sadly. "All I can tell you is that I miss Jonas like crazy and I wish he was here with me right now."

"So you had a good time, huh?" George said, glancing at the bedside clock. It was clear he was not listening.

Blue just looked at him. "Yeah George, I had a real good time. That's why I've been in bed all day... because I had such a good time," she said sarcastically.

"Hey man, we'd better get goin'. It's almost five o'clock," Denny yelled from downstairs.

"Fuckin'-A. Let's do it," he yelled back. He gave Blue's breast a squeeze. "Later, girl – just you and me. Keep the bed warm."

Blue disregarded his advance. "Where are you going in such a hurry?" she asked.

"We got some business to take care of – down at the club," he lied. "Don't expect me till late," giving her no time to probe further.

"We got everything we need?" Blue heard Denny ask.

"No, man. I gotta get the..." George said, lowering his voice so Blue was unable to hear. A few minutes later, she heard the front door slam and her car drive away. What's he driving *my* car for, she wondered.

"They're up to something," she said to Muss. "I just know it."

"Let's check our equipment, Den. We got two pairs of gloves?" George asked. They were parked in an alley, a safe distance from the factory.

"Yep," Denny replied.

"Blue's nylons?"

"Yep."

"A crowbar?"

"Uh... I don't see it."

"You dumb fuck. Didn't you bring it?"

"Here... here it is."

"A flashlight?"

"Yep."

"The blow torch?"

"Yep."

"The bag for the money?"

"Yep."

"You got the combination to the safe, George?"

"Shit! Where'd I put it?" he said, looking at Denny helplessly.

"*Now* who's the dumb fuck," Denny retorted.

George searched frantically through everything they'd brought with them. "Goddammit, where is it? Wait a minute... my Kools," he said, reaching in his shirt pocket. "I slipped it in my cigarette pack."

"Jeezus." Denny breathed a sigh of relief.

"All right," George said. "Let's boogie. Remember our plan. As soon as the security guard goes on dinner break, that's when we make our move. *Comprende?*"

"Got it."

"You watch for him," he instructed. "When he walks into that restaurant, you signal me. Then we know we've got exactly twenty minutes to do the job."

"What if he decides to eat somewhere else?" Denny asked. "Or what if he brown bagged it today?"

"Will you put a clamp on it?" George told him. "This guy's as predictable as piss. You worry like a woman!"

The two split up. George waited by the back door and Denny walked to the front of the building to watch for the security guard. In a few minutes, he gave George the signal. The back door was locked, as they'd expected. Both men were strong, especially Denny, from daily weightlifting. The taut muscles in his neck strained as he pried at the lock with a crowbar. Veins in his rock-hard biceps popped out as he used everything he had to prevail against the metal door. It wouldn't budge.

"Time for the blow torch," George said, aiming the hissing blue flame to the lock. After a few minutes of heat, the door's lock gave way. With gloved hands and heads encased in Blue's nylons, the two men ran straight for the offices on the second floor. "How in the hell do women wear these things?" George complained as they climbed the stairs. "I can't fuckin' *breathe.*"

"They don't wear them on their *heads*, asshole," Denny quipped.

George laughed. "We'd better get serious, man. We only have thirteen minutes before the guard finishes his break." Denny forced the office door open with the crowbar. This one was much easier, a cheap, hollow wooden door with a single lock. It surrendered with little resistance.

"Okay. Now to the safe." George pulled out the piece of paper with the combination on it. "Here Den, hold the flashlight so I can see." He read the numbers as he turned the safe's lock. He overshot the last number and the door to the safe would not release. "Fuck!" George said, spinning the dial to start over. "How much time do we have left?"

Denny was getting nervous. "Nine minutes, pal."

He tried it again. This time the door swung open. Denny shined the light into the dark space. There it was – all that money in neat, tidy bundles. Both men stared, wide-eyed. "Wow – just like in the movies, man," Denny said.

"Yeah, well, you may be watchin' movies in the *slammer* if you don't hurry up and give me the money bag," George said sarcastically. Still in shock, Denny didn't move. "Don't just *stand* there, fool! Hand over the bag!" Together they shoved the bundled money into the sack. "Let's split!" George said.

They sprinted down the stairs and across to the hallway that led toward the back door. George pulled the black nylon off his head as he ran. "This thing's too fuckin' hot, man." He hastily stuffed it in the back pocket of his jeans. Or so he thought. As he pulled his hand out of his pocket, the nylon came with it and floated gently to the floor.

"We got two min..." Before Denny could finish, they heard someone whistling. Then footsteps. They ducked around a corner. The footfalls stopped, as if the person was listening very intently to something. George and Denny held their breath. Then the footsteps and the whistling started again, growing fainter as the guard turned down another hallway.

They looked at each other. Beads of sweat had broken out all over Denny's face, making a strange, eerie pattern underneath his nylon. "God dang," George laughed. "I wish I'd brought my camera. You are one *ugly* mother under that stocking!"

"Fuck you, man," Denny retorted, pulling off his nylon as they ran to the back door and out onto the street. The sky was darkening and no one seemed to be around.

"The gods are with us," was George's comment. They threw their equipment and themselves in the Volkswagen and took off. "Blue would be pissed if she knew I was usin' her precious Saffron as a getaway car," he chuckled.

"Just don't get us a ticket, man," Denny told him.

After driving a mile or so, neither one could stand it anymore. They locked eyes at the same time. "Far fuckin' out, man!" they yelled in unison. George had to pull into a parking space, they were laughing so hard. "I knew we could do it!" he exclaimed. "When you've been through Nam, robbing a safe is easy-schmeezy!"

"I was sweatin' it," Denny admitted. "I didn't know if that son-of-a-bitch metal door was gonna budge! And I thought for sure the guard heard us. Shit man, my heart was in my mouth!"

They had tucked the bag of money safely in a large toolbox in the front-end trunk of the Volkswagen. Nylons and gloves were off. Now they were just a couple of guys out for a spin "Hey, Den. I could use a T-bone steak – rare. How about you?" George asked. "You wanna hit that... uh, place... what's it called?"

"Kansas City Chop House?" Denny offered.

"Yeah, that's it."

"I could eat a whole cow."

A half a mile down Kellogg Avenue, they wheeled into the parking lot of the restaurant. "I still can't believe what we just did," Denny said as George cut the engine. "Besides dope, I haven't done anything this illegal for a long time. My pop would *kill* me if he found out I stole this much money... or anything for that matter!" he told his friend. "He'd introduce my ass to a two-by-four!"

"Your pop *won't* find out," George said firmly. "We left no fingerprints and nobody saw us. It was a perfect heist." They were silent. "Are you sorry you went in on this with me, Den?" George asked.

"Nah. This ain't no big thing. The only situation I've ever regretted was watchin' my buddies die in Nam – and not bein' able to do jack about it," Denny said without hesitation. "And wipin' out a whole village of slant-eyed kids and their folks. *That's* what I'm sorry about," he said. "Not this."

George reached over and squeezed Denny's hand. "I know, man – only too well." They got out of the car, realizing that going further with their conversation would just bring them down. The two walked into the crowded restaurant and took a seat next to a window to keep an eye on the booty in Saffron's trunk.

The two friends consumed their steak dinners with a relish – complete with salads, garlic bread, fried potatoes and sides of cottage cheese. The taste of money, after all, couldn't help but enhance the already flavorful meal. They washed it all down with a few beers. Denny belched. "Bed's gonna feel real good," he said, wiping his mouth with a napkin.

"Yeah, no shit," George agreed, lighting up a Kool. "But first, I got a reward waitin' for me when I get home. I get to poke ma woman before I turn in."

"I dunno where you find the energy, man. Just the *thought* of pokin' somebody peters me out." Denny's mouth took on a slow grin, enjoying his play on words. "When are we splittin' up the money?" he asked.

"Tomorrow, partner," George replied. "I'm feelin' rich already. Nashville, baby, here I come!"

The pictures arrived on a Saturday. George and Muss were napping on the couch. Blue let out a whoop that could be heard all over the neighborhood. Tearing open the envelope, she seized the photographs like someone who'd been starving and just found food.

"Shit, Blue," George complained, awakened by the noise. "You woke me up! What the hell's going on?"

"Far out!" she exclaimed, ignoring his complaint. "They sent the pictures of Jonas and me! Oh, wow, look at these. Here's the one of us at the park... my beautiful boy, and me" Blue said proudly. "Oh G.G., don't you think he's just the handsomest, most wonderful little guy in the world?" she exclaimed. "I can't believe it's been only two weeks since I saw him."

"Put a lid on it, will ya?" George growled. "I gotta get my beauty rest." Blue was so excited she hardly noticed his irritation. Lately, she was immune to George's verbal slights. Ever since Jonas, she'd even thought of leaving him.

She spread the pictures out on the coffee table like precious gems. God, seeing my boy again makes me happy, she thought. I'll make a Jonas and Blue scrapbook – one for him and one for me, she decided, examining the array. After looking at the photos, she put them away carefully.

As she straightened the coffee table, her eye caught the front page of the Saturday paper lying in disassembled sections. She picked it up. The headline read, "Investigation Of Heist At John Deere Company Continues." She scanned the first paragraph and realized it was the company George worked for that had been robbed. The article said that two men had successfully cracked the company's safe and had taken as much as $100,000. The article further stated that the police and a group of employees from the company were conducting the investigation, but so far, they had no suspects.

"Gee zooey!" Blue said, shocked by what she read. This happened just about the time I came home from Ponca City. I wonder why George didn't tell me? She questioned. Wait a minute, she thought. The night George and Denny were at the house they were anxious to

111

'take care of some business.' Then George came home late that same night, she remembered, in an unusually cheery mood and woke me up for sex.

"Oh, Blue. C'mon. George is slick, but he's not a thief!" she exclaimed. But it *does* seem like he's been spending money more freely lately, she mused. He even bought me a dozen roses the other day. And for no reason. George *never* does that. She tore out the article and stuck it in between page fifty-eight and fifty-nine of *Lady Chatterley's Lover*. And in the book is where it stayed because Blue put the whole thing right out of her mind.

"It feels to me like you're getting stronger," Love Mae said with a smile. Blue had called for an appointment to talk about Jonas. It was clear to Love Mae that she had become a surrogate mother to her client... the only older woman Blue could talk to about her life.

"I *feel* stronger," Blue said confidently. "I think I'm starting to realize there's more to life than George. I have my son now."

"Oh?" Love Mae questioned. "What do you mean you have your son?"

"Well," Blue said, backtracking. "He's not *with* me, but I visited him a few weeks ago. Oh, Love Mae, Jonas looks just like *me*," she said excitedly. "He's got hazel eyes, just like mine, with the longest eyelashes." She pulled the photographs out of her 60's looking cloth shoulder bag. The colorful, shabby bag was covered with buttons, each one touting a different slogan – "make love, not war", "freak freely," "flower power." Blue thrust a photo in front of her. "See, here we are... the two of us."

Love Mae saw that Blue was in love – with a son she couldn't have. "Are you glad you went to see him?" she asked gently.

"Oh, yes! But when I left I got so sad, I felt like hurting myself," she said, her voice lowered in shame.

"So you wanted to hurt yourself because you were sad?" Love Mae asked.

Blue nodded yes and hung her head. Two tears dropped on her short, chartreuse polyester skirt. "I wanted to hurt myself because I was mad that I gave him up in the first place. The feeling that I wanted to take him home with me was so strong. It just seemed... you know...

natural. He's *my* baby, after all. I brought him into this world," she said. Blue looked at Love Mae, eyes full of defiance.

Love Mae's heart sank. She realized in dismay that encouraging her client to find her son could've been a mistake. Blue's fantasy about reclaiming him was all about filling the void in her life.

"Blue honey, look at me," Love Mae said. "I know we talked about how important it was that you find Jonas, so that you could let go of your shame about how he was conceived. And it sounds like you had a wonderful time getting to know him. You must've felt real joy for the first time in your life."

"I *did* feel joy, Love Mae. I really did." Blue replied.

"That's wonderful, my dear. You're probably going to get mad at me for saying this, but you can only offer him the love of a friend. Down the road, if and when his parents tell him he's adopted, he'll understand that you are his biological mother as well as his friend.

Remember, Blue, Jonas is not *your* little boy anymore," she emphasized. "He's a baby you conceived and gave up after three weeks – to two people who love him and are raising him until he grows up and leaves home. The only real connection you have to Jonas is that you gave him life and he's fifty percent of your gene pool."

She watched for her client's reaction, her eyes compassionate. Blue looked like she'd been shot. Her face blanched, then flushed with anger. "How can you say that to me? You were the one who told me to *find* him!" she exclaimed, tears in her eyes. You tricked me!" she accused her therapist. "I thought *you*, of all people, would understand! I asked George and *he* said I could get a lawyer and get Jonas back if I wanted!" She paused, her face crimson with intensity. "I've got rights as his real mother!"

"Are you thinking of his welfare – or yours?" Love Mae challenged.

Blue glared at her, refusing to answer the question. "You're just like my *mother*!" she said, jumping out of her chair. "She doesn't want me to be happy either." Gathering up her photos, which had spilled onto the floor, she stomped out of the office. "I'll *never* see that damn bitch again," she mumbled audibly, as she stormed by the receptionist. "Never!"

"Miss Spencer?" the receptionist called out to her.

Blue slammed the door, especially hard, behind her.

Love Mae leaned on the secretary's desk, addressing her bewildered assistant. "Don't worry, Beatrice. She'll be back... when she lets what I said to her sink in."

Blue flew out the front door of the building and marched down the street like a little napoleon. Red-hot anger was all over her face and she was mumbling under her breath. "Shrinks reel you in. Tell you what to do. And you trust them. Then they fucking betray you! She tells me to go find Jonas and after I do, she tells me 'he's not my son anymore.' She's a goddamn liar!"

Blue was so upset; she forgot she'd driven to her appointment. She walked all the way home in a fury – at least five miles or more. Once inside the house, she collapsed in a torrent of tears. "What have I done?" she wailed. "Tortured myself by being with a son I can never have?"

She tore at her clothing, scratching her arms with her fingernails, revisiting the pain of a decision made years ago that she couldn't undo – and it was making her crazy. Love Mae's words swirled in her head. *"He's not your son anymore... he's not your son anymore."* Truth came crashing down around her, and she couldn't stand the sound of it.

Three weeks had passed since the robbery. Rumor now had it that someone from inside the plant was the ringleader. The employees had been assisting the police in their investigation. George was one of the first to volunteer – to make himself look good. He also had an alibi. That's where Blue came in.

The security guard on duty the night of the robbery had been questioned repeatedly. All he could tell the police was that he thought he heard something, but didn't see anyone. He confessed he hadn't looked very hard. He was fired for negligence of duty. George caught him on his way out the door of the factory. "Geez man, I'm sorry they fired you. It's not fair. I'd like to find the scum bags who did this!"

"Yeah, you and me both! I'd still have my job if this hadn't happened," the man answered.

"Did you see *anything*?" George asked, trying to determine whether he and Denny had gone unnoticed.

"Nope. Nothin' and nobody. I guess I just screwed up," he said, looking down at his shoes. "That's a real bummer! I've got three kids to feed, and no job now."

"Good luck, man," George said slapping him on the back. He didn't respond. George watched him walk away, feeling a second of guilt. He hadn't anticipated an innocent man would be fired because of this. Well, he rationalized, shit happens.

Poor Olivette was questioned as well. After all, she was the only one, besides the president of the company, who had the combination to the safe. She was horrified at being interrogated by the police. One question the police had asked was keeping her awake at night. *"Did you ever give anybody an opportunity or tell anybody about the fact that you have the combination to the safe?"*

"Not that I recall," she had answered. The fact that she lied to protect George was making her so nervous that she had broken out in hives all over her body. She was literally covered with the ugly, red bumps.

It was obvious George had wrecked havoc. A security guard lost his job. One hundred thousand of the company's money was missing.

Poor Olivette was besieged by hives. And not only that – she'd fallen for him and he'd broken the poor woman's heart.

George felt an additional moment of guilt. He'd used Olivette to get the combination, and now she was smitten. Jeezus! I'm a real cad, he thought. But I can't worry about any of them, or I'll do something stupid, like take the money back.

I gotta plan for Nashville, he thought, and the best way I can make it big in the music business. I've got fifty thousand dollars in my duffel bag at home, just waitin' for me. Another couple of weeks and this town will be history. In the meantime, he thought, I've gotta firm up my alibi with Blue...

"Hey girl. How about you and me going out to eat somewhere," George asked Blue, walking in the front door and throwing his lunch bucket on the chair. She was stretched out on the couch reading, Muss asleep on her stomach. No answer. "Lady Chatterley? It's your red-hot lover. Got any time for *me*?" George came over and took the book out of her hands.

"Dammit, George. Now I've lost my place," Blue complained. As he took the book from her, the newspaper article fell from its' hiding place on page fifty-eight. They both looked at it. George picked it up. "What's this?" he asked, turning it over.

Blue tensed. "Oh, that? I just tore it out of the paper the other day, to show you. I forgot I put it there."

"Investigation of Heist At John Deere Company Continues," he read. Oh, this is old news," he said smoothly. "A couple of idiots decided to rob the plant. I'm on the investigation team. Didn't I tell you?" he asked.

"No," Blue said. "You didn't. Has the team uncovered any clues yet?"

"Just one," he replied. "A woman's nylon. The police figured they wore them over their heads. They didn't find the other one, though. Oh, they're hot to solve this case all right. It'll be a feather in the cap of the WPD, cracking a case for the John Deere Company." George paused, lighting a cigarette. "Some of us are helping the cops question the employees," he said candidly. "They get pretty nervous bein' questioned, even when they're not guilty."

"Are... are they going to question you – even though you're helping with the investigation?" Blue asked hesitantly.

"Without a doubt, my sweet. Everyone is a suspect. But when they do, I'll have a solid alibi," George said confidently.

"What is it?"

"I was here with you, babe. Don't you remember? We were fuckin' each other's brains out – all night long." He gave her a kiss to seal his story. "So if the police decide they want to talk to you, just tell them we were together that night. Okay?"

"But... but, we weren't together until late that night. You woke me up, G.G.," she protested.

"Spence. Listen. Do you know *exactly* what time I came in? Do you?"

"Well, no. I didn't look at the clock," she confessed. "But it must've been after midnight, because you woke me out of a deep sleep."

"You nitwit!" George said. "You have no concept of time. Denny and I went out to get something to eat and came right home. Den hung around here for a while, and then split. I ended up staying downstairs for two or three hours. Smoked a joint, watched some TV, then came upstairs... and made sweet love to my baby," he said, nuzzling her. She giggled. "Do you think you can remember to tell the cops that?" he asked. "Can you?" He began tickling her.

Blue was an extremely ticklish girl. She let out a yelp. "Stop it, Georgie. Stop! I'll pee my pants if you don't quit!" she threatened.

"Promises, promises," he said, launching into more tickling.

"Pleeease. Stop. I can't take any more. You're hurting me!" she squealed.

George looked at her for a moment and quit. "All right. I can see that my old lady doesn't want to have any fun!"

"It's not that, G.G," she protested. "You just don't know when to stop."

"So," he said, holding her face in his hands. "Are you going to give the cops an alibi for your man, or do you want to see him go to jail for something he didn't do?"

"I'm going to tell them the truth – that you were with me, like you said."

"That's my good girl. You know, even when a person doesn't have an alibi, it *don't* mean he's guilty," George said.

"What exactly *is* an alibi?"

"An alibi, my love, is a corroboration by another person that somebody was with them at a specific time at a certain place."

"Oh." Blue paused. "You wouldn't... I mean, *steal* would you?"

"Baby, the only thing I've ever stolen in my life is your heart," George said, kissing her.

"Oh you think so, huh? You didn't steal it. I gave it to you.

"And that was your big mistake. Right?" George said, assured she would disagree.

She looked at him, as if searching for something to say. An unfamiliar voice inside her spoke. "There *are* no mistakes, George. Only lessons."

George reached for his Kools. Searching for his lighter, he said, "You might be right 'cause I've sure made plenty of mistakes in *my* life. So, that must mean I've learned all my lessons by now."

"And when the lesson's finished," she continued, "that's when you leave the other person's life." Blue was shocked by her own words. Where's this coming from? she wondered.

"Well, aren't we the philosophical sage today?" George said sarcastically. "If you wanna leave me, Blue, you know where the door is. Ole' George won't stand in your way."

"I'm famished," Blue said, changing the subject. "Your offer still good for dinner?"

Sure enough, George was right. Two officers showed up at the door a few days later, around 3:00 in the afternoon. Blue was home alone when she saw the cruiser pull up in front of the house. "Oh *shit*," she said. She didn't trust the police. George had convinced her they hated hippie-types and were always looking for reasons to arrest them. She glanced around to see if there was any drug paraphernalia in sight. A dried-out, half-smoked joint was in the ashtray and George's favorite pot pipe was lying next to it. She ran to the bathroom, flushed the joint and jammed the pipe in a box of cereal that was sitting open on the kitchen counter.

There was a knock at the door. Sliding into leather sandals and pulling her hair back with a barrette she answered it, a little out of breath.

"Wichita police, ma'am," they said. "We're here to ask you some questions. Can we step in for a minute?"

"Oh, sure. Come right in," Blue said graciously, opening the door. Mussels chose that moment to make a mad dash for the outside, right between one of the officers' legs. Blue made a dive for him, grabbed his tail and pulled him back in. He yowled in protest at his humiliating capture. "That's enough out of you, young man," Blue said, shutting him in the bathroom as the two men watched.

"Sorry. He can be an escape artist sometimes," she apologized. "Would you like to sit down?"

"No thanks, ma'am. We just need to ask you a few routine questions," they responded politely. "About the robbery down at the John Deere farm equipment company on June 13th. Have you heard about it?"

"Yes. I read about it in the paper," Blue answered. "What a shame. Do they...?"

"Were you at home that night?" one officer interrupted Blue.

"Yes sir. I was here all evening," she replied nervously.

"Alone?" the other officer asked.

"No sir. I wasn't alone." She'd been rehearsing her answer since George instructed her. "My boyfriend George was with me. All evening. We live together... that's not against the law, is it?" she asked innocently.

The officer half-smiled as he wrote down Blue's words. "We're not here to investigate your living situation, ma'am. So the two of you were here together all evening?" he reiterated.

"Oh, yes sir," Blue lied. "George always comes straight home after work... because I'm such a good cook." The officers looked amused. "I'm very domesticated," she informed them. "I know he expects supper – and it's there, on the table, every night. You know, they say the way to a man's heart is through his stomach..." Blue was nervously rambling.

"Did he leave at any time during the evening – *after* supper, for instance?"

"Well, sometimes he does. But not *that* night," she said, thinking fast. "You see, it was our anniversary and well, after fixing his favorite meal, it was *so* good and he was *so* appreciative that he carried me up to the bedroom and..."

"That's okay, Miss Spencer," the policeman interrupted. "We don't need to know the rest. We just wanted to confirm what Mr. Garret told us about his whereabouts that night. Thank-you for your... uh, generous cooperation." The officers put on their hats and started to leave.

"Sure," Blue replied. "Anytime."

One of them turned around as they were leaving. "What *did* you fix for dinner that was so good?" he asked curiously.

"Oh, just one of my fabulous specialties – meat loaf with twice-baked, cheesy potatoes, almond green beans, flaky buttermilk biscuits and double-fudge chocolate cake with mocha icing," she answered, her eyes sparkling in response to his interest.

"He's a lucky man," he said.

"Let's go, Mike," the other officer advised.

"Thanks for the compliment," Blue beamed at the inquisitive cop. "I think he's lucky too." She watched them pull away and closed the door. He was cute, she thought. Too bad I had to lie to him. Muss was meowing to be released from his lavatory prison. She freed him, scooped him into her arms, flipped on the television and flopped on the couch.

120

I was fibbing like a teen-ager, she thought… like that story about it being our anniversary. She stared at the television disinterestedly, worrying that what she said to the police would come back to haunt her somehow. She ruminated about George, wondering if what *he* told her about that night had been a lie, too.

I *don't* know exactly what time George came home, she fretted, but I'm positive it was late, long after I went to bed. Recollections of the evening flooded her memory. She remembered George and Denny stopping at the house and being in a big hurry to go "take care of some business." She remembered how they lowered their voices so she couldn't hear what they were saying. She recalled several pair of black nylons, washed and hanging in the bathroom, that conspicuously disappeared.

"But why would G.G. take my nylons?" she wondered out loud. The answer rolled across her mind like spring thunder… the newspaper article… the black nylon the police found. "Oh, my god, George… you couldn't," she said to the four walls. "You just wouldn't…"

Olivette squeezed the final drop out of the dented, now empty silver tube. She dabbed the ointment the doctor had prescribed on the last hive she could reach, the one amidst all the cellulite on her right buttock. A bottle of anti-anxiety medication was sitting on the kitchen counter waiting to be refilled. She downed the last one with a swig of canned pineapple juice.

She left the office early because work had been hell lately. She couldn't concentrate, knowing George was downstairs in the plant. She itched constantly and everywhere, scratching herself, embarrassingly, in her most private places. She was in constant fear the police were going to know she'd lied to them.

To keep from pacing the floor, Olivette called her friend Phoebe. "What if the police find out I didn't tell the truth… that I was covering for someone?" she asked in a worried tone.

"I don't know, Ol. Do you suspect the guy did it, I mean – robbed the company?" her friend questioned.

"If he did, I'm the biggest sucker on the block!" she retorted. "I was passed out cold after three margaritas. Anything could've happened and I would've never known it. Even though the locket was around my neck when I woke up... and the combination was in it, he could've copied it."

"Ollie, you *never* drink. The condition you were in, he could've done *anything* to you!" her friend exclaimed.

"I know," Olivette admitted. "Phoebe, I have a bigger problem. I think I'm in love with George. I haven't been able to stop thinking about him and the way he makes me feel. I've gotta find a way to..."

"Vette!" her friend interrupted. "You sound like you're obsessed with this guy. You'd better come to your senses. He's probably already got a woman – maybe two!"

"I don't care," Olivette told her. "I'm going to find a way to get that man into my bed, if it's the last thing I do!" She was dogged in her determination and desperately horny. "He's going to make love to me, hives and all! And if he refuses, I just might have to stop protecting him and go to the police."

"This doesn't sound like you at all, Ollie. This guy could screw you and you might end up dead! You don't know *what* he might do," her friend warned her.

"It's just that I've never been in love before... never had a man pay attention to me like he did," Olivette whined. "Now that someone has, I want more – a lot more! I've waited all my life for this."

Phoebe was silent. Finally, she spoke. "Can I say something to you as your best friend?"

"Of course you can, Bee."

"You're pretty naive when it comes to men, Ollie. You know that. So *please*, be smart about this guy," her friend pleaded. "Try and read between the lines. I don't believe he's all you think he is... and I don't want to see you hurt."

"I know you don't, Phoebe, but I'm *sick* of my dull, boring life! It's time I take a chance... go after something I want! Listen. I know you love me, but don't worry," she reassured her friend. "I'll be okay."

"Famous last words, Ol. Hate me if you must, but I don't think this guy has any intention of loving you..."

"Hey," Olivette interrupted, "I've gotta run to the pharmacy to get my scripts refilled. I'll call you later."

As soon as she hung up, Olivette called George at work. "George Garret, please," she said, disguising her voice.

"I'll have to take your number and have him call you back during his break. We can't pull people off the line," the receptionist said politely.

"My number is 978-0052," she told her. "Please have him call me at his earliest convenience. Thank-you." She hung up quickly, and then hurried to the pharmacy and back, hoping she wouldn't miss his call.

Olivette heard the phone ringing as she opened the door. That's him! she thought. She rushed to answer, slinging her purse, its contents and her purchases in all directions. "Hello?" she said, trying not to sound breathless.

"Hello." The voice on the other end *was* his. "This is George Garret. What can I do for you?" She could tell he didn't recognize her voice.

"Mr. Garret?" she said, her heart pounding. "This is Olivette Hudson. I'm calling you in regard to the robbery investigation. I need to talk to you about it. I thought perhaps you could help me – since you're on the investigation team."

"What can I help you *with*?" George sounded puzzled.

"Well, I really can't tell you over the phone. Would it be possible to meet this evening? At my home?" Olivette held her breath, waiting for his answer.

"Uh... well," he stammered. "I'm working overtime tonight, but I guess I could come over after I get off. Around nine."

"Oh, good. That would be perfect. You remember where I live, don't you?" she asked sweetly.

"Yeah. I can find it again. No problem," he said, still sounding perplexed.

"Okay. I'll see you at nine then."

"Okay." They hung up.

Olivette raced to the bathroom to examine the current state of her hives and to begin the arduous task of covering them with make-up. I'm gonna be ready for him this time, she thought. I've got a pair of tight cigarette pants I've never worn and a low-cut blouse. And I'll wear that push-up bra my sister gave me. I'll wash my hair, shave my legs and polish my nails. "What else, Ollie?" she asked, peering at her reflection in the mirror. "What else can I do to tempt this man?"

123

She left her question unanswered, trusting that further inspiration would reveal itself at the appropriate time. By eight-thirty she was ready. The house was cleaned, a pitcher of vodka Collins was chilling, Frank Sinatra crooned from the stereo, and a fog of sickeningly sweet perfume trailed after her. "Okay, George Garret," she said. "You're in for an unforgettable evening – and this time I'm gonna be completely conscious!"

It was nine o'clock straight up. There was a tentative knock at the door, as if the person knocking hoped it wouldn't be heard. But it was. Sitting next to a door makes *not* hearing a knock highly unlikely. Olivette waited for the sound again. Then she answered, opening the door with a dramatic, sweeping gesture. "Mr. Garret. Please come in."

George looked at her, shock registering on his face. "Olivette?" he asked stupidly.

"The one and the only," she replied gregariously. An earlier vodka Collins was having its desired effect. "Thank you for coming. I know you must be exhausted, working overtime."

"Nah, you get used to it," he said, unable to disguise the uneasiness he was feeling. George was obviously uncomfortable returning to the scene of a previous misdeed. She motioned for him to sit. "What, uh... is this meeting about?" he asked, sitting down and crossing his long legs.

For the moment, Olivette ignored his question. The tables are turned now, Mr. Garret, she was thinking. You're playing in *my* court tonight. She disappeared into the kitchen and returned with a tall glass of vodka Collins, garnished with an orange slice and a cherry. "Here you are," she said proudly. "I taught myself to make this just for you."

"Thanks," he responded, accepting the libation hesitantly. Just my luck she added strychnine to it, he thought.

"It's a vodka Collins," she volunteered, noticing his reluctance. She poured herself one and sat down on the edge of her chair. "Cheers," she said, reaching over to clink their glasses. "Now. You asked me a question and I've gone and forgotten what it was."

This was a new Olivette, George noticed, – a woman who spoke with certainty and self-assurance. He cleared his throat and repeated himself. "Exactly what's this meeting about?" he asked, dragging on a Kool and still avoiding his first sip.

"Oh, yes... of course. I suppose you know that the police have questioned me about the robbery," she informed him. "It seems I'm a key figure, because I'm the only one, besides the president of the company, who knows the combination to the safe."

"Uh-huh," George mumbled, flicking the ash off his cigarette into the nearby ashtray Olivette had placed by his chair.

"You haven't touched your drink," she chided. "You don't believe I can make a decent Collins, do you?"

"Oh, no. It's not that at all. I'm just not very thirsty right now," George fibbed. "I'm sure it's more than decent," he said, taking a sip.

"Well? What do you think?"

"Extraordinary," he replied, giving her a wink.

"Why thank-you, Mr. Garret," she laughed, lapping up his praise. "Where was I? Oh, yes. I thought you might want to know that the police asked me if I had ever given anyone the opportunity or told anyone that I had the combination to the safe."

"What's that got to do with me?" George asked, shrugging his shoulders.

"Nothing I hope... other than I told *you* where I kept the combination. And I *did* pass out the evening you were here... so, uh... what I'm saying is... I don't really know *what* happened that night," Olivette said coyly.

"Are you implying I had something to do with the robbery?" George asked, sounding insulted.

"Not at all. I'm sure you wouldn't have done a thing like that. You don't steal money, Mr. Garret. I can tell. But... nevertheless, when the police asked me that question, I lied. I told them I hadn't let *anyone* know where I kept the combination. But I had." Olivette paused dramatically. "And now I know why I lied to the police."

"You do?" George asked, leaning forward in his chair.

"Uh-huh. I was *protecting* you."

"*Protecting* me? From what? I had nothing to *do* with the robbery," he stated flatly.

"I know you didn't. Even so, I couldn't tell them that you knew where I kept the combination," she explained, "because of what happened the night you were here. You know, sometimes information leaks out..."

"Look, Miss Hudson, I don't need your protection," George said coolly. "Thanks for the drink, but I've gotta split." He uncrossed his legs and stood up. "I'm pretty beat and I have to get up early tomorrow."

"Oh I understand," she responded quickly. "But how about another Collins before you leave? For the road. I spent *hours* learning how to perfect these. Please, just one," she begged.

"All right," George acquiesced, not wanting to piss her off. "I guess one more can't hurt." Olivette poured the remainder of the mixture into his glass. She walked to the kitchen, moving her hips freely inside her snug cigarette pants. The alcohol was making her feel very sexy and self-assured.

"George, I think I'm in trouble," she blurted as she poured his drink. "Big trouble. And the *real* reason I asked you over tonight was to help me get out of it." I'm pulling out my big guns, she thought. I hope he buys it.

Shit! I've really gotta get *out* of here, George thought. Pronto.

"What kind of trouble?" he asked cautiously, sitting down again, this time on the edge of his chair.

"*Man* trouble," she answered, sauntering over to him and plopping herself on his lap. She loved the bravado drinking gave her. She could say anything – do anything. "You see, I'm in love with a guy who hardly knows I'm alive. And I don't have any idea what to do to get him to pay attention to me. So I was hoping you could give me some tips. How *does* a woman like me get a guy to notice her?" she asked, sliding her arms around his neck, her misshapen proboscis only a few inches from his.

"Olivette," he said, grimacing and pulling away from her. "I'm no good at things like that. Why don't you ask a girlfriend?" He got up, almost dumping her from his lap. "I really have to go now. Blue's waiting." The words slipped out before he could stop them.

"*Blue? Blue who?*" Olivette's face darkened as she spoke, the corners of her eyes narrowing.

"My old lady. That's who." Maybe that'll stop her, he thought, irritated with her unwanted advances.

"You have a *girlfriend?*" she asked, visibly hurt. "You got me drunk the other night, seduced me, had me take my clothes off – and you have a *girlfriend?*" Her voice was laced with anger and disbelief.

How could I be so stupid, he thought. I should've *never* agreed to this meeting. He began to make his exit. Olivette cut in front of him, preventing his escape by flattening herself against the door. Oh, god, he thought. I've got a real drama queen here.

"If you have nothing to say to me, George Garret, I've got something to say to you!" She lowered her voice to almost a whisper. "You know *how* I'm gonna get that guy I'm in love with to notice me? I'm gonna tell him that if he *doesn't* notice me, in fact if he doesn't *make love* to me when I ask him to, I'm going to have to tell on him.

"Now *what* am I going to tell?" she said in a threatening tone. "And *who*? For one, I'll have to call his 'old lady' and tell her that he's been unfaithful. And for two, I'll have to tell the police that someone *did* know where the combination to the safe was kept besides me – and his name is George Garret. And he's been a *bad boy*," she said, pushing out her bottom lip in a pout.

George knew she had him. "Are you *blackmailing* me?" he protested anyway. "The innocent, shy, sweet accountant who..."

"Shut up, George! It's my game now. I'm horny, lonely and hung up on you and I *will* have my way. Unless, of course, you'd rather talk to the police down at the station than stay here and make love to me..." she said, sidling up to him.

He wanted to wallop her, knock her out, make her stop talking. You'd really get your ass in a sling if you did that, Garret, he thought. The best thing for me to do is play along. Give her what she wants. "Didn't you know, Miss Hudson, the *only* thing I'm interested in," he murmured, slipping one hand underneath the cup of her push-up bra and the other between her legs, "is making your pussy happy?"

That was all Olivette needed to hear. "Oh, George..." she sighed, putty in his hands. Suppressing a groan, George picked her up and carried her to her bedroom. Nothing could've prepared him for what happened next.

As soon as her body touched the bed, Olivette was a woman of purpose, flinging clothes everywhere. Before George had the chance to undress her himself, she had stripped off her pants, pulled her blouse over her head and relieved herself of her underwear – all in a single motion.

She practically ripped her panties in her hurry to remove them. And her bra went flying across the room, landing in a corner to rest there until morning. The bed became a trampoline – stark naked, her lemon-sized breasts bobbed and bounced with every movement. She literally jumped onto George and began making strange, animal-like sounds, biting him indiscriminately and tearing at his shirt.

George was amazed, especially since he'd seen and heard just about everything that could happen in a bedroom. She bit, she clawed, she growled, she snorted, she panted, she writhed, and she drooled. Falling to her knees, she reverently worshipped his erect member. I guess this is what it's like when someone hasn't had any for thirty years, George concluded.

Olivette surrendered her body to him like a young virgin. She offered her breasts, presenting them like succulent fruit to be devoured. She squirmed and moaned, demanding he caress her sumptuous buttocks. Arching desirously toward him, she was a dam bursting, a flower opening, a geyser gushing... a woman in heat.

Olivette's antics in bed were laughable, but George played along. "You're some chick," he said, trying to keep from cracking up. He knew better than to make fun of her. If this woman's not sexually satisfied in every way, he thought, her threat about going to the police is gonna stick around like a bad hangover. I've gotta do this, for my future – for Nashville.

After several hours of copulation in every conceivable position and numerous, noisy orgasms, Olivette was satiated. When it was all over, her body continued to make involuntary movements – jerking and twitching. George lay on his back, sweaty and spent. "Oh... Mr. Garret, you were *wonderful*," she crowed. "I could get addicted to this. I've never... never had..." A noise made her stop mid-sentence. She looked over at George. He was snoring.

How can he fall asleep... the nerve! Oh well, she thought, I don't care. I got what I wanted – and there's more whenever I have the urge. You've made a deal with the devil, Mr. Garret, she thought. We have an agreement. I keep my mouth shut as long as you service me. Ollie honey, you've struck gold!

She was tall with stringy, dishwater blonde hair. Blue barely noticed her or her live-in lover before today. But she *had* noticed the couple's white German shepherd dog, who routinely used their lawn as a bathroom. Blue liked dogs, but not their droppings on her grass. This morning was the last straw. The leggy blonde was out with the dog, watching him defecate on the edge of their front lawn. "This is gonna stop, dammit," she complained to George, peering out the living room window.

"Aw, Blue. Leave 'em alone, for god's sake," he told her, sipping his Saturday morning coffee. "They seem like okay people. Don't start with neighbors. Things can get ugly."

"*I* wasn't the one who started it!" Blue yelled as she marched out the door. By this time, the dog had finished and owner and canine were heading back toward their front porch. "Excuse me. *Excuse* me!" Blue shouted. The woman stopped and turned around. "My name's Blue Spencer and I'm absolutely *certain* you know that your dog uses our front lawn as a toilet."

"You're *kidding*," the woman answered sarcastically. "Well, it's only been a couple of times. And your old *man's* never complained about it," she continued, walking back towards Blue. As she got closer, Blue saw needle marks on her arm. The woman noticed her stare and folded her arms across her chest.

"My old man doesn't complain because *he's* not the one who mows the yard," Blue retorted. Now face-to-face, she noticed the woman looking at her in a peculiar way – almost as if she was sizing her up. "Please try not to let your dog use our yard as a bathroom – okay?" Blue felt her face flush with embarrassment as the woman's eyes traveled up and down her small frame.

"Sure, no problem," the woman said smiling. "Look," she offered, putting out her hand. "My name's Sonnie. Sorry about the dog. We'll do better. Hey, why don't you come over for a beer and some munchies later today, around 5:00? I'll make it up to you... fix my outrageous nachos." Her offer caught Blue off guard and she accepted the invitation before she knew it.

Walking back home, she thought, I don't even *like* this woman. Why did I say yes? She opened the front door, still wondering what just happened. "George, will you come with me to the neighbor's house for a beer?" she asked. "She invited me over today at 5:00 and I don't want to go by myself. I saw track marks on her arm. I'm sure she's shooting up."

"You're having a beer with the woman you just wanted to punch?" he chuckled. "Sorry babe, you're gonna have to do the neighborly thing without me," George said, between bites of toast. "I got rehearsal from 4:00 until whenever we're done."

"Great," Blue pouted.

"Listen Spence, Sonnie and Jimmy are heroin addicts. They go to the clinic every day to get their methadone. She's not gonna hurt ya," he told her.

What am I doing? Blue thought, as George was talking. I'm living with a guy who smokes pot every day, raped me, probably sleeps with other women and treats me however he wants. And *now* I find out I'm neighbors with a couple of heroin addicts. This is *not* what I had in mind for my life, she lamented.

Blue started cleaning the house to get her mind off her troubles. She absentmindedly washed the dishes stacked in the kitchen sink, barely noticing the dishwater turning a pinkish color. Then came a stinging pain. She jerked her hand out of the water to see blood dripping from a cut on her finger. "Damn," she cursed. She ran to the bathroom, holding the bleeding appendage under cold water.

Her bloody finger was the last straw. I just can't *take* this anymore," she cried, as tears tumbled over her eyelids. "This is no life, no life at all..."

After a good sorry-for-herself cry, several cigarettes and a nap, Blue kept her reluctant promise to her neighbor. After all, she thought, I *am* a woman of my word.

"Come on in," Sonnie yelled from the kitchen as Blue knocked, peeking through the screen door. "Door's open." A white German shepherd bounded into the room and was nose to nose with Blue, barking and snarling. Sonnie came striding toward the dog and hit him so hard, he yelped. "Stop it, Wolfgang!" she yelled. He slinked away, tail between his legs. "Sorry. He thinks he owns the place. It's the

Shepherd in him," she said, holding the door open for Blue.

"Does he bite?" Blue asked cautiously.

"Not usually. He went after Jimmy once, when he and I were fighting. I guess he was trying to protect me. Another time I got so mad at him I threw him down the stairs. Nearly killed the poor dog. But that's when I was still shootin' up… before methadone – when we were crazy," she said with a laugh. "Hey, how about a beer?"

"Thanks. I think I need one," Blue said gratefully. Between the dog's snarling and Sonnie's accounting of her violent tendencies, Blue felt like she was playing a bit part in a low-budget movie. Sonnie brought in a tray of nachos, piled high and dripping with cheese, with an accompanying six-pack of Rolling Rock beer.

"This ought'a keep us happy for awhile," she said, sitting on the couch too close to Blue for comfort. "My old man won't be home for hours, so we can play."

Blue wondered what she meant exactly. "Where *is* Jimmy?" she asked.

"Oh, he's at work. He just got a job. The people at the clinic helped him find one after he got off heroin. You know, it's pretty hard to keep a job when you're so high you don't know where your job *is*," she said, laughing and slapping Blue on the knee.

By her second beer, Blue was inching down the couch, away from her too-neighborly neighbor. Sonnie had already downed three beers and hardly touched the nachos. Blue was about to politely excuse herself and flee to safety, when Sonnie leaned over and whispered. "You are truly a *babe*. Why don't the two of us get nude and explore the possibilities?" She stuck her tongue deep in Blue's ear.

Blue jerked away from Sonnie's inquisitive probing like she'd been stuck with a hatpin. She stood up. "Are you a junkie *and* a lesbian?" she said angrily.

"So what if I am?" Sonnie retorted defensively. "You against lesbians?"

"No. Not that's it's any of your business *what* my sexual preferences are," Blue shot back. "This has nothing to do with what I think about lesbians. It's that you didn't bother to ask me whether I *wanted* your tongue in my ear!" Blue started to walk out.

"Wait. Please. I'm sorry. I didn't think you'd get so upset. I just figured you... well, you might be interested," Sonnie said lamely.

"What in the hell gave you *that* idea?" Blue asked.

"Well, everybody I know is bi – they go both ways. It seemed like you were that way too. Just something about you..." Sonnie was disturbingly frank.

"You know, something told me not to come over here," Blue said. "Now I know why. Keep your hands *and* your tongue to yourself!" Blue opened the door with a jerk. "And for your information," she said as she left, "if I ever *do* go both ways, it certainly won't be with you!"

"No skin off my nose, chick. You'll just never know what you missed," Sonnie retorted. "Hey, I bet you don't know your old man came on to me," she yelled after her departing neighbor. Blue stopped in her tracks and came back into the house.

"He *came on to* you?" she asked.

Sonnie simply smiled. " 'Bout a month ago," she said. "You must be a *real* cold fish."

Blue's body began to tremble. She could feel her anger rising like a fever as Sonnie's words delivered their impact. "So, did you *fuck* him?"

"Let's just say we did everything but," she informed her bluntly. "My advice is that you'd better try a little harder to please him in the sack."

"Don't tell me what to do with George," Blue said angrily. "It's none of your damn business!"

Sonnie continued on as if Blue hadn't spoken. "I bet," she said with a sly grin, "that we could make him jealous by getting it on with each other... or, better yet, the three of us could..."

Blue cut her off. "You know, Sonnie. I feel sorry for you because the only thing you believe you have to offer is your pussy! I used to be convinced of that too, but I know now that I'm a helluva lot more than my privates!" She turned on her heel and with a toss of her head, made her final exit.

"Well, at least I know what to *do* with my cunt," Sonnie yelled after her. "That's more than I can say for you!"

Blue stomped home and burst through the door. George's lucky he's not here, she thought, entertaining fantasies of killing him. Muss only had to look at her face to know there was something very wrong. Blue noticed the cat's stare. "Don't *even* ask!" she told him, as she went up the stairs to the bedroom.

She slammed the door, locked it, turned around and kicked it. Plucking a pillow from the bed, she threw it across the room, screaming as loud as she could. Then, grabbing a ceramic heart George had given her from off the nightstand, she pitched it, shattering it against the wall. "That's what you've done to *my* heart, George Garret," she screeched.

"And as for *You*, God – where have *You* been all my life? *You* don't seem to give a shit about my heart *either!*" she accused. "*You* furnish a mother who doesn't know if she wants me. Then *You* take my father away from me. Then *You* make it impossible for me to keep my baby. Then *You* put an alcoholic in my life to smack me around for a while. Then *You* let crazy George rape me. Now *You* permit some junkie-lesbian chick to come onto me… Do You just need a little *amusement* at my expense – is that why You're allowing all this to happen to me?" Blue felt nothing but miserable. She tumbled onto the bed, sobbing.

Muss had been listening to Blue's rantings outside the bedroom door. *I don't like it when she yells like this,* he was thinking. *My ears are very sensitive. Not only that – I never know what she's going to do when she gets like this. She could throw me down the basement stairs. She could stop feeding me. She could strangle me, like she did to Ruby that day. Oh, dear... thinking about all of this upsets my stomach... ack, ack.* Muss started throwing up, heaving bits and pieces of cat food all over the hallway carpet. He padded to the bathroom and hid behind the sink, abandoning his vomitous deposit for later discovery.

Blue came out of the bedroom, only to step in slimy, slightly curdled cat puke. "Geez Louise, Muss!" she complained. "I'm always cleaning up half-digested food you leave on the carpet. Can't you throw up on the linoleum? Would that be too much to ask?" Already in a foul mood, this only made it worse.

She cleaned Muss's upchuck from the drab, green carpet. Marching into the kitchen, she picked up a nearby plate and hurled it against the wall, leaving the broken pieces on the floor. "George can clean up this mess," she said, "when he comes in at 3:00 a.m. What I'd *really* like to do is take his precious guitar and smash it into a thousand pieces and let him clean *that* up!"

Blue opened a beer, flipped on the television and flung herself on the couch, petulant and angry. She lit a joint, inhaling deeply as she eyeballed whatever came onto the screen. It was what she needed to shut down the pain.

As she began to space out, a voice coming from the television startled her. "God loves you," were the words. "God's love is so powerful it sets you free. All God is asking is for you to turn your life over to Him by surrendering your will to His..." Blue heard every word and kept watching the television evangelist preaching fervently to thousands of people. The charismatic figure was her mother's favorite man of God – Billy Graham.

Transfixed, she watched as Reverend Billy gave the call for worshipers to get out of their seats and come to the stage to accept Jesus Christ as their Savior. The parade of people began with twenty-five, fifty, one hundred... then more, until there were several hundred making their way to the front. Some stood, most were on their knees. Many were crying. The organ began playing a hymn she remembered from childhood, *Just As I Am, Without One Plea,* – her mother's favorite. Blue sang along with a trembling voice, fighting back tears of confusion and pain.

Something was tugging at her heart, closed long ago to anyone who suggested letting go of your own will to follow God's. Religion crammed down her throat as a young girl, the whole idea was repugnant. But watching this procession of believers moved her. Silent tears streamed down her cheeks. She felt a yearning... an ache and a desperation.

Joining the faithful on television, she got down on her knees in the living room. Billy was talking to the "people at home" – encouraging them to get up out of their recliners and come to Jesus. And there on her knees, in front of the television, she beseeched the God of her childhood. "Help me, God. *Please* help me," she implored. She would've heaped burning coals on her head if she'd had them.

She rolled over onto her back on the floor. Her mind wandered to the time when she joined her father's church at the tender age of ten. She remembered her dad weeping as he baptized her in the lukewarm, cloudy baptismal water. He'd hugged her and given her a brand new Bible with her name inscribed in it.

"Where *is* that Bible?" she said, sitting straight up. It became imperative to find the gift given from a father to his young daughter. After ransacking the house, she found the treasure. Climbing into bed that night, Blue slept like a ten-year old – with the Holy Scriptures tucked under her arm for security.

George fell into bed as the sun was peeking over the horizon. "Don't get me up," he said to Blue, rousing her briefly. Three hours later she awoke, something compelling her to ease out of bed. I want to get away from here, she thought. Take a walk... be alone. Dressing quickly, she downed a cup of coffee and went out the door into the already warm Sunday morning.

Cars passed as the slight, young woman moved slowly down the sidewalk that lined a major city street. Blue's eyes were downcast; her hands jammed in her jean pockets. Occasionally, a car would honk at her. Someone whistled once. She startled when bells close by rang a welcome to churchgoers. She looked toward the sound. It was coming from a large church across the street. The front doors were wide open and people were streaming in.

Without looking in either direction, Blue crossed the street toward the church – almost like she was being led. She heard brakes screeching, but kept right on walking. She felt self-conscious in her blue jeans; afraid someone would tell her she was not dressed properly. But no one did. Instead, people stationed at the doors welcomed her and handed her a program.

I didn't plan on coming here, she thought. What am I doing in a damn *church* service? The surging crowd seemed to be pushing her toward the middle of the sanctuary. Resisting the crowd's momentum, she stepped into one of the back rows in case she needed to make a quick exit.

There must be five-hundred people here, she thought, as she looked around at a sea of faces. The familiar hymns caught her off guard and flooded her with memories of Sundays in her father's church. The minister, who was a tall, sophicated-looking man with slightly graying hair, had a commanding and benevolent presence. Blue was drawn to him. He reminded her of Soaring Hawk.

Singing the last hymn, she noticed a sudden, overwhelming warmth filling her body. The minister had given the "altar call," inviting worshipers to come to the front of the sanctuary to accept the Lord. A sensation in the middle of her back felt like a strong hand, pushing her to move. It scared her. "Don't," she said out loud.

Whatever you are – leave me alone! she thought. Not only did this "force" *not* leave her alone, it pushed her out of the pew, commandeered her down the aisle to the front of the church, and placed her directly in front of the minister. Blue dropped to her knees, shaking and in tears. She covered her face with her hands.

The minister's prayerful voice soon began to soothe her. The warmth that had overtaken her body earlier now enveloped her heart. She felt a heat unlike anything she had ever experienced... and indescribable peace. Kneeling there, something inside her soul was healing.

When she stood up, the young girl was instantly barraged with people, hugging her and telling her that God loved her. It was too much for a former preacher's kid who thumbed her nose at anything resembling religion. She nearly raced out of the church, stopped only by the minister at the front door. Reaching for her hand, he held it warmly with both of his. She tried to think of something complimentary to say about his sermon, but nothing came. She was tongue-tied in the presence of someone so compassionate.

"What's your name, young lady?" he asked with a benevolent smile.

"Blue – Blue Spencer."

"Well, Miss Spencer," he said gently, "anytime you want to be a part of our church family again, please come back. I could see you were having a few God-moments today."

"God-moments?" she said inquisitively. "What's that?"

"Just a phrase I use that means someone is having a direct experience with God," he replied. "And you were."

"I was?"

"Oh yes. Don't be surprised if within the next twenty-four hours your thinking will begin to change. Don't let it frighten you, though. It's just God's spirit altering your brain chemistry, so to speak. You've opened yourself up to God's love and that can do some pretty amazing things," he said with a knowing smile.

"No sh... Wow," Blue corrected herself.

The minister laughed. "Pretty cool, huh?" he said, using her vernacular.

"Yeah... I guess," she stammered.

"God bless you, Blue," he said warmly. "If you ever need anything, please call me here at the church and I'll be glad to help."

She thanked him and walked out the door, feeling strangely happy and strong-minded. She heard a voice, almost as if it was coming out of the air. *"There are many doors to walk through. Ask and you will get the help you need to enter the one that will change your life."* The audible words gave Blue a shuddering chill in the morning sun. She felt goose bumps rising on her arms. She listened as Soaring Hawk's message came to her again. *"No matter how things look around you, trust Great Spirit..."*

Blue felt light as a feather. She had made a decision. She was going to leave George and free herself to choose a better life. She felt full of resolve as she arrived home, tripping up the porch steps. She opened the door – only to see her house crammed with people – most of whom she didn't recognize.

George and the band were there, as well as Sonnie and Jimmy. Two rough characters, who looked like they had just been released from the penitentiary, were rummaging through the refrigerator in the kitchen. Three or four young groupies were hanging around the guys in the band. And everyone else was just a blur...

As Blue panned the room, she saw beer cans, empty bottles of tequila and rum, food, and ashtrays full of cigarette butts. The thick odor of hashish and pot penetrated the house. Iron Butterfly blasted from the stereo. George saw her, walked over and planted a big kiss on her mouth. He was as high as she'd seen him for a while.

"Hey Spence, welcome to the party," he said, grinning. "I sort'a forgot to tell you I invited some friends over today. But I'll make it up to you. It's the drummer's birthday... he's twenty-six today. You know, Kevin, don't you?" He rambled on. " I wanted to do somethin' special for him. Want a hit?" he asked, offering her a very fat joint.

"No thanks," Blue said, disgusted. She was feeling as if she would explode. It was all too much – from Sonnie coming on to her, finding out about George's unfaithfulness, her "God-moment" at the church, and now her sensibilities assaulted by a roomful of potheads!

I don't want this anymore! she thought. But I haven't figured out what I *do* want. I feel so lost! she realized, looking around at the people who'd invaded her space. From the other side of the living room, Sonnie interrupted her thoughts. "Hey, Blue. You know I dig you girl," she yelled obnoxiously. Blue forced a weak smile and bolted.

She made a beeline for the stairs, barely speaking to anyone. In the privacy of the bedroom she sat, thinking – rocking her body back and forth, like a small child. If I leave George now, where will I go? She wondered. Maybe Laura? No, she just moved in with her mother to take care of her. My mom's brother, Clyde? No. He's a religious nut. He'll wanna convert me.

I feel like an orphan. I have no one, she thought. Well, there *is* my mother. A chill shook her body. Oh god... Ruby. We haven't spoken since I called to apologize for trying to strangle her. But what have I got to lose? She questioned. It would be a place to crash for a few days until I decide what to do. She picked up the receiver and dialed her mother's number.

"Hmm... yello," Ruby's voice answered.

"Ruby?" Blue's heart was pounding.

"Who is this?" she asked, not recognizing her own daughter's voice.

"It's Blue, mom." Silence. "Mom?"

"What do you want, Patti?" Ruby asked, her voice flat. She had never accepted Blue's name change, nor much of anything else about her only child.

Blue took a big breath. "Mom, I watched Billy Graham on television the other night and, well... I had some kinda conversion. He was telling people that God loved them. I felt like he was talking to me... and I started to cry."

"This is why you called – to tell me about a religious experience you thought you had watching Dr. Graham on TV? You must've been on dope," Ruby said mockingly.

"No, mom. It wasn't that," Blue replied, ignoring her mother's sarcasm. "I *know* God was speaking to me that night. That's why I slept with the Bible dad gave me."

"Well, sleepin' with it isn't gonna do you any good," Ruby said caustically. "I thought you would'a pitched that Bible by now. I'm sure you've never read it."

"Yes I have," Blue defended herself.

"*Nothing* we ever tried to teach you about being a Christian amounted to a hill of beans, Patti," her mother continued. "I guess your father and I failed. All we wanted was for you to be a fine, young woman," she said with resignation. "But you were always so defiant, so rebellious. You just wouldn't listen to us." She paused. "It's *your* life though," she said. "And you're living it the way you always wanted to."

Blue felt an old, familiar heartache – the one that reminded her she'd always been her mother's black sheep. She hated when Ruby talked to her this way. "Mom, I need a place to stay for a few days," she said, disregarding the lump in her throat. "I'm trying to leave George and I don't have any place to go."

"I hope you're not asking to stay with me," her mother said. "Because I just don't have the space anymore. I've turned the guest bedroom into a sewing room. So, there's really no place for you to 'crash' as you put it."

"Oh," Blue said softly. "I could sleep on the floor, mom. I'll stay out of your way. I promise." She could feel the bitter warmth of embarrassment in her cheeks.

"Patricia," her mother's tone was weighty. "Frankly, it's very hard for me to be around you because of the way you are. I need to think of myself now. I've already raised you – and failed," she told her. "So, I'm begging you to please not ask to stay with me. I just couldn't handle the stress of it."

Blue felt a sadness so profound there were no words. She had invited her mother's rebuff – reopening the already cavernous wound in her heart. Unable to respond to Ruby's cruel honesty, Blue simply hung up the phone. She sat for a long time, staring at the floor.

"Well, Great Spirit," she said finally. "You're all I have, so it's up to You to get me out of this mess." Help came immediately. Blue began to pack her suitcase as sadness transformed into sheer determination. "I don't know where I'm going or how. But I'm going!" she said.

Yanking clothes off hangers, pulling out dresser drawers, gathering underwear, tops, belts, shoes, shorts, bellbottom jeans – she jammed them all into her suitcase. Sitting on it to get it closed she thought, wait a minute. Those nude pictures George made me pose for... where are they?

"Where did you put them?" she said, frantically rifling through the closet. "I'm *not* leaving them here with you, George!" Muss was delicately sniffing the heap of George's dirty clothes on the closet floor. "They've *gotta* be here someplace."

Tucked in the back of the closet in a corner, she spied a brown leather duffel bag. Unzipping it, she beheld, not nude photographs, but hundreds of neatly packaged bills. Money. Lots of it. More than she had ever seen in her entire life. "Oh, my god," she said, feeling lightheaded. "Where did all this money come from?"

Footsteps. Up the stairs. Two at a time. Shit, she thought. It's George. Shoving the money back into the bag and zipping it, Blue scrambled out of the closet.

"Blue?" George called out. He burst through the door. "Hey, where's my party girl? Why aren't you downstairs?"

"I've been looking for some pictures you took of me," she answered, thinking fast.

He noticed the closet door was ajar and slammed it. "*What* pictures and what *for?*" he asked, his face darkening. "I thought I told you *never* to mess with my stuff, miss busybody! Did you get into anything in there? *Did you?*"

Blue froze. "No," she answered thinly. She could hear Muss meowing and scratching at the closet door to get out. Too afraid to anger George further, she didn't move to free the trapped cat.

"Hey, Garret," someone shouted to him from downstairs. "Everybody's splittin' for the Purple Onion. You comin'?"

"Man, just go ahead. I'll catch up with ya later," George yelled back.

"Git your old lady and come on," the male voice persisted.

George stuck his head out of the bedroom door. "Blue and I got some business to take care of first," he said, with a 'leave us alone' tone.

"Gottcha."

George all but dived into the closet. After a few seconds, he came out looking relieved. Good, Blue thought. He hasn't noticed anything.

"Now," he told her. "Let's get back to the business at hand. Your jaws've been tight ever since this afternoon. What the hell's wrong with you? You got somethin' stuck in your craw?"

Blue stared at him, wondering if she should say anything about Sonnie.

"Speak up," he said impatiently.

"Okay, George. I'll speak up if that's what you want. I just found out from Sonnie that you put the moves on her. I'm figuring you probably screwed her!" Blue was angry, but frightened enough of George to move to the other side of the room as she spoke. He looked at her without saying a word. "Well?" she demanded. "Is it true? And don't lie to me!"

"That bitch came on to *me!*" he fibbed. "You'd better get your story straight, Spencer, before you go accusing me of something I didn't do!" His eye caught the corner of her open suitcase. "Oh, *I* see," he said slowly. "You think you're leavin' me, huh. Packin' up?"

"What's it to *you?*" Blue asked "You don't care about *me*... you just use me for whatever you happen to need at the moment. Why should I stay with a man who treats me like a servant while he's screwing any woman with a crotch?"

"Dammit, Blue! I didn't fuck Sonnie. Are you gonna believe a *junkie* over me?"

"Oh, you call her a *junkie* now, when it's to your advantage," Blue said sarcastically. "Look, George. If it were only Sonnie's pants you'd gotten in to, it'd be one thing. But you've had your hands in a lot of chicks' underwear since I've been with you. And don't *even* try to deny it!" Blue could feel years of wrath unleashing itself.

I've gotta change my approach, George thought. She's my alibi. He walked toward Blue cautiously, trying not to scare her. He gently took her hands in his and held them. "Baby," he called her. "What can I do to make it up to you? I'll do anything. I *love* ya, Spence. Don't you know that by now?"

"No, I *don't* know that." Blue jerked her hands away from his hold.

"How can I prove it to you then?" he implored.

"The only thing you've proved to me is that you're an asshole, George!"

"No. I mean it," he pleaded. "How can I prove it?"

"Are you serious?" she asked.

"Dead," George replied solemnly.

"I'll tell you what you can do then. You can see Dr. Montgomery with me, to work things out between us. If you'll do that, I might decide to forgive you."

George had *no* interest in changing his ways. But he needed Blue for an alibi and wasn't about to endanger his dream of Nashville. "Sure, Spence. For you – I'll do anything." He gave her a quick kiss. "Thank-you, baby... for givin' me another chance. You're a real doll!" She nodded, giving him a slight smile. "I'm goin' to the club. You sure you don't wanna come?" She shook her head no.

Blue, wearied from all the emotion, fell into bed after George left and didn't get up until 9.00 a.m. George was still sleeping as she tiptoed downstairs. After two cups of coffee, she felt awake enough to make the doctor's appointment. On the second ring, Beatrice answered the phone. "Good morning. Dr. Montgomery's office. May I help you?" she asked politely.

"Hi, Beatrice. This is Blue Spencer. I was wondering if I could get in to see the doctor – and bring my boyfriend."

The receptionist paused. "I'll have to check with her, Blue... since you haven't been in for awhile. Hold the line." After several minutes, she came back on the phone. "I'll let you talk to Dr. Montgomery about it."

"Hello Blue," Love Mae's voice was welcoming.

"Hi Dr. Montgomery," Blue said nervously. "George has... well, he's agreed to come in with me to see you."

"Oh? What prompted this?" she questioned.

"Well, we had a fight and I told him that the only way I would forgive him for what he did was if he would come in with me to see you," Blue told her.

"What did he do?" she asked. "My god, Blue, did he *rape* you again?"

"Oh, no... no. He, well... I think he had sex with our neighbor, Sonnie," Blue told her hesitantly. "She told me he came onto her. When I confronted him he denied it, but I don't believe it. He says he'll do anything to make it right."

Love Mae was silent for a moment. "You won't want to hear this, Blue, but I need to caution you that George agreeing to see a therapist to keep you happy won't do a *damn* thing for him. He's not coming here to change. He's coming here to keep the peace with you." Blue wanted to interrupt, in his defense, but kept quiet. "And don't be surprised if he tries to charm *me*. When that doesn't work, I predict he'll get real pissed off. He's a consummate manipulator, Blue."

"Does that mean you won't see us?" Blue asked.

"No. I'll see the two of you," Love Mae assured her. "I just wanted to give you fair warning. I'd like to be wrong about George, but I don't think I am," she told her. "I'll let you talk to Beatrice now. She'll set up a time for you."

"Wait," Blue interrupted. "I wanted you to know that you were right about Jonas and me. I didn't want to hear it though... about Jonas, I mean. I wanted to believe that somehow I could make it up to him... for leaving. That maybe by some miracle, he'd come back into my life and I could be his mother again."

"I'm glad, my dear... relieved that you saw through your illusion," Love Mae said. "It's already painful enough giving up your own child. I didn't want you to go through more heartache."

"I know you didn't, but I was so furious at you I could'a spit nails at you," Blue confessed. "I've gotten over it though... and I just wanna thank you for caring enough about me to give me your honest opinion. You're the closest thing to an angel mother I've ever had," she said tearfully.

"You're welcome, darlin'," Love Mae said. "You deserve all the love in the world. You just don't know it yet. Now, I'm gonna let you talk to Beatrice. She'll take care of you. Bye-bye."

Beatrice came on the line. "How's the day after tomorrow sound. Around five?"

"That's okay. We'll be there. Thank you, Beatrice."

Blue's stomach growled irritably. She often 'forgot' to eat, ignoring her hunger pangs. But today she listened. I could eat a horse, she thought. She peered into the scantily stocked refrigerator. It was an exercise in futility – with only a package of dried-up lunchmeat, milk on its way to becoming cheese, and several unrecognizable leftovers inhabiting the barren shelves. I'll just go out, she thought, eyeing the unappetizing menagerie.

Blue had anxiously worried about her weight since giving birth to Jonas, drinking nothing but Metracal for months afterwards. She always despised her female form, envying instead the male physique. Even though she was petite, Blue always inspected her body with a critical eye.

After abandoning the chocolate liquid, she began eating real food. She carefully restricted how much she consumed, using a cheap, plastic food scale to weigh meager morsels. It gave her a feeling of control. Her pregnancy had been so *out* of control. Eating constantly, she watched her body balloon into clothes three times her usual size.

Now, ninety-two pounds dripping wet was Blue's heaviest weight. Just a slip of a thing, Blue could wear clothes from the children's department. Her intense fear of getting fat was a mystery to her. No one in her family was overweight. She often wondered if wanting to stay thin was her way of refusing to grow up.

A neighborhood burger joint was not far from the house. I'll walk down and get a burger, she thought. The odor of hamburger grease filled her nostrils as she opened the door of the restaurant. "Just one?" the hostess yelled. She nodded and sat down.

Gee zooey, I need a phone book to sit on just to reach the table, she thought as she sank into the booth's seat. She slid her cloth purse under her, adding a few inches to her perch.

"Whad'll it be today?" the dyed-black coiffure with a woman's face under it asked. The name *Fran* was sewn onto the waitresses' uniform pocket. Blue must have been staring at her inky-colored hair, because the woman prompted her. "We got vegetable soup on special today. You git a bowl of soup with two slices of homemade bread for two dollars and fifty cents. Want the special?"

"Hmmm... no. I want the hamburger platter, medium well. Hold the pickles, please," Blue said politely.

"Suit yerself." She scribbled on a pad with a pencil, and then stuck it behind her ear. "Burger platter – medium, hold the pickles," she called out to the cook. After what seemed like forever, Blue had her food. "There ya are," Fran said, plunking down the platter in front of her, the one that had been sitting under hot lights for the last ten minutes.

Several French fries lost their position on the heap and slid onto the table, making the floor their final destination. The waitress started to walk away, but turned and came back to the table. "I hope ya don't mind my askin', but do you need somethin' to sit on? You're 'bout to disappear there."

"Oh no, ma'am," Blue said, amused the waitress had noticed her plight. "I've had this problem for years. You see, both my parents were midgets... so there's nothin' that can be done. I'll never get any bigger," she said, straight-faced. Fran, perhaps for the first time in her life, had nothing to say. She just shoved the order pad into her uniform pocket and turned on her heel. Blue chuckled and dug into her food.

She looked up and noticed an older woman who bore a strong resemblance to Ruby. Blue's stomach knotted immediately, like a reflex. Recalling their recent phone conversation, she felt a wave of sadness. My own mother can't tolerate being around me, she thought, dragging the last French fry through a mountain of catsup and dropping it in her mouth. Some of the catsup plummeted to her chin. She noticed her mother look-alike staring at her with distaste. Blue smiled at her sheepishly as she wiped off the catsup with her napkin. The woman quickly averted her eyes.

Blue called George when she got home – to tell him about their appointment with Dr. Montgomery. His comment was predictable. "Just remember one thing, Spence. I'm doin' this for you."

"Yeah, G.G., I'll keep that in mind." They hung up. This'll either get us back on track or it'll be a bust, Blue thought. I don't think I even care *which* way it goes anymore. Distractedly, she got the vacuum cleaner out of the broom closet and began pushing it from room to room. The house hadn't been cleaned since the party and Blue could no longer stand the mess.

Muss eyeballed his mistress from one corner of the room. *Here I go complaining again, he thought, but I wish that sucking machine she's pushing around would self-destruct. It reminds me of that metal death machine she makes me ride in when we go to Ruby's. That's bad enough, but this thing scares me silly! I just know that someday, she'll mistake me for an oversized dust bunny and I'll disappear into the guts of that monster. Time for me to remove myself,* he thought, leaping from the rug to higher ground.

Blue heard the phone ring and shut off the vacuum. She grabbed the receiver. "Hello?" she said.

"Hello, Blue?" the voice answered. "This is Naomi."

"Oh, hi. How are you?" Blue was surprised to hear from her.

"Well I'm fine, but Jonas has been asking about you."

"He *has*?" Blue was shocked.

"Yes," Naomi replied. "He's been asking when Boo is coming back."

"Boo?" Blue laughed.

"Yes. He can't quite manage the *L* sound, so your name comes out Boo. Would you like to talk to him?"

"Sure," Blue said excitedly. Naomi put Jonas on the phone. "Hey, my little goose. Do you know who this is?"

"Uh huh," Jonas said. "Can you ride the bus and come to my house again?"

Blue laughed. "I'd love to, goose. You're my most favorite playmate in the whole world. I can't come today, though. I'll have to wait awhile."

"How long?" he asked plaintively.

"Oh... not very," Blue told him, longing caught in her throat. "I'll talk to your mom about it, okay?"

"Okay. Bye." Just like that and he was gone.

Naomi came back on the line. "Would you like to come for a visit again?" she asked.

"Oh yes, for sure. I have some things to take care of here first, though," she answered, referring to her situation with George. "As soon as that's out of the way, I'd love to see Jonas again."

"Well, just call us when you think you can come," Naomi said.

"You've got our number."

"I will – and thank-you," Blue said appreciatively.

She continued clutching the receiver after they hung up. A sudden melancholy dampened her spirits. She wanted to turn around and see Jonas standing there, so she could grab him and embrace his little body. Knowing he wanted to see her made Blue more determined than ever to return to Ponca City. *This time I'll drive*, she thought, *so Jonas and I can be alone together. I'll take him to a zoo...*

Her daydream was interrupted – by a simultaneous clap of thunder and the sound of crashing glass. Racing toward the din, she saw her prized red lava lamp and its contents spreading in every direction all over the hardwood floor – with Muss sitting on the mantle looking down, dispassionately, at the evidence. "Dammit Mussels! That was my favorite lava lamp of all time! I could just *kill* you!"

Oops, Muss thought, as he sat, curling his tail around him protectively. *All I did was walk behind it. I guess there wasn't room on the mantle for me and that... ugly thing. Hmm... she looks pretty mad. I'd better make my apologies.* He jumped down from his perch and rubbed against Blue's leg, repentant, as she cleaned up the mess – while outside, the darkened sky emptied a generous measure of rain.

Blue dumped the last of the glass in the garbage. *So much for that lava lamp*, she thought. Another thundercloud burst directly over the house, causing Muss to seek safety underneath the couch. She walked out on the porch to the old, upholstered chair occupying one end of it. She pulled it close to the porch railing and sat down in its lumpy depths.

Propping up her feet, Blue watched the storm. Lightening was always terrifyingly plentiful in Kansas. Brilliant streaks of electricity illuminated the late afternoon sky, charging the air. She almost wished one of them would strike her – not enough to kill her, just enough to make her feel alive.

"George, hurry! We're gonna be late for our appointment. We have to be there by 6:00," Blue yelled from the upstairs bathroom. He had been playing his guitar ever since he'd come home. It'll take an act of God to pull him away, Blue thought. No answer. "George!" She was starting to panic. "Come on!"

Taking his sweet time, George climbed the stairs, a hacking, cigarette cough accompanying him. "Will you get a move on?" Blue said, peering over the banister.

"Leave me alone, woman! I'm sure 'Lovely Mae' will be there, whether we're on time or not," he scoffed. George was irritable and hung-over from drinking with Denny the night before.

It had been a disturbing evening with his friend, George was thinking. By the third beer, Denny was talking about the war again. But this time, he was saying things about how hard it was to live in the world. How the 'kill or be killed' philosophy he learned in Vietnam was the way he survived, but here at home, it was killing him.

"What the hell are you talkin' about, Den?" George had asked him.

"I'm talkin' about the fact that's it's the same over here – kill or be killed," he had replied bitterly. "Except it's not blowin' somebody's fuckin' brains out. It's slimier than that. Here, you either 'kill' the guy who's trying to get ahead of you on the ladder, or he 'kills' you. You do whatever you have to do to make it, no matter who you get rid of along the way. The whole American thing is about greedy bastards who want to stay at the top!"

"You all right, Den?" George had inquired. He didn't like the negative tone his friend's conversation was taking.

Denny had just looked at him. "I don't know, man... even havin' $50,000 doesn't seem to make me happy. I feel guilty as hell 'bout the way I got it."

"Shit, Denny. You wouldn't look a gift horse in the mouth even if your head was in it!" George had been irritated his friend brought up the subject of the stolen money. It made him feel guilty about persuading his reluctant buddy to be a partner in crime. The guy's just never happy with anything, he concluded, squeezing a gob of pink-striped toothpaste on his toothbrush. Blue's voice yanked him out of his thoughts.

"George, you'd better be ready, because I'm about a minute away from leaving," Blue yelled, as she pulled on her well worn, cherished bellbottoms – the ones with the "peace now" patch sewed on the rump. Tucking in a blue work-shirt, she decided it would be more ladylike to belt her jeans today, rather than wearing them without a belt and low on her hips like she usually did. "Let's go," she announced, fluffing out her curls with a pick.

Still brushing his teeth, George grunted his reply. He had beautiful teeth and routinely spent an inordinate amount of time studying them in the mirror. Blue walked by him on her way downstairs, yanking on his sleeve. "Your teeth are disgustingly perfect. Now let's get outta here," she said.

"Okay. Okay. I'm coming," George replied, speeding up his pace. They took the stairs at a good clip, ran out the door, hopped in the VW, made a U-turn in the street and headed toward Love Mae's office. Saffron and her passengers made it into the parking lot with only a minute to spare.

"She's usually running late anyway, G.G. – so we'll be on time," Blue informed him as they rode the elevator to the sixth floor. She was apprehensive about their appointment, babbling nervously all the way to the office. In contrast, George hadn't said more than two words since they left the house. *I'm starting to have a bad feeling about this,* she thought, noticing his silence.

But there wasn't time for Blue to pursue her nagging feeling. Love Mae was on time today and took them right in. Offering George her hand, she introduced herself. "George, I'm Love Mae Montgomery."

"Yeah," he mumbled, keeping his hands in his pockets.

She pulled back her extended hand. "Well hello, Miss Spencer. Where have I seen you before?" she teased.

"Hi, Love Mae," Blue responded nervously.

"Sit down. Sit down," she said, gesturing toward the couch. George sat at one end, legs crossed and arms folded over his chest. *Hmm... revealing body language,* Love Mae thought. Blue sat at the other end, legs drawn up protectively against her body. She looked no older than five – scared and uncertain. George was staring straight ahead, not looking at either woman. Oh boy, Love Mae thought. This is going to be a long hour.

George was the first to speak. "Mind if I smoke?" he directed at Love Mae.

"Certainly not," she replied. "I'm a smoker myself. I'll have one with you." They both lit up. Love Mae pulled the standing ashtray between them. George seemed to relax a little after his first drag. "Would it be accurate to say that it wasn't your idea to come here today, George?" she said, smiling.

"How'd you guess?" George responded, laughing at his own sarcasm.

"I get lucky sometimes," Love Mae replied, exhaling a long stream of smoke. "Have you ever been in a psychologist's office before?" she asked.

"No, I can't say that I have," he replied. "Wait a minute. I *did* go to see a shrink, after my brother was killed. I was havin' bad nightmares about him bein' decapitated."

"Oh, that must've been horrible," Love Mae said genuinely.

"Yeah... it was," he told her. "He worked for the railroad. I was helping him fix track one day. A train came up on us at a pretty good clip, blowin' its whistle. I started runnin' toward the embankment on the other side. But Dave, stupid show-off, took his good ole' time gettin' off the tracks. Then his fuckin' boot got caught between the ties. The tracks were on a bridge over a river, so he had nowhere to go." George's eyes moistened and his voice quavered. "Shit... I didn't come here to talk to a stranger about this." Blue reached over and squeezed his hand.

Love Mae was silent for a moment. "Where would the two of you like to begin?" she finally asked.

"Well, it wasn't my idea to come here, but I wanna do whatever it takes to make things better at home," George volunteered.

Blue spoke up. "I asked George to come with me today because we haven't been getting along," she said diplomatically. "Have we, G.G.?"

"No, I guess not," he replied. "I'm still not convinced how talking to a shrink is gonna help us."

"Well, *we* certainly don't have the answers," Blue told him.

"Maybe she does."

"Look, Blue. Doctors have always tightened my jaws, ever since I saw the one about my brother," George informed her. "She's been seein' you since forever, so I'm the odd man out here. And besides, I'm no idiot. I know the two of you have already made up your minds about me. I'm a condemned man." he said matter-of-factly.

Love Mae knew then that she and George were going to be dancing on a tightrope with no net below – both of them trying to keep from falling by pushing the other one off.

"How so, George?" Love Mae questioned.

He seemed amused at her inquiry. "This must be a trick question," he said, lighting another Kool. "Let me see. I'm sure Blue came running to you crying rape. I know she told you about Sonnie. In your eyes, I'm *already* the ultimate bad guy. Does that satisfy your curiosity?" he asked acerbically.

"No, actually it doesn't," Love Mae fired back. She knew as soon as the words came out of her mouth, she had said the wrong thing.

"Well then, I'm outta here," he announced, starting to get up. "I don't have to answer your questions or listen to your fuckin' psychological bull-crap!"

"Wait, George. Don't go. Please give this a chance," Blue pleaded.

"You know, Spence, your Dr. Montgomery has a smart mouth. She needs to realize just who she's dealin' with." He put his cigarette out in the ashtray like a bug being squashed.

"You're right, George," Love Mae said. "I *don't* know who I'm dealing with. What would it take for you to stay so I can find out?" she asked.

George walked around behind the couch. He looked at Love Mae, disdain shadowing his face. "I don't know you, lady – and I don't like you," he told her. "You know why? Because you're like every other woman I've ever met. You think you know it all, so you believe you're better than me. All I have to say to you is *this*. If you keep trying to turn Blue against me, so help me Joseph and Mary, you'll be one sorry-assed woman! Now, do you still want me to stay?"

Blue's face was ashen. Love Mae's was flushed with anger. "Are you threatening me, Mr. Garret? I just want to know for the record."

"You can stick your records where the sun don't shine! I'll let *you* decide whether I'm threatening you or not. But let me tell you something, doctor. I killed lots of people in Nam – some of 'em women. Blowin' away a female is *nothin'* to me. So I suggest you watch your back!" He turned to Blue. "Are you coming with me or staying here with her?" he demanded.

Blue didn't give even the slightest suggestion of going with him. "I guess that's my answer," he said, walking out and slamming the office door. As soon as he was gone, Blue burst into tears. Love Mae sat next to her, putting an arm around her shaking shoulders.

"I had a bad feeling about this," she said between sobs. "And I was right. I'm sorry. We shouldn't have come in together."

"Blue, this was very revealing," Love Mae told her. "I left my professional demeanor behind, pissed him off and saw, first hand, what you deal with *all the time*. Look at me, Blue," she told the sobbing girl. "What happened here makes it crystal clear that George has a serious problem with women. And I'd be willing to bet it started with a mother who dominated the *shit* out of him," she said. "So that makes *any* woman a target of his anger, especially one in a position of authority, like me," she told Blue, giving her a tissue.

Blue dried her tears and blew her nose. "I'm beginning to see how George takes his anger out on women – by having power over them, like when he raped me. He charms them, then uses them... whatever it takes for him to feel in control.

"You're absolutely accurate, Blue. Now, do you want to stay with a man like that – a man whose modus operandi with women includes *violence*?" Love Mae challenged her.

"No," Blue replied sadly. "I don't. I'm gonna have to let him go." She wanted to tell Love Mae about finding the money. Too fearful of George's wrath, she stopped herself – afraid he would 'know' if she uttered a word to anyone. "I guess I have a lot to think about. I'm sorry he acted like such a jerk," she said, as if his behavior was her responsibility.

"I've had worse, believe me," Love Mae reassured her. "The only thing I want you to concentrate on is mustering the courage to get yourself out of the headlock you're in with a man you absolutely cannot trust. You're not safe with him, Blue," she warned. "He's full of rage and unpredictable."

"I know," Blue said. "I'll be careful. You know what? Deep in my heart, I don't really believe George loves me. I think I've just convinced myself that he does by taking whatever crumbs he throws me. Why do I *do* that, Love Mae?"

"I'll tell you why. It's because your pain is *not* only about your mother," she replied. "It's been at the hands of your father as well."

"What do you mean?" Blue asked. "He didn't put me down or slap me, like mom did."

"He did something far worse, Blue. He used you."

"What do you *mean*?" Blue asked defensively.

"For his own selfish reasons. He deserted the family and replaced you with his church concerns. And that left your mother a lonely, unhappy woman. She resented the hell out of him and withdrew her affection," Love Mae continued. "I believe that's when he turned to you, his young, vulnerable daughter, for attention – all the things he wasn't getting from her."

Blue was silent. She reached into her purse and pulled out a worn piece of paper. "Can I read this to you?" Love Mae nodded yes. "I carry this with me all the time. It's something I wrote to my dad. He died before I could give it to him."

"A letter to my father... Dear father– You have lived a sheltered life – young boy fantasies pushed aside by the hidden flow of your guilt. How little you knew of your own inner self – the shadow of your dark side so neatly wrapped within the viscera of your small body.

You have been like a slippery fish – scales beautifully silvery and shiny in the light... with blue eyes, slightly downcast and seductive. I could see you enchanting hungry women in the congregation with those eyes. After all, you were their shepherd. Did you seduce me too?

What do you need, daddy? You look so sad. What can I do to please you? I don't please momma – how can I please you? I see your beautiful smile and those sad eyes when you come to my bed in the morning to wake me for school. I know you're lonely, but what can I do? I'm your daughter, remember? I just want to be your little girl... I love you."

"That's a disturbing letter, Blue... touching too," Love Mae told her. "And beautifully written. It spells out your confusion about who you are to your father. And it verifies what I was saying about him using you to take care of his own emotional needs." She paused. "Did he ever touch you sexually?" she asked.

"No," Blue replied. "Not that I ever remember. His was the only affection I got at home... it never came from my mother," she said sadly. "She stopped being affectionate when I wasn't her little girl anymore... the little doll she could dress. That's why I'm so glad you're my therapist. Thank you for being here for me," she told her, throwing her arms around Love Mae's neck.

"You're welcome, Blue. Let me tell you something," she said, pulling away to look at her. "I hope someday you won't even *flinch* at being labeled a black sheep. Because you know what?" Blue shook her head. "Being different, standing apart from the rest of the herd, is a blessing. It means you're almost *guaranteed* to make a stellar contribution to the world. Just remember that, especially when you're questioning your value as a person."

"I could make a contribution? That's cool..." Blue mused.

"It takes great courage to confront your demons and put the pieces of your life together. There aren't many of us who are willing to do what it takes to make that happen," she said, opening the office door for her young patient.

"Bye doc," Blue said. Love Mae gave her a wink.

Her last appointment for the evening over, Love Mae sat in her comfortable, rose-colored armchair, looking out the window at the Wichita skyline. She lit another cigarette. What a day, she reflected. George is a scary character. He's killed and I believe he could kill again. He threatened me and I need to take steps to protect myself, she thought. She flipped on the intercom. Beatrice answered. "Bea, before you leave, would you get the police department on the line?"

"Yes ma'am. Right away." In only minutes, Beatrice patched the police through to her office.

"Wichita police department. Can we help you?"

"Well, I hope so," Love Mae answered. "This is Dr. Love Mae Montgomery. I'm a psychologist located in the 505 South Main building. "What kind of protection is currently available to me when a client blatantly threatens my safety?"

"What was the threat, ma'am?" the officer asked.

"He implied he could kill me and told me to 'watch my back' – that I'd be sorry if I didn't stop influencing his girlfriend," she told him. "She's my client. My concern is, this guy has a crazy, angry streak in him and directs it toward women. He's a Vietnam vet and a drug user. He made a point to tell me in the session that he'd killed many people in the war, some of them women. Now doesn't that sound like a threat to you, officer?"

"Yes ma'am, it does," the officer replied. "But there's not much we can do about it, unless he actually tries to carry out his threat. What I *can* do is beef up security around your building in the morning and at night."

"Well, you're not telling me anything I don't already know," Love Mae said. "I was hoping policy had changed – new legislation, perhaps. But it sounds like your hands are still tied unless some act of violence is actually attempted."

"Right. I'm sorry, Dr. Montgomery. Nothing's changed, I'm afraid. But I *will* see to it that I have extra officers over there in the morning and evening. You have a protection service in your building, don't you?" he asked.

"Yes," she replied.

"I would suggest, doctor, that you give your building security a description of this guy, so that they'll be on the look-out for him if he comes into the lobby."

"Yes, I'd already planned on doing that," she said.

"Even though we can't take action right now, let me get some demographics on him." She gave the officer a full description of George as well as his address and phone number. He thanked her and they hung up. She let out a long, weary sigh. "Honey, you should've gotten out of this business a long time ago... and opened a fashion boutique," she said. "In Paris."

Blue was so angry with George for the way he'd treated her therapist that she stopped speaking to him. And he made no attempt to get her to talk. The tension between them was so thick that Muss camped out behind the bathtub whenever George was home. One day, when George went to work early, Blue stayed in bed as he left, pretending to be asleep.

As soon as the front door closed, she scrambled out of bed. I'm gonna see whether that duffel bag full of money is still in his closet, she thought, or if he's moved it. She peered into the darkness and saw the bag exactly where it had been before. Upon closer inspection, Blue noticed it was now secured with a lock.

Lying beside the bag was a torn newspaper clipping. Blue picked it up and brought it into the light of the bedroom. It was a recent article about the robbery. "Investigation Continues As Police's Only Clue is Woman's Black Nylon," the headline read. Why is this torn out? she wondered. I'd bet any money those are *my* missing nylons they're talking about. The phone interrupted her thoughts. She picked up the receiver.

"Blue, I just got to work and..." the voice said.

"What do you want, George?" she said icily.

"I wanted to apologize for actin' the fool the other day," he said. "It's just that... I felt ganged up on by the two of you."

"That wasn't the idea, George," Blue replied. "Love Mae was just trying to get to know you, but you took it the wrong way."

"Yeah, well... I'm sorry. But I still think she has an unprofessional mouth on her... it wouldn't take much for me to give her a fat lip."

Blue was silent as she tried to contain her rage. "Look, *George*," she seethed. "Your apology doesn't mean a damn thing to me, especially when you talk about giving my therapist a fat lip in the same breath. Love Mae told me you hate women and she's right. You think we're beneath you and therefore, you can lord it over us," she asserted.

"Well, no more! I'm giving you one week to get your shit together. That means treating me with respect for once in your life. If I haven't seen any changes by the end of the week, I'm leaving you!" Blue told him, in no uncertain terms.

"Baby, wait a minute now... you're not giving me a fair chance," he protested.

"Fair? You have *no* right to talk about fair! You raped me, George Garret! Was that *fair*?" she asked, her voice laden with outrage. "I should've pressed charges against you, but I *didn't* because I loved you! You've *never even* said you were sorry for raping me! I believed I deserved it – like it was *my* fault! Well, guess what! I *didn't* deserve it – in all *fairness* to me!" She slammed down the receiver before he had a chance to say a word.

George hung up the phone and went to the men's room. He glanced at himself in the mirror, and then walked to the open restroom window. Lighting a Kool, he stared at the world outside, watching the smoke from his cigarette meander through the screen. She's right. I should'a never done that to her, he thought. Jesus, why did I force myself on her like that? he wondered. What was I so goddamned angry about?

Blue's a good woman, he thought. She's done a lot for me... but she's changed since she's been seein' that psychologist. And if I'm not careful, that bitch's gonna take Spence away from me, especially when she's filling her head with talk about me hating women. Suddenly, an idea came to him.

George finished his shift and walked out of the John Deere plant at exactly 5:00 p.m. He stopped for a few quick beers and an order of take-out ribs from The Pig-Sty. Sitting in his car in front of Dr. Montgomery's office, he finished off the last, barbecue-soaked rib. He looked down at the boxful of bones on his lap, idly licking his fingers. Damn, I was hungry, he thought. He had parked so he could easily view anyone who came out of the front of the building.

He turned on the car radio and settled back in the seat. An hour went by. She's gotta be coming out soon, he thought. "Speak of the devil," he said slowly. Love Mae, carrying a briefcase and an armload of papers, walked out of the building toward the parking lot. She passed by his car, not noticing him.

Digging deep in her purse for the car keys, Love Mae heard a noise. Startled by it, she looked up and saw George. He was dropping a box of what looked like greasy, mostly eaten rib bones on her car and smearing them over the surface of the hood.

"What the *hell* are you doing?" she asked incredulously.

"Just making sure we have an understanding," he told her, smiling wickedly. "Cause if we don't, I'll do this and more – except the next time, it could be something more than your car."

"What *understanding* are you talking about?" she asked, trying to keep from shrieking as she watched barbecue sauce and rib bones making slimy patterns on the hood of her brand-new, 1974 silver Porsche.

"Stop trying to turn my girlfriend *against* me," he threatened. "You tell her to hang in there *with* me. If you're a good girl and you do that, I'll never bother you again. Take it or leave it, 'Lovely Mae'," he said derisively.

"Do you think, Mr. Garret, that you can just go around threatening people when you feel like it?" Love Mae replied, as calmly as she could. "You're *not* in Vietnam anymore and I'm *not* the enemy." She unlocked her car door and started to get in. George came around to the door and pretended to hold it open for her. When she tried to close it, he wouldn't let go.

"Please let go of my personal property," she said firmly.

"I will if you promise to let go of Blue – *my* personal property," George said just as firmly.

"I'll consider your concerns, Mr. Garret. Believe me, I will. But if you don't stop harassing me, I'll have to call the police." She looked him dead in the eye and he let go of the car door. The idea of cops snooping around and asking questions made him a little queasy.

"Drive carefully," he said contemptuously, as she started the engine and drove out of the parking lot, rib bones sliding off her hood in all directions. *Very* carefully, he thought, walking toward his car. I need a drink... gotta plan my next move. He headed to The Watering Hole, a bar he often frequented.

Things are heating up a little too much for my comfort, he thought, pouring his bottled beer in the cloudy bar glass and watching the bubbles swirl in the yellow liquid. Blue's given me an ultimatum, the police are hot to solve the robbery, Olivette's blackmailing me, and I just had an altercation with my old lady's therapist in a public parking lot.

Fuck, man – you're pushin' it, he was thinking. If you don't watch

160

it Garret, some bad shit's gonna come down. He finished his beer. I'm goin' out to Denny's, he decided. Smoke a little reefer. I've gotta chill.

On the way, George started planning his escape. *First of all, I'd better get that money out of the closet. I don't want it anywhere Blue can lay her hands on it. Then, I'm gonna give notice at work... tell them I've been offered a job where I can move up in the company. No... maybe I'll just split for Nashville without telling anyone. The only problem is, if I do that, the police are gonna suspect that I was connected with the robbery. I'll run it by Den... see what he says.*

He turned in his friend's driveway. Shutting off the engine, he slouched down in the seat and gazed at the stars crowding the night sky. God, there's nothin' more beautiful than Kansas stars, he thought. He looked at the house, which was dark, except for a light in the kitchen and the bedroom. Good, he thought. Den's up. He got out of the car and walked to the house. He knocked. No answer. The door was unlocked, so he let himself in.

"Den?" he called. George went over to the refrigerator and opened it. I'm not even hungry, he thought, eyeing the barely stocked icebox. A roasted chicken, with only a leg missing, was sitting on a plate. He ripped off the other. "Hey, you lazy fuck," he said, taking a bite of the bird. "What does a guy have to do to get a little company?" Venturing into the living room, he inquired again. "Denny? Hey, you crazy fool – get up!" But there was no sound, no sound at all.

He looked around. A Wichita newspaper was still in its rubber band; unopened and unread. Lying on the coffee table was a piece of paper. George picked it up. He recognized Denny's handwriting – "Call George, ASAP!" A partly empty quart of beer was sitting on the floor. George reached down and took a swig. He made a face. It was flat.

"Oh, so that's how it is," he quipped, referring to the bottle. "Ya got drunk and passed out again. You can't drink late at night, Den. You're gonna get a beer gut." Finishing off the chicken leg, he tossed it into a nearby trashcan. He walked toward the bedroom. The door was slightly ajar. "Get your drunk ass out of bed, man," he said, giving it a push.

Denny was lying on the bed. Beside him was a written note,

splattered with blood. He was on his back, wearing only briefs and socks. His military dog tags were stuffed in his mouth, part of the chain hanging from his bottom lip. A handgun rested in his palm. The room was in total disarray. His beloved posters were torn down and the telephone cord was pulled out of the wall. His dresser drawers and their contents were strewn everywhere, as if he'd been looking for something. The money from the robbery was scattered all over the floor.

"Oh, my god! Oh, my god! *NO!*" George screamed, his face contorted in horror at the sight of his friend. "You *motherfucker*! What have you *done!*" he said, running over to the bed. "Dammit, we went through *Nam* together. We kept each other *alive*! After all that, how could you *do* this to me?" he yelled, shaking his friend's lifeless form by the shoulders.

Denny's body was cold and his face had started to discolor. The feel of his clammy skin made George jerk his hands away. He vomited. Then he cried – deep, gut wrenching sobs that doubled him up in a ball on the floor.

The bullet had successfully found its way to Denny's brain. One shot to the temple. He had been a superior marksman in the war. Sadly, it was a skill he used in the end, on himself. Bright, red blood from the bullet hole spread a poppy-colored stain on the yellowed sheet. His blue eyes were open – staring blankly at nothing.

George read the suicide note, tears running down his cheeks. *"To whoever finds this miserable excuse for a human – I don't know if I've done the right thing, but it's too late now. I figured I'd better not fuck this death thing up, since no one would want to take care of another helpless vet in a wheelchair. So, I tried to be accurate. Dad, I know I let you and mom down. Didn't come home with any medals. Sorry I couldn't make you proud. I just guess I wasn't cut out to be a soldier like you, dad. George, take the money. It's yours. I want you to get to Nashville. And tell Blue she was the first girl I ever met who genuinely seemed to like me. Make sure she keeps you in line, buddy, if that's possible. I won't miss this crazy, fucked-up world, but I'll sure miss the people I love. Say a prayer for me, cause I don't know where I'm gonna end up. Good-bye, D."*

George burst into a renewed torrent of tears and curses. "Damn you,

Den! You were so hot to trot off to that stinkin' war... and look what it did to you. You just couldn't fuckin' handle it! You *had* to go and blow your brains out!" he lectured to the still corpse on the bed. "I tried to tell you this country's fucked up and to just forget it and go on with your life! But no! You had to try to figure it all out."

George collapsed on the floor, exhausted with his tirade. He glanced up at Denny "You were a good guy, Den... I'm so sorry about the way I got pissed at you the other night, when you were tellin' me how bad you felt about the money we stole. I should'a never asked you to go in on it with me. It just wasn't you. You're a better man than me... you *were* a better man. *Motherfucking jesus Christ*... I wish you hadn't done this," George cried, putting his head between his hands, his broad shoulders shaking with sobs.

It was with a heavy heart he made the appropriate phone calls – to the police and Denny's parents. He must have smoked two packs of Kools waiting for everyone to arrive. The police came first, then the parents. When Denny's mother and father saw him lying in a pool of blood, they were horrified. His mother was inconsolable and insisted on cradling her dead son in her arms while her husband tried to comfort her.

She sat, in the middle of the bed, holding her son's head on her breast, her face smeared with blood from kissing him. George couldn't stop watching the agonizing scene. No words could describe the deep grief he experienced that night. In his mind, George had lost the only two men in his life he'd ever really loved – his brother Dave and now, Denny.

Four a.m. and George was heading home with the stolen money stuffed in a paper bag and Denny's dog tags around his neck. Couldn't leave the loot there, he thought. Evidence for the police. I was sweatin' it just being in the same room with them.

He stopped at an all-night restaurant for coffee, sat in a booth and stared out the window. The waitress refilled his cup silently, somehow sensing his despondency. He downed three or four cups, slapped several bills on the table and walked out.

George drove home in a trance. He pulled up in front of the house and slowly got out of the car. An incredible heaviness was overtaking him – like a two-ton weight on his chest. He unlocked the front door quietly, tiptoed up the stairs and into the bedroom. Blue was sound asleep, snoring delicately. Muss was curled up flush against her backside. George undressed and crawled in beside her. His lungs were on fire from an endless stream of cigarettes. His body ached and his eyes were swollen from crying.

Blue stirred, rousing from sleep. Muss relinquished his place next to his mistress for roomier territory. And, for the first time in months, George and Blue embraced. He began kissing her more passionately and lovingly than she could ever recall. The smell of tobacco was strong on him and there was another odor she couldn't recognize. But it reminded her of death...

The next day their shaky union made a comeback, like someone dying of cancer who rallies briefly before passing away. George told Blue about Denny's suicide. She was shocked and dismayed. A tenderness and compassion surfaced for George she hadn't felt for awhile.

Life took on a brilliant edge, like the ribbon of light that outlines an early morning cloud. Everything previously labeled mundane now assumed special significance. With the shroud of death wrapping itself around their life, the fact they were both alive was what mattered. For George, even $50,000 of stolen money couldn't touch that. At least for the moment.

Funerals were something Blue had grown up attending. Her

minister-father had conducted hundreds. She and her mother would often go along, out of respect for the family of the departed one. Seeing a dead body in a casket, and hearing about how wonderful the deceased had been was just part of Blue's life.

For George, funerals were something to be avoided. He hated the ceremony, the procession of the casket, and most of all, the morticians. "They're slimy, little con-artists," he told Blue, "who prey on grief-stricken families, when they are most vulnerable to handing over their life savings to a stranger."

Blue and George walked arm and arm out of the sprawling cemetery. Blue had tossed a last bit of dirt on top of the casket before they lowered it into the ground. A cold, drenching rain accented the somber occasion. George's flared-bottom black suit pants were getting wet. Blue could feel her flats filling with water from the soggy ground. Not thinking to bring an umbrella and not really caring, the two of them were getting soaked.

Huddled in George's car, chilled and wet, they fell silent. Others who attended the service walked to their cars. "Well, that's the end of Denny as we knew him," George said, watching people go by. "I guess God needed him more than we did. You know, Spence," he reflected, "I took Den's dog tags out of his mouth and put 'em around my neck, so I could always have a part of him with me. I'm never gonna take them off," he told her, unbuttoning his shirt to pull out the tags. "I really loved that guy..." he said softly, examining them

Blue looked on. She was seeing a different side of George – a gentler, more humble side. There's still the fact he's taken the money, she thought. How can I stay with somebody who's committed a felony? But... I don't want to deal with that right now. She reached over and massaged his shoulders. "Wanna get high and have a few laughs on Denny?" she asked.

George considered it for a moment. "Nah. I don't feel like laughin' right now. Maybe in a couple 'a weeks. And besides, I've been hittin' the reefer and the cigs too hard lately. My lungs feel like somebody poured gasoline in 'em and lit a match."

He started the engine and pulled slowly onto the gravel cemetery road that led to the highway. "You know, G.G.," Blue said. "Death really makes you think about things, doesn't it? Like your life, and all.

And God. And how fragile we are... but livin' life like there's an unlimited supply of tomorrows."

George took his eyes off the road for a second to look at Blue. "Right on, babe. We all take too much for granted." Blue reached over and took his hand. They both looked straight ahead and drove the rest of the way home in silence.

Some honeymoons are short-lived. The next day was the beginning of the end of theirs. Denny's sudden death had served as a pause in their decidedly crumbling relationship, like the space between breathing in and breathing out.

"He *what*!" Blue's voice exploded into the receiver. It was mid-afternoon. George was at work. Love Mae and Blue were in conversation on the phone.

"He threatened me with rib-bones in the parking lot," Love Mae said bluntly.

"This *has* to be a joke," Blue exclaimed, not wanting to believe what she was hearing. "What are you *talking* about?"

"George dumped his leftovers on my car," Love Mae explained. "Apparently, he must've had a yen for ribs that day. He smeared half-eaten, greasy, barbecued ribs all over the hood of my new car. If I didn't believe he was a danger to you, I'd be laughing my ass off about it," she said chuckling. "But it's not funny."

Blue sat down gingerly on the edge of the bed. "I don't believe this," she said quietly. "I thought he was starting to make an effort to behave like a decent human being. But I can see it's too much to ask of a jerk like him. I feel bad, Love Mae," she said solemnly. "I should'a never brought him to the session."

"I'm a big girl, Blue," Love Mae told her. "I told him if he didn't stop harassing me, I'd call the police. That seemed to work. I think he wanted to scare me because I'm a threat – someone who's trying to take you away from him. The reason I'm telling *you* about this, Blue, is because I'm concerned for your safety," she said with a worried tone. "He sees you as his possession, and that means he'll do anything to keep you. Even kill you. *Please*, if you feel frightened, just leave... get away from him. Go to a woman's shelter."

"Okay, I will. I promise," Blue replied, remembering when she and the priest had taken Laura to the shelter.

"I have a patient waiting, so I need to hang up now," she told her. "Don't hesitate to call me if you need me."

"I won't. Bye, Love Mae." She sat with the receiver in her lap, numb with anger and disbelief. Now George had four black marks against him – raping her, committing a burglary, screwing Sonnie, and now threatening her therapist. *I should have known the last day and a half with him was too good to be true,* she thought disconsolately. "Dammit, George, I was starting to forgive you... even feel love for you again," she said sadly.

Blue walked downstairs and into the kitchen. She opened the refrigerator and took out a beer. Uncapping it, she grabbed one of George's cigarettes and went out on the front porch. Muss was sleeping, curled up in a perfect sphere on the chair's cushion, his whiskers twitching as he dreamed. He startled awake when Blue's foot hit the chair. He looked up at her, squinting. *I would have to be stuck with a mistress who's a klutz!*

"Move over, Muss," she instructed. "I'm depressed." She picked up the previously napping cat and placed him on the ground. The spot on the cushion where he had been was still warm. She propped her feet up on the porch railing and hunkered down in the chair, taking periodic swallows of cold beer.

The day had started out sunny, but clouds were forming and the smell of rain was in the air. A brown-feathered sparrow landed on the railing, cocking its head first to one side then the other. Muss noticed the bird and began to move his mouth in an odd, repetitive way – making predatory cat sounds.

Absorbed in the interaction between the two, Blue didn't see a car pull up in front of the house. The door opened and a woman got out. That's when she noticed and began wondering who the woman was and why she was coming up her sidewalk. She was plain looking, with medium dark hair, sloping shoulders and ample hips.

"Is your name Blue?" she asked, red lipstick not only covering her mouth, but streaking her front teeth as well. A pair of horn-rimmed glasses framed her square-shaped face.

Blue sat up. "Yes. How do you know my name?"

She didn't answer the question, instead introduced herself. "My name's Olivette. I'm looking for Mr. Garret. Is he here, by any chance?" she asked.

"No, he's not," Blue replied, with a questioning tone. "He's supposed to be at work. What do you want with George, may I ask?" This has gotta be business, she thought. He certainly didn't take *this* chick to bed.

"You're his girlfriend?" Olivette inquired.

"Yep. For the moment," Blue said flippantly. "Why are you asking?"

"I work with him at the John Deere plant and he's mentioned you before. That's all," she explained. Her hand was shaking as she pulled an envelope out of her purse and handed it to Blue. It had George's name on it. "I have to go back to work. Would you please give this note to Mr. Garret when you see him?" she asked. "It's important."

"Sure. No problem." Blue took the sealed envelope from her.

"Please be sure and give it to him for me," she said. "Thank-you." As she stepped off the porch, her heel caught on the step. Her body pitched forward. Grabbing the railing, she was able to catch her fall, but Blue could tell her pride was damaged.

"Are you okay?" she asked, feeling sorry for the strange woman.

"I'm fine... just fine," Olivette said as she winced. Blue watched her as she limped to her car and drove away.

Blue looked at the envelope. Well, this is an interesting development, she thought. She held it up to the light. It wasn't a check. It wasn't a letter. It looked more like a note – a brief note. She considered her options. I can give this to George, unopened and unread, she thought. Or I can read the note and give it to him, resealed.

The temptation was too great. Blue opened the envelope carefully. She pulled out the note and read it. *"Dear George – You're not keeping your end of the bargain with me. I'm WAY PAST DUE for servicing. I strongly suggest you make an appointment to see me immediately or, god forbid, I'll have to go to the police and spill the proverbial beans. Waiting impatiently, horny and hot – Olivette."*

Aghast, Blue read the note twice – just to make sure she wasn't hallucinating. "Okay, George," she said. "This is the last straw... the one that's gonna do you in. This note tells me two things. One – you're in deep trouble with the police. And two – you're in deep trouble with me!" She stormed into the house, taking the stairs two at a time, picked up the phone in the bedroom and dialed George at work.

"John Deere. May I help you?" the receptionist answered.

"Yes, please. This is Blue Spencer. I need to speak to George Garret right away. It's an emergency," she said urgently.

"I'm sorry," the woman replied. "I can't pull him off the line. But I will make sure he gets this message. Does he have your number?"

"Yes. And please hurry!" Blue hung up. Her fury was boiling, like scalding water in a pot – agitated, rolling and churning. It's over! she thought. That jerk has been nothing but a constant heartache. She waited, fuming. Finally, the phone rang.

"Hello," she said curtly.

"Spence? What's wrong?" George asked apprehensively. "Lottie said it was an emergency."

"You're damn right it's an emergency! I'm leaving you!" Blue yelled into the receiver.

"Oh, christ almighty! You called me to the phone for *this*?" he said, irritated with her.

"Yes – *this*! Wanna know why? Your floozy Olivette came by the house today with a note for you."

"What the *hell* are you talking about?" George retorted angrily.

"I read it. That's what the hell I'm talking about! She says, and I quote, *'I'm way past due for servicing.'* She also says if you don't give her what she wants, she'll have to *'go to the police and spill the proverbial beans.'* So, now I know it was *you* who robbed the company. Apparently, she knows it too and she's blackmailing you. Looks like Olivette keeps her mouth shut as long as you fuck her! *Christ*, George! What kind of vermin *are* you?" Blue was screaming into the phone.

George was silent, his mind racing. "Blue, *sweetheart*," he said

169

smoothly. "Calm down. You just ran into a crazy woman today – we call her 'owl-face' around here. She's after anything with a cock! And her latest conquest happens to be me. She's been on my ass for months and it's almost cost me my job," he told her convincingly. "She's a pathological liar, Spence. I've tried *everything* to discourage her. I even told her you were my wife."

"That's *bullshit*, George, and you know it! She seemed perfectly sane to me," Blue retorted. "If she's desperate enough to show up at your house to make sure you get her letter, then I imagine you've probably fucked her and now you're avoiding her like she's a disease. I know you, George," she told him. "I think you've agreed to be her sex toy to keep her from going to the police!"

"So you're gonna believe *her* over *me*?" he asked.

"Oh, I've heard *that* one before! Yeah, I *am* gonna believe her over someone who lies to me with every breath. Not only are you a liar, you're a thief 'cause I'm lookin' at stolen booty right now – in that duffel bag of yours," Blue retorted, then wished she hadn't.

"What makes you think there's money in there? If I remember correctly, I put a lock on that bag," George told her. "Unless you busted it!"

"Yeah, there's a lock *now*," Blue fired back. "But I saw what was in there *before* the lock... and it was green and there was lots of it. You shouldn't have been so careless, George," she said sarcastically.

"If you as much as *breathe* on that money, I'll kill you!" he threatened.

"*I* won't, but the cops'll be happy to! Because you know what I'm gonna do? I'm takin' this money and my big mouth down to the Wichita police station and turnin' you in!" Heart pounding in her chest, Blue couldn't stop her words.

"*YOU STAY PUT!*" George ordered her. "Don't leave that house, do you hear me? I'm comin' home."

"You can't stop me," Blue said bravely.

"Oh, yes I can. I'm only going to say this once, so you'd better listen," George said evenly. "If you so much as step *one foot* outside that house before I get there, I swear to you, you'll be the sorriest bitch alive!"

"What do you mean?" she asked.

"I mean I'll go after the one person you truly love – your precious Jonas. And I might hurt him. Or I might kidnap him. I might even *kill* him. And the thang is, sweetheart – you won't know *which* of those I'm gonna do." George's deadly words were daggers piercing her heart. He was raping her again – this time through her son.

A fearless, mother-bear instinct washed over Blue as George leveled his threat. The sensation was beyond fear. Beyond anger. "If you so much as touch *one hair* on his head, I will *cut your heart out!*" The words came rushing up swiftly, like a geyser erupting in the very depths of her womb.

Click. George had hung up. "*Shit!*" she said, slamming down the phone. "I'm not letting him get away with this. He's *not* keeping that money and he's *not* getting near Jonas! The only way I can be sure of that is to go to Oklahoma myself!" She grabbed her already packed suitcase and an overnight bag, throwing in toiletries and other necessities. Double-check the closet, she thought. Only empty hangers remained.

Adding a few keepsakes, she zipped her bag. "Damn! He'll be home any minute. I've gotta get out of here!" She started to leave the room. "The money!" she remembered, dashing back to the closet. She dragged the heavy duffel bag down the stairs, along with her luggage.

"Oh, my god! Muss!" she exclaimed, realizing he was somewhere in the house. She ran the rest of the way down the stairs, calling for him. I can't forget his things, she thought. She scooped up the kitty litter box, toys, cans of Friskies, and the bag of Smell's Gone cat litter. "Mus-sels?" she called. No Muss. She frantically looked in his favorite hiding places. "You pick the *worst* times to make yourself scarce!" she said, unable to find him.

She carried the bagful of money, her suitcase and overnight bag out to her car. Throwing them in the back seat, she raced back into the house to get Muss. She opened the front door to see if he was on the porch when George's car squealed to a hard stop. He leaped out of the car and sprinted toward the house.

When he saw Blue, he yelled, "Don't move!" She closed the front door and backed into the living room, bracing herself for the worst.

In the meantime, Muss had appeared and was sitting on the coffee table. *What's all the commotion about?* he yawned.

George threw the door open, so that it banged against the wall behind it. The look on his face was a mixture of panic and fury. He went straight for Blue's slight body. Grabbing her by the shoulders, he shook her until her teeth rattled. "You and that money are not going *anywhere*! Do you understand?" He let go of her, pushing her backward onto the couch.

"I'll lock you in the goddamn basement, *bitch*!" he cursed, spit flying from his mouth. His eyes were as crazed as the day he'd raped her. Blue felt terror, like flaming arrows, burning holes in the pit of her stomach. "You fuck with me, Blue, and I *will* hurt you – and your son! Matter of fact, I'll show you what'll happen to your son if you try to screw me! He reached down for Muss, who was now hiding behind a chair, and grabbed him. "I've always *hated* this cat anyway!" he snarled.

"Put him down! *Right now*!" Blue jumped to her feet. She lunged at George, who had the cat by the neck. Muss was struggling to get free from his vise-like grip. He clawed his captor by lifting his back feet and sinking them into George's chest.

"Ow!" George yelled, as bright, red blood appeared from Muss's hold. "That was the *wrong* thing to do, you mangy feline! You're payin' for that!"

"*NO!*" Blue shrieked. She lunged at George, biting his arm. That's when he let go of Muss. Not by dropping him to the floor, but by throwing the cat across the room – much like a batter throws his bat after hitting a home run. Muss crashed into the wall, fell to the floor limply and did *not* get up.

"*Muss? Muss!*" Blue screamed hysterically. She ran over to where he was lying. "Oh, my baby... Mussie," she cried, bending over him. She turned around, eyes filled with fury. "Well, *do* something, you *murderer!*" she ordered George. "*You* threw him, now *you* save him!"

George was in shock. He hadn't intentionally meant to *kill* the cat. He just wanted to get his point across. His gaze suddenly shifted beyond Blue to something outside. "It's the fuckin' pigs, man!" he exclaimed, as two cops got out of a cruiser. "You called them, didn't you?"

"You killed my Mussels, you *bastard*!" was all she could say. "He's dead. You broke his neck!" She convulsed into sobs. George

172

raping her had killed off something inside Blue. Now he'd killed her best friend as well. Loud knocking accompanied Blue's crying. The police were at the door.

"You mention *one word* to the cops, about anything, and you won't be able to get up for a week," George threatened. He composed himself and answered the door. "Hi, officers. What can I do for you?"

Blue tenderly wrapped Muss in a towel and gathered him in her arms. "Oh, Muss. I love you so," she said, weeping. She held him close; hoping somehow the strength of her love would bring his life back. The sleek, gray body was motionless.

She was sobbing when she heard a voice in her head. *"Look, I'm already dead. There's nothing more you can do for me. Just get away from him, while you still can."* She knew instantly it was Muss's spirit giving her a warning. Blue looked to see if George was still occupied. He was. I'd better sneak out now, she thought, keeping an eye on him as she moved through the kitchen toward the back door.

"No matter how things look around you, trust Great Spirit." Suddenly, her friend's words blasted into her thoughts again, like meteorites hurtling through space. Blue repeated them, mantra-like, as she left the house and climbed into Saffron. She placed Muss gently on the front seat. A sick feeling overwhelmed her as she felt his body losing warmth.

Starting the engine as quietly as one could a Volkswagen beetle, she backed out of the driveway. She knew she had George in a bind. The police were still there, so he couldn't go after her. Blue beeped the horn as she passed by them – just to needle him. I hate him so! she thought. When he saw her whiz by, he blanched. Good, she thought. He knows I'm leaving with his precious money!

She drove straight to Ruby's, sobbing and glancing over at her towel-covered companion. Blue had decided to leave Muss with her mother. I want him to have a decent burial, she thought, one where I can put his toys and a picture of me beside him. Blue knew her mother would take the cat and bury him as if he were her own. Over the years, Ruby had buried all her dead pets in the back yard. And Muss would be no exception.

Somehow, sharing the cat's death with her mother was Blue's way of trying again for her love – through her cherished Muss. She pulled in the driveway and shut off the car. Ruby was out in the yard, pulling stray weeds that were making their last attempt at life before the first frost. She looked up, squinting from the late summer sun. Cradling Muss in her arms, Blue walked toward her mother.

With no greeting for her daughter, Ruby resumed her weed yanking. "You'd better not be comin' here for any hand-out – or a bed," she said, not bothering to look up.

"No, mom. I don't want anything but a shovel," Blue said quietly.

"A shovel? For *what*?" Ruby replied, refusing to stop what she was doing.

"I'd like you to help me bury Mussels," Blue said, her voice catching. "He was killed an hour ago." The weeding stopped – abruptly.

Ruby stood up, disbelief blanketing her face. "This had better not be a joke, Patricia Ann," she said. Blue opened up the towel to reveal Muss's ever-stiffening body. Ruby gasped when she saw the cat's motionless form. "Oh, my goodness. My sweet baby... he's dead," her mother's voice was tearful.

Blue held out her arms and Ruby took the bundled cat from her daughter. It was a deja-vu... a moment of remembrance when she had handed her son over to another woman. For the first time Blue could ever remember, her mother lovingly looked her straight in the eye and said, "I'm so sorry, Patti. I *know* you loved Muss. I loved him too."

So strong was Blue's hunger for her mother's compassion, her eyes filled with tears. "Thank you, mom," she said gratefully. "Then can we bury him here, with the other pets, so he won't be alone?"

Her question must have melted Ruby's icy heart. She leaned over and gave her daughter a kiss on the forehead. "Of course we can," she replied. "I'll get the shovel."

The officers left after an hour. Finally! I thought they'd never leave, George thought. I'm sure they bought my story since I've been helping with the investigation. "Sorry boys," he said, as if they were there. "But I'm blowin' this town. I've got $50,000 to recover!" The police had instructed him not to leave the city until the case was solved. "*Nothing* and *nobody* is going to stand in the way of getting my money," he said, taking the stairs two at a time.

George threw a few things in his travel case, made sure he had some reefer, a carton of Kools and ran out the front door. He grabbed a map on the way, just in case there was a route that could get him to Ponca City in less than four hours. He turned the engine key, expecting the car to start. It didn't. "Shit! What the *fuck...*?" he exploded.

Raising the hood, he began checking the guts of his red Ford Galaxy. Testing for loose wires, he tried starting it several times. No luck. Every second I diddle with this car, he thought, Blue is getting farther on down the road! "*Damn!*" he cursed. He checked the battery, a new one that had been installed recently. Looks like one of the battery cables vibrated loose, he thought. He got his tools from the trunk and tightened the cable. He tried the engine again. It turned over. Slamming the hood down, George jumped in the car, put it in gear and gunned it.

Blue had been driving for an hour – in deep reflection. It feels like Muss had to die, she thought, so mom and I could bury him together. His dying actually brought us closer. And I couldn't believe it when she kissed me on the cheek and told me good-bye when I left. Oh God, I hope we've turned a corner, she prayed silently.

She periodically checked for George's car in her rear-view mirror. Glancing at the gas gage, she saw it was below empty. And she was on a long stretch of road with no gas stations in sight. "Rats!" she exclaimed. She felt Saffron slowing down and pulled off on the side of the road. George'll probably get there before me now, she thought, getting out of the car and looking around. The wind was whipping dust into mini-tornadoes that ran along the ground, picking up homeless tumbleweeds in their path and tossing them in the air.

In the distance, Blue could see something moving on the road. It looked like a pick-up truck. As it got closer, Blue began waving her arms and yelling. "Hey! I need help!" The pick-up slowed to a stop. A man and a woman were in the cab of the truck. The woman was driving. She looked to be about fiftyish, with a knot of long salt-and-pepper hair perched atop her head, threatening to cascade down her back any minute. Her face and hands had the weathered look of outside work, but her brown eyes sparkled like a young girl's.

"I bet yer outta gas," she predicted. "We females are famous for that. Let 'er run right down to the last drop and then wonder why we can't get 'er to go." She laughed at her own joke. "I do it all the time. Makes Bodey here so mad he'd jus' as soon shoot me as he would look at me."

"I *am* out of gas," Blue admitted. "How far's the nearest gas station?" she asked, wiping her forehead with her hand.

Bodey, bearded with a face sun-lined like his wife's, pointed a tanned finger. "Thar's one jus' down the road, 'bout four miles from here. You could'a walked it, if you'd known. Whar's a young girl like you headed all alone?" he asked.

"Ponca City, Oklahoma," Blue informed him.

"Oh, well then," he said. "You don't have too fer to go."

"Hop on in, missy," the woman said. "Me and Bodey are the only taxi service you got 'round these parts!" Bodey got out and let Blue climb in to sit between the two of them. "You got valuables in that car?" she asked, eyeing the bags in the back of Saffron.

"Oh my gosh, yes." Blue replied, suddenly remembering the duffel bag full of money. Practically climbing over Bodey, she got out of the truck and put the bag in her trunk and locked it.

As Blue got back in the cab, the woman introduced herself, "My name's Harriet and this here's my husband Bodey," she said. "We're the Prescotts. We live jus' down the road apiece – on a big cattle ranch. The hired help's there now, runnin' the place while we go to town. What's yer name?"

"I'm Blue. Blue Spencer," she said, nodding to both of them.

"Nice to meet 'cha," Harriet said, extending her hand. "Where ya from, Blue?"

"Wichita, Kansas." Everyone got quiet as they bounced along in the shiny black Chevrolet truck.

"Home of the Wheatshockers," Bodey eventually piped up.

"Yep," Blue responded, surprised he knew of the University of Wichita basketball team.

"Me and the herd listen to their games on the radio when I'm out in the barn," he said, pulling on his stubby beard.

Blue started to say something, but Harriet made a sharp right turn into the gas station, causing Blue to pitch towards Bodey. "Harriet, for god's sake, will ya slow down? We got a rider!" he criticized his wife. She screeched to a stop, dust flying everywhere.

"This girl needs some gas, Sam," Bodey called to a tall, sandy-haired man wearing an oil-stained uniform and a purple bandanna around his forehead. "Her car's down the road bout two miles thata'way. Can ya lock up fer a minute and take care of her? We gotta get on to town."

Sam looked at Blue and smiled. "Sure, Bodey. Always glad to help a fine lookin' woman," he said. "I'll get your gas for you, miss. My truck's over there, next to that stack of tires. You can go ahead and get in if you want."

Harriet and Bodey pulled away and Blue was alone with Sam. He's handsome but I'm not sure I can trust him, she thought. This guy could smile at me, and then kill me for all I know. Sam saw her expression and read her mind. "You're *not* with an ax murderer. I'm a Harvard man." Blue laughed, embarrassed at being so transparent. "How I ended up out here between the Kansas and Oklahoma state line owning a run-down gas station is a mystery to me."

"Is that true? You went to Harvard?" she asked, getting in the front seat of the truck.

"Sorry, the seat's kinda dusty," he apologized, brushing it off. "Yep. I went to the best school in the county – and ended up here," he said wryly, backing the truck onto the road. "Got my degree in law and moved back here to my home state of Oklahoma. I bought some land and had a house built on it – called it Rainbow Acres.

I just needed some space," he continued, "you know, earth instead of concrete. Oklahoma's Indian territory is all over this state... sacred ground for the Potawatomi, Shawnee, Ponca, Pawnee, Kickapoo.

There's hundreds of tribes," he informed her.

"Really?" Blue replied, thinking suddenly of Soaring Hawk.

"Opened a law office," he went on. "But after a while, I got disgusted with the greediness of most lawyers and didn't want to be labeled a shyster myself. So, after four years practicing law, I sold my practice to a Harvard buddy of mine from Texas. Bought this gas station and I've been operating it ever since – about six years now."

"Are you happy?" Blue asked.

"Happier than I was," Sam told her. "But this isn't all I do. I'm a playwright... I write plays. Just got one published recently."

"Cool," Blue said, awed by his success. "A real playwright. I'd like to write someday. I've done poetry and stuff, but nothin' that anyone would ever want to publish."

"Take my advice and stay with it, whether you're ever published or not. You'll never be sorry. Writing's like havin' a good friend around. This your car?" he asked, as Saffron came into view.

"Yep. That's my girl. I let the poor thing run completely dry."

"I used to have a VW bus, back in Boston – it was orange. I loved that thing. It was a blast to drive. Sold it for a song." He made a U-turn in the highway, pulling up behind her car. "Where're you headed, if I may ask?"

"Ponca City," she told him. "It's about a hundred miles from here, I think. I saw a sign a few miles back."

Sam filled her gas tank and told her if there was anything else he could do, just to let him know. "Here's my phone number, in case you run into any trouble." His blue eyes were penetrating and kind. He handed her a slip of paper with his number on it.

"Thank you." Blue looked up at him. "You've been a life-saver." Unable to resist the impulse, she stood on her tiptoes and kissed him on the cheek. Without hesitation, he encircled her in his arms and they embraced. "Good luck with your plays," she said, pulling away, surprised at their instant rapport. "You'll probably be famous someday." She gave him one of her million-dollar smiles.

"Aw shucks," Sam said, mimicking a southern drawl.

"I'd better go."

"Okay, Blueflower," he said warmly. "I don't know you or what you're up to, but I have a feeling you need to be careful. You're a woman alone," he warned her.

"I will," she promised. God, if he only knew who and what I'm up against, she thought. "See ya," she said with a wave as she drove away.

Glancing in her rear-view mirror, she could see Sam watching her. He looks lonely standing there, she thought. And he called me Blueflower... what a sweet name. She wondered, as he disappeared from sight, what it would be like to be the woman in *his* life.

George was making good time, with no cops in sight and a straight stretch of road. He picked up the map lying on the passenger seat. With his knee guiding the steering wheel he studied it, checking his location. Two more hours on route thirty-five he thought, and I'll be in Ponca – and hot on Blue's tail! He floored the car, just thinking about the fact that she had his money. "That bitch's gonna wish she'd never met me," he said, lighting up a joint – "especially when she tries a double-cross. If she wants to see her son again, she'd better hand over the money without a hitch!"

Welcome To Ponca City – population 26,000 the sign read. Thank god, Blue thought. I don't know if George is behind me or in front of me, so I'd better go straight to Jonas's day care center. She asked for directions at the first gas station she saw. The cashier told her the Lots of Tots day care center was on the corner of Shawnee and Pine streets and pointed her in the right direction. When she pulled up in front, there were a handful of children on the playground. One of them was Jonas.

He's by far the cutest one out there, she thought, admiring him. She walked over to the fence. "*Jon–as*," she called. Her heart skipped a beat with his look of happy recognition. He ran over to the fence where she stood. "Hi," Blue said, smiling.

"Boo! Hi, Boo," he said excitedly. His hazel eyes sparkled and his cheeks were flushed from play. "Come and meet Stewie," he told her. "He's my best friend."

"Okay, Jonas. I'm going to go in the front door. Come inside and I'll meet you there," Blue instructed. The large playroom was alive with the noisy activity of children. The center was overpopulated and understaffed, with only three adults that she could see and well over twenty children. Jonas ran toward Blue when he saw her, his arms outstretched in anticipation. She picked him up in a warm embrace and began swinging him around. "How's my little goose?" she asked, kissing him on the cheek. "I've missed you so much!"

One of the staff was watching their display of affection. Curious about who this pretty young woman was, she approached the two of them. "Hi. I'm Suzanne. Are you Jonas's big sister?" she asked. Blue laughed, deciding in that second to make the woman's innocent question her story.

Still holding Jonas, she answered, "Yes. How'd you guess?"

"Well, you both look so much alike," she replied. "I've never seen you around here before, though."

"That's because I don't live here. I moved to Kansas to go to school and hardly ever have a chance to come home," Blue continued her effortless fabrication. "I'm so busy with my full-time job and college. So, I don't get to *see* this boy much," she said, giving Jonas a squeeze. He looked at her, his expression puzzled. He knew what the word *sister* meant, and that he didn't have one.

"You're not my sister," he said.

"Don't mind him," Blue told Suzanne. "He sees me so infrequently, he forgets who I am." Blue put Jonas down before he could say anything else that could be incriminating. "Do you want me to meet Stewie?" she asked him.

"Yeah!" he exclaimed. He reached for Blue's hand and pulled her toward the door.

"Is it okay for us to go outside?" Blue asked Suzanne, as she opened the door for Jonas.

"Of course. Stay as long as you'd like," she replied cheerily.

"Thanks," Blue said. Once outside, she scanned the play area. Unable to locate an opening in the six-foot fence, she realized that taking Jonas from the playground would be impossible. Jonas tugged her playfully toward his friend. "Hi, Stewie," she said to the little boy, who looked surprisingly like Jonas. She knelt down and gave him a hug. "Any friend of Jonas's is a friend of mine," she said warmly.

At the moment Blue was embracing Stewart, George was watching it all from the privacy of his car. If I hadn't broken into that attorney's office, he thought, I would've never known to hang out here. He recorded in his memory what he'd just seen and drove away unnoticed by Blue. This'll be easy, he thought. Like takin' candy from a baby.

Blue played outside with the two boys until one of the staff announced it was snack time. As she was taking them back into the building, she had an idea. I'll fake a phone call to Naomi and Robert

181

under the pretense that *I'll* be taking Jonas home this evening, she schemed. Then I can leave with him and avoid any questions from the staff.

The only obstacle to carrying out her plan was the little boy's father. Robert had left work early and was at the day care center to pick up Jonas when they walked in from the playground. The staff was busy passing out snacks to the children when Blue, holding Jonas's hand, ran straight into him. "Blue! What are *you* doing here?" he asked, a surprised look on his face.

"Daddy!" Jonas announced happily. He let go of Blue's grasp and ran toward his father.

"Hello son," Robert answered, picking him up and kissing him.

"Oh, hi!" Blue said, hiding her alarm. "Well, you all invited me back to visit Jonas sometime," she explained. "I just decided that... uh, sometime was now. Sorry I didn't call first, but it was sort of a spur-of-the-moment thing." Seeing Robert unexpectedly caught her off guard and she could feel her face reddening.

"Oh... well then... why don't you join us for supper tonight?" he asked, tousling his son's hair, then putting him down. "We'll just set another place at the table." Jonas, in the meantime, was having great fun playing between his dad's legs. His infectious laughter tugged at Blue's heart. I wish *I'd* been the one to provide Jonas with a father, she thought sadly, watching the two of them.

"Oh, I can't. I, uh... have some other business to take care of. I have a cousin who lives here and I told him I'd have dinner with *him* tonight," she fibbed. "But you know what I'd *really* like? I'd love to pick up Jonas tomorrow morning for day care. Would it be all right with you and Naomi?'

"It's fine with me. It would save me a trip. But I'll have to confirm it with Naomi," he replied.

"Can I call you later tonight to find out?" she inquired.

"Of course. I'm sure it'll be okay with her. Jonas, shall we go home and see mommy?" he asked. "She'll be surprised we're so early today." He picked up his small son like a sack of feed and swung him over his shoulder. The boy squealed with delight.

"Bye, Jonas," Blue called out, watching Robert carry him away. "Maybe I'll see you tomorrow."

"Bye, Boo." He could hardly get the words out, he was giggling so. Blue blew him a kiss, remembering Love Mae's prophetic words. *"You can only offer him the love of a friend... Jonas is not your little boy."*

George drove to the nearest payphone he could find. This might be like looking for a needle in a haystack, he thought. Opening the Ponca City phonebook, he ran his finger down the list of motels. After ten dimes, ten motels and no Blue, he began feeling frustrated. I've *gotta* find her, he thought.

A block away from the payphone, he spotted a bar. Hell, give yourself a break, he thought. You'll find the bitch. He walked down the block toward the bar and entered the darkened establishment. A red, green and yellow revolving light splashed primary colors on the bar top. A country western tune he didn't recognize was the jukebox's current play. The place was dead, with only a fistful of customers – four men and a woman. George slid onto a barstool and ordered a draft and some beer nuts. He noticed the bartender staring at him, like he thought he knew him.

"You look familiar. You from around here?" the barkeep finally asked.

"No, man. I'm a Kansas boy," George replied.

"What'cha doin' here?" he inquired further.

George took a drag off his Kool thinking, who is this guy – an undercover cop? "I came after my old lady," he said, exhaling smoke as he spun his yarn. "We had a terrible fight yesterday on our anniversary, and she split. I knew she was headed this way. I couldn't risk losing my woman, so here I am. The problem is, I can't find her. I've called almost all the motels in the city and... no luck. I'm gettin' worried."

The bartender shook his head slowly. "Females," he said. "My wife of twenty-nine years divorced me a year ago. Tore me up. Said she just wasn't happy. I didn't have a clue... I thought everything was fine."

"What a bummer," George replied. "Yeah... chicks have a way of sneakin' up on ya when they wanna dump you."

"Boy, ain't that the truth! You a war vet?" the bartender asked, noticing the dog tags around George's neck.

"Yeah," he told him. "These aren't my tags, though. They're my buddy's. After he died, I decided to wear 'em... makes me feel better."

"Oh, I'm sorry," the barkeep said. "That Vietnam thing was a goddamn fiasco. Everybody lost, in my opinion," he said, then paused, staring into space. "Yeah, war is hell. I served in World War II and lost a lot of buddies – too many."

"Yeah, I know man. Losin' *one* is too many," George agreed. "I never really wanted to kill anybody either, but you had no choice over there. It was you or the other guy," he remembered. "Well, gotta go," he said abruptly, polishing off his beer. "You wouldn't know any motels that aren't listed in the phonebook, would ya?" he asked as he tossed down a couple of bills for the beer and nuts.

"Seems like I'm always tellin' out-of-towners about motels," the bartender laughed. "Yeah, there's one called Millie's Motel over on State Street. It was here before practically anything else, except maybe the refinery. Serves up the best breakfasts in town. And another one's out on the East end of town. It's a brand new Holiday Inn," he said. I think Millie's is mos' likely in the directory, but I'm not sure about the other one. It's only been open a week."

"Hey, thanks for your help, man. Keep the faith, brother."

"Take 'er easy," the bartender yelled. "I hope you find your wife!"

"Thanks," he yelled back. You and me both, George thought. And she'd better have my money!

Millie's Motel was George's first stop. Pulling into the parking lot, he thought, Blue wouldn't stay here... too humble for her taste. She likes the high life too much... especially when she can use *my* bread to pay for it.

The clerk on duty was Millie herself, white hair piled high and secured with a beaded hair comb. Her blue denim shirt was adorned with a heavy turquoise and silver necklace and her arthritic fingers were covered with rings. "Howdy," she said with a drawl. "I'm Millie, owner of this place. Can I help you?" She smiled broadly, revealing a set of perfect dentures.

"I hope so," he replied. "I'm lookin' for my wife."

"Well, is she lost?" she asked with a chuckle.

"No ma'am, she's not," George replied, poker-faced. "She ran away from home yesterday, after we argued, and I've gotta find her so we can make up," he told the wizened woman, sounding desperate. "By any chance, has she checked in here?"

"Sir, I can sure see you're pretty upset. As proprietor of this place, it's my prerogative not to give out information I consider confidential," she informed him in a serious tone.

"But it's my *wife* we're talkin' about. Doesn't that make a difference?" George pleaded.

"Nope. 'Fraid not" she said flatly. "You could be the man in the moon paradin' yourself as Mr. George so and so. 'N'other words, I don't know you from Adam, or what your intentions are or if you're married, or what. I'm real sorry. It's jus' policy." The phone rang and Millie excused herself, all the while keeping an eye on George.

He strained to get a glimpse at what looked like the guest check-in list lying on Millie's desk. Shit! Can't make out a thing, he thought. She's probably using an alias anyway so it wouldn't do me any good. Striding out of the motel, he jumped in the car and drove to his next destination.

I'm gonna have to be a lot more convincing with the next person, he thought. That old bitch was too smart. I've gotta put on the Garret charm. "Flowers!" he exclaimed. "I'll bring my 'wife' some posies."

He stopped at a convenience store and bought a semi-wilted, paper-wrapped bouquet of flowers and a six-pack of Coors. Throwing the flowers on the front seat, he barreled out of the parking lot. He opened one of the beers, keeping it out of sight between mouthfuls.

Five miles later, the Holiday Inn sign appeared on the left. George pulled up in front of the lobby doors. The bartender was right, he thought. This motel's as new as a baby's butt! The clerk should be a pushover. Just hired, and probably green as hell. Show time, Georgie boy! he thought. Grabbing the flowers, he walked in wearing a look of heartache and panic. The clerk was a young, pimply, horn-rimmed glasses kind of guy. This boy doesn't have a chance with me, he thought.

"May I help you, sir?" the pushover asked politely.

"You're my last hope," George replied solemnly. He placed the flowers on the counter for the clerk to see. "You see, I've lost my wife and I believe she might be here," he told him anxiously. "We had a silly argument yesterday, on our anniversary, and she split. I was beside myself. I hate to admit it, but I cried all night long," he said, feigning tears. "I love this chick so much. She's my best friend." The clerk gave him a sympathetic look.

"Anyway, she called me early this morning and said she had checked into the Holiday Inn just outside of Ponca City. And then she said the magic words," he continued his story. The clerk was mesmerized by this time. " 'I'm sorry about yesterday, baby,' " he mimicked a woman's voice. " 'Please meet me at the motel. I'll be waiting. I love you.' "

"So I jumped in my car," George continued. "Didn't even change my clothes. And I drove four hours straight to get here – so please… please tell me she's checked in," he implored the young man, who was obviously moved by his story. "I want to give my woman these flowers, kiss her sweet lips and tell her how sorry I am. Her name's Blue Spencer. She's petite and very pretty… with dark hair," he told him, pulling a fifty-dollar bill out of his pocket.

"Uh… well… I'm new here and I don't think I'm supposed to…" the clerk stammered, eyeballing the money.

George shoved the bill in front of the clerk's face. "This is yours if you'll just take me to my wife's room so I can give her these flowers and make it up to her."

The clerk looked at the money, glancing furtively around to see if anyone was looking. He took the fifty. "There *is* a woman here who fits your description," he said, checking the register for her room number. "But her name's Elizabeth Spencer," he told him, looking up at George.

"That's her!" George said, guessing. "Elizabeth Blue Spencer. She's my honey!" Signing your name was fairly *stupid*, Blue, he thought.

"I can't leave the front office sir, so I'll have to give you the key to her room. But you've got to bring it back in ten minutes, or I'll be in big trouble," he told him nervously, handing the room key to George. "It's around back, first floor – room 143."

"Oh, no problem, man. I'll bring it back before you know it's gone," he promised. "Hey, thanks a million. Peace," he said, giving the clerk the two-fingered sign. Quickly exiting the lobby, he followed the clerk's directions and located the room. Dumping the flowers into a nearby waste can, he inserted the key and opened the door slowly.

"Bingo! This looks like her hideout," he said. Blue's things were there, but the room looked unused. He checked the bathroom. No one. She's probably hidden the money around here somewhere, he thought. He began ransacking the room, pulling out drawers, rummaging through her suitcase, looking under the bed, to no avail. "Fuck!" he cursed. "You *cunt*! Where's my money?" In a fit of rage, he tore the bedclothes off the bed and dumped the contents of her suitcase and overnight bag on the floor.

A tube of lipstick fell out of the overnight bag and rolled across the carpet. She's not only gonna *know* I was here, he thought, grabbing it. She's gonna *worry* that I was here – because I'm gonna write her a little "love" note. He began scrawling words on the mirror above the dresser with the coral-colored lipstick. His message was undeniably clear. *GEORGE WAS HERE AND WANTS HIS FUCKING MONEY!* it read. He ran out of space on the mirror, so he used the motel stationary to finish. *"He knows where your kid is – so meet him at 11:00 p.m. in the parking lot of the Ponca City Tavern, six blocks from this motel with the money – or else!"*

Meanwhile, Blue was driving back to the motel from the day care center. She was worrying about George's whereabouts. I know he's in town, she thought. But where? And I'm sure he's furious. Oh god, why did I take that money? Why didn't I just leave it? What was I trying to prove? What if he gets to Jonas? Unanswerable questions... unthinkable consequences. Blue was paralyzed with fear.

Blue realized she was on a street she didn't recognize. "Rats! she exclaimed. "I think I'm lost." I turned left when I was supposed to turn right, she thought. Making a U-turn in the street, she drove to a gas station and got directions.

She lit a cigarette and took a deep drag. Smoking nervously as she drove, she carefully followed the directions. Within minutes, she saw a sign telling her that the Holiday Inn was only three miles further on the left.

George put the finishing touches on his message and checked the room again, looking for any possible hiding place he might have missed. She must have the money with her in the car, he concluded.

A knock at the door and an inquiring voice startled him. "Mr. Spencer? The clerk told me to come and get the key. We have to have it back now." George didn't answer. "Uh... sir, if you don't cooperate with us, we'll have to call the police," the voice continued.

That was all it took. The mention of the law sent chills down George's spine. He opened the door, an apology on his lips. "I'm sorry, man," he said, shutting the motel door behind him and handing over the key. "My wife's not here and I just thought I'd wait awhile for her to come back," he lied.

"We understand your dilemma, but you'll have to leave now, sir. The motel can't allow you to stay in the room," the message-bearer said anxiously. "You can wait in your car or in the lobby if you'd like." George resisted an impulse to wrap one hand around the skinny neck of this kid and squeeze.

"Hey, no problem," he said nonchalantly. "I know your job is not to clear up domestic disputes. I'm splittin'." He got in the Galaxy, backed out of the parking space and careened out of the motel lot. "This is a fucking stone bummer," he said angrily. Just as he turned out onto the street, Blue pulled up to the stoplight in front of the motel.

In her vigilance, she recognized George's car. "Oh, my god," she gasped, her breath becoming shallow. "He knows where I am." Thankfully, George hadn't seen Blue. She spun into the parking lot and bolted out of Saffron like someone being chased. Running to her room she unlocked the door, only to be assaulted by the aftermath of George's fury. "Oh no!" she exclaimed, surveying the jumbled mess.

"*How* did he get in here?" Blue scanned the room, feeling angrier and more violated by the moment. Her belongings were strewn everywhere, the bed was torn up, and there was something scribbled on the mirror. The lipsticked words were not hard to distinguish.

"He wants his money? It's never been *his* money!" she said angrily. "I'm sure he charmed the shit out of some young, gullible employee and they let him in here." Her eyes fell on the note George had written. She picked it up. "Oh, dear god. He knows where Jonas is!" she exclaimed, frightened by the prospect.

Blue felt all the blood drain from her face. "Think," she told herself. "Just sit down for a minute and think." She felt lightheaded as she sat on the edge of the bed. I'm gonna turn the money over to the authorities, she thought, so they can arrest him. But... what about Jonas? If I don't cooperate with George, I don't know *what* he'll do to Jonas. Blue's heart was racing.

No – I'd better do what he says, she decided. I'd just *die* if anything happened to Jonas. The motel clock said 10:30 p.m. I've only got a half an hour to pull this off, she thought. "Okay, Blue girl," she challenged, looking at herself in the mirror. "It's time to discover what you're made of." She opened the door and looked out into the night. There wasn't a soul around. Like a featherweight boxer charged for a fight, she tripped lightly down the stairs and headed toward a ravine behind the motel.

About halfway down the sloping hill and to the left was an abandoned Tappan range, partially hidden in some bushes. Earlier in the day, Blue had stuffed the bag of money in the rusting stove. Now, as she opened the oven door, it squeaked, making an eerie sound in the darkness. Afraid to reach her hand into the once vacuous metal cavern, she felt for the leather bag.

The soft cowhide welcomed her grasp and she pulled it toward her. Clutching the bag against her body, Blue climbed the hill and ran to the car. Her watch said 10:45 p.m. "Gee zooey... I've gotta get out of here to make it by 11:00." Saffron started right up, as if knowing it was on an important mission. She put it in reverse and backed up.

Within seconds, Blue knew the car felt lopsided, like one tire was flat. Oh damn! she thought. She got out and peered at the tires. The back right one was flattening by the second. Panicked, she opened the hood and pulled out the spare. She ran into the motel lobby, asking the clerk if someone could help her change a tire.

"Please," she said breathlessly, " it's very important that I meet someone at exactly 11:00 tonight. I need help right now!"

"You've only got ten minutes then," the clerk volunteered. "I can't leave the desk, but the manager's here." He called for Tim, and a balding, middle-aged man with dark circles under his eyes, appeared. "Can you help one of our guests with a flat tire?"

"Sure," Tim said tiredly. "You have a spare?" he asked.

"Yes I do," Blue replied urgently. "I've *got* to leave in five minutes to meet someone or I'm in big trouble."

"I'll do the best I can," he assured her, walking quickly toward the door. Blue followed him out. "Where's your car?" he asked.

"Right over there," she told him. "It's the little yellow Volkswagen, the one with the sunflower on the antenna."

"My tools are in my car. It'll take me thirty seconds to get them." He was as good as his word. In a minute, he was on his knees changing Blue's now completely flat tire. "Looks like you got a good-sized nail in it," he told her.

She looked at her watch. "Oh, my god. It's a minute before 11:00... I've gotta leave *now*!"

"Just need to tighten this last lug. There you go," he said. Gesturing gallantly, he opened the car door for her.

"Thank you," she said, flashing a quick million-dollar smile. "Don't know what I would've done without your help." She started the car and peeled, tires squealing, out of the motel parking lot. It was 11:02. I'm so scared, she thought. What if he's not there? She sped toward the appointed meeting place.

Lurching to a stop in the parking lot of the tavern, she got out with the bag of money in hand and looked around. But nowhere did she see the Galaxy or George. "He *can't* be gone," she said. "He just *can't*! Couldn't he have waited?" she fumed. "You would've made it on time if you hadn't had that damn flat!" Blue was regretful and frantic. If he's not here, she thought, then he's hot on his trail of revenge... right to Jonas.

"No matter how things look around you, trust Great Spirit." The words literally flew out of her mouth. Shocked by the spontaneous reminder, Blue realized that Soaring Hawk had come... to offer his help. She took a deep breath and raised her eyes to the Oklahoma night sky. Even with the glare of street lights, a shooting star made it's debut for her to see. Okay, God. I'm not alone, she thought. You're right here beside me.

Blue drove to Jonas's house – just to make sure he was okay. The house was dark and the family car sat in the driveway. She looked around for George, but didn't see him. I'll park down the street so I can keep an eye on things, she thought. I wouldn't put anything past George. She positioned herself a half block away and kept an all-night vigil, alternately dozing and rousing.

She was awakened by sunlight streaming through the windshield. "Oh... aaah, my back," she said, feeling stiff from sleeping upright in the front seat. Blue's first groggily sad memory was of Muss. Oh, Mussie. I miss you... she thought. I'd give anything to hear you complaining… about riding in Saffron or being hungry, she mused, staring out the car window. I can't believe that you're buried under the dirt in Ruby's back yard instead of being here beside me.

Lost in her thoughts, she looked up to see that Robert's car was now gone. "What time is it?" she asked, looking at her watch. The hands read 8:30. "Jeesuz!" she exclaimed. "I've got to get to the day care center. George doesn't have his money, so he's gonna try to get his hands on Jonas," she predicted. "I've *got* to get to my boy before he does."

Finding her way back to Lots of Tots was not an easy task. It took asking two people, one who was nice enough to draw a map for her. "I couldn't find my way out of a paper bag," she scolded herself, attempting to follow the directions. Maybe someday, when you're all grown up, she thought, you'll find your purpose and your path in life, Blue. Then reading a map will be a piece of cake, because you'll already know where you're going...

Blue *did* find her way that morning. It was imperative. Jonas's safety was at stake. When she pulled up, there were three state police cruisers parked in front of the day care center. "What the...?" she said, immediately alarmed. She ran in the building, fearing the worst. The officers were talking to a man and a woman. The woman was crying and the man looked ashen. She spotted Suzanne and pulled her aside. "What's going on?" she asked anxiously.

"One of our children was abducted early this morning by an

192

unknown man," she replied.

"Oh, god!" Blue exclaimed, pulling on Suzanne's arm. "Was it Jonas?" she asked, even though she didn't see Naomi and Robert anywhere.

"No, honey. It wasn't your little brother," Suzanne reassured her, seeing the fright in Blue's eyes. "It was his friend, Stewart. He lives a half a block down the street and walks to the center with his mother every morning. But he came alone today, for some reason. The guy must've been waiting for him."

"Where's Jonas?"

Suzanne pointed to the playroom. "He's in with the other children. He had an asthma attack a little while ago, so we had to give him his atomizer. This morning has been pretty upsetting for him. He doesn't understand why his friend isn't here today," she said, her eyes full of concern. "We've explained to the children that Stewart was taken by a bad person and the police are here to find Stewart and bring him back to his parents."

Did George take this child? Blue speculated as she walked away. Why would he do a stupid thing like that? She went over to Jonas, who was standing at a window, as if waiting for his friend to arrive. "Hi, goose," she said tenderly, kneeling behind him. He turned around, eyes full of questions.

"Why did that bad man take Stewie away?" he asked her. "Did he need a playmate?"

"Oh Jonas, sweetheart. Only *you* would ask a question like that..." Blue replied, kissing him on the cheek. "No, he didn't take Stewart because he needed a playmate. It was because he just wanted to do a bad thing. But that's what the police are for, to catch people who do bad things." The little furrow between Jonas's eyes relaxed slightly.

"You mean, they'll bring Stewart back so I can play with him?" he asked, with an innocence only a child could demonstrate.

"Angel, that's what we're all hoping," Blue said, hugging him tightly. "In the meantime, why don't you play with some of the other children," she suggested, knowing it would take his mind off his friend. "I'll be back later to visit you, before your mom picks you up. Okay?" She started to leave, but Jonas clung to her. She hugged him, hard. "I love you, goose. Everything will be okay."

"I'll be back later," she told one of the day care workers as she left. I've got to make sure Jonas is safe, she thought, driving back to the motel. The only choice I have is to kidnap my own son. It's the only way. I can't let Naomi and Robert know he's in danger, because they'll go to the police. That's just too risky with George around. Absorbed in her plans, she almost drove by the motel. I'm gonna find a way to prevent him from getting to Jonas *and* the money, she determined, turning sharply into the parking lot.

When Blue got to her room, a courtesy morning newspaper was hanging in its plastic cocoon on the doorknob. A note was taped to the door. She removed the newspaper and ripped the folded piece of paper off the door. It was from George, as she suspected – his words cold and unfeeling. *"How's my favorite bitch?"* it read. *"Since you didn't bother to show up with the money last night, your son had to pay the price. It's up to you. If you want Jonas back unharmed, you'd better be there tonight – same place, same time. Peace, baby – You Know Who."*

A chill ran down her spine, giving her a shudder. He thinks he took Jonas, but he didn't! He abducted the wrong child! Oh god, she thought, when he realizes he has the wrong kid, he's *really* gonna be pissed. He'll double his efforts to find Jonas, she predicted. I can't take the chance of *anyone* screwing this up, including the police. I've got to do this myself and I've got to do it *now*!

It was getting close to noon. Four hours had passed since George snatched the little boy. Confident he'd been successful, he didn't even bother asking the child his name. "Hey, kid. You hungry?" he asked, looking over at the little boy. "You wanna eat something?" Stewart didn't answer. In fact, he'd barely said anything since George grabbed him and put him in the car. "Well, I'm havin' an attack of the munchies," he quipped, snuffing out his joint in the car ashtray. "Let's go get us a couple of hamburgers. You like burgers?"

Stewart looked down at his lap. George scrutinized his diminutive captive for a moment. "Lighten up, kid. I'm not gonna hurt you," he told the frightened child. "I'm just gonna keep you for a little while. It'll be like a vacation. No parents to tell you what to do. No school. No early bedtime. Just the two of us, cruisin' down the road." George

194

playfully punched the boy's arm.

"I wanna go home," Stewie finally said, looking at George with big tears cascading down his cheeks.

"You can't cry, kid," he said, giving his hair a tousle. "I don't have anything to wipe your nose." He was touched by the child's distress. But only for a moment. I can't let this kid get to me, he thought. He's the only leverage I have. I gotta be a hard ass, or I'm gonna end up without my $50,000 – or in jail!

They pulled into a McDonald's. "You're comin' in with me, so keep your mouth shut," he said firmly. "And I don't want you tryin' to run away either." They walked into the busy, fast food restaurant. George headed for the men's restroom, shoving the boy in the door first. "You stay in front of me, you hear?"

Poor Stewart was so petrified, he just nodded numbly. George stood him next to the urinal he was using. The child watched as his captor relieved himself, the yellow stream banking off white porcelain and finding its way down the stainless steel drain.

"You gotta go?" he asked.

"No," Stewart said softly.

"Let's split then," George instructed. "I want some food. And I don't give a rat's ass what it is, as long as it's dead," he said, laughing at his remark. He approached the counter, arms folded across his chest, and ordered. "Give me three big macs and a double order of fries," he told the female employee. "To go." He looked down at his hostage. "You want a milkshake?" Stewart just stared at the floor and shook his head.

"Well, I'll get ya one anyway," he told him. "You're probably real hungry." He ordered a strawberry shake, paid for the food and turned to leave. As they headed toward the door, George spotted two officers getting out of their cruiser. Shit, he thought. They're either here for lunch or for me. He took Stewart's hand and quickly exited through the door on the opposite side of the restaurant. He looked back to see that the officers were just there to eat.

Three in the afternoon. I'd better get back to the day care center, Blue thought. Naomi will be there to pick up Jonas soon. I've gotta get there before she does. She had been soaking in a tub of now lukewarm water in an attempt to relax. I'd better have my wits about me tonight, she thought. She stepped onto the bathroom floor and toweled herself dry. "You have to stay cool, Blue," she said to the image in the mirror. "There's an actress in you, so play your part well today. You can do this... just remember what's at stake and use your head."

She dressed, deliberately conventional. Pulling a pink, knit dress over her head, it dropped down easily over her slim hips. Pink was a good color for her, but not one she wore often. And only occasionally did she wear a dress. But today, it was important to look the part – the older sister coming to pick up her little brother. She smoothed her curly hair back, away from her face, outlined her lips with wild rose lipstick and slipped into her singular pair of black flats.

Now I'm the person my mother always wished for, she thought, gazing at her reflection in the mirror. Ruby had wanted her daughter to be sweet, girlish – and perfect. "Well mom, you'd be pleased today," she said. "Here's your flawless little doll – in the flesh." Grabbing the duffel bag of money, a change of clothes, her purse and a jacket, she took a deep breath and walked out of room 143.

Get ready for a wild ride, Blue, she thought. I just hope to get out of this alive. Resting her head on the steering wheel, she prayed. *"Great Spirit, I know you're with me, no matter what things look like, but please, I need some serious guidance today. Show me what to do and loan me a couple of your biggest, baddest angels because I have a feeling I'm gonna need them..."*

Blue felt a sudden infusion of courage that streamed through her body like electricity. "I *will* protect my son from this monster, whatever it takes," she proclaimed. "Only if I do *nothing* will I be making a mistake." It was a young woman's declaration and a mother's war cry.

"All we have to do now is wait, young man," George told Stewart. "And I'm not gonna worry about a thing 'cause Blue's gonna bring me my money tonight, like a good girl. Then I'm takin' off. Headin' for Nashville," he said dreamily. "Oh *mamasita*, it'll be a pretty sight – all that money!" The two of them were in a room at the Ponca City Star Motel. George was stretched out on the bed. Stewart sat on the floor watching television and eating a Snickers bar George bought him.

A news bulletin interrupted the afternoon cartoons. The tone of the newscaster's voice communicated the seriousness of his report. *"This morning, a five- year old boy was abducted on his way to the Lots of Tots Day Care Center."* George sat straight up in bed. *"No one has been able to identify the man who did this heinous crime, but police are diligently gathering any evidence they can find about who this man is and his whereabouts. The little boy who was abducted has dark hair, brown eyes and a small scar on the right side of his face. His name is Stewart Benson. If you see..."*

George didn't hear the rest of the newscast. He was too busy cursing. Stewart ran to the bathroom for safety. "Goddammit! Son-of-a-bitch! Motherfucker!" The epithets catapulted across the room like stones launched from a slingshot. "I've got the *wrong fucking kid*!" he yelled, picking up a lamp and throwing it. The television was next, his foot aimed at the head of the bearer of bad news. It fell backwards off its metal stand with a crash.

"I'm fucked!" he continued. "This kid's worth nothing. And I'll bet my right *testicle* Blue knows I got the wrong one. She doesn't have to do a thing now... except turn me in to the police. She's got her precious Jonas and I've got... *Stewart*!" He sat down on the edge of the bed. "Calm down, Garret," he said. "You've had to figure out situations more complicated than this in Nam! So use your head, man!"

Blue walked through the front door of Lots of Tots, a vision of traditional loveliness. The day care staff was waking the children from their afternoon nap. She waited patiently for a staff person to notice her, however she was anything *but* patient. Naomi could walk in here at any moment, she worried. I've got to take Jonas – *now*.

Suzanne happened to look in Blue's direction. "You look so pretty today," she declared, walking over to her. "Special occasion?"

Her question gave Blue the perfect opening. "Yes, there's an occasion today. I'm taking my little brother out to his favorite restaurant for an early dinner. Mom and dad are going to join us after work. We're celebrating just bein' a family," Blue lied.

Suzanne smiled. "Oh, that's wonderful," she exclaimed. "Family's so important. It just seems lately like families don't stick together the way they used to. Everybody's so busy." Her voice trailed off as she realized Blue had stopped paying attention to what she was saying.

"I'm in kind of a hurry, Suzanne. Is Jonas ready to go?" she asked anxiously.

"Oh, I'm sorry. Of course, I'll get him."

"Hi, goose," Blue greeted Jonas, as Suzanne brought him and his belongings to her.

"Hi, Boo," he replied, happy to see her.

"Me and you, my little man, are going to your favorite restaurant and have some supper. Would you like that?"

"Yeah!" he said, shaking his head vigorously. "Are mommy and daddy coming too?"

"Yep," she fibbed. "They sure are."

Jonas started jumping up and down in excitement, as Blue attempted to put his jacket on him. "Hey wiggle worm, stand still for a second," she said laughing. Jonas giggled, enjoying their tug-of-war. "Tell Suzanne good-bye," she instructed as they left.

He waved good-bye with one hand, holding onto Blue with the other. Once outside, Blue took a quick look around, then picked Jonas up and ran to the car. "Wheeee," she said, laughing and whirling him around. He laughed delightedly at being whisked away in Blue's arms. She started Saffron and took off without looking in her rear-view mirror. Just outside her range of vision, the Ford Galaxy crept along behind her.

There was only one person in the Galaxy. George. He had dumped Stewart, telling his young captive he would take him home if he would be a good boy and keep his mouth shut about what happened. He threatened poor Stewart that if he told on him, he would find out, come back and take him away for good. Only minutes before Blue and Jonas exited the day care center, George had dropped Stewart off a few yards from his house, unhurt, then sped off down the street. And now he was following the two, both of them oblivious to his sinister presence.

"Where's my boy?" Naomi said cheerfully, as she walked into the day care center. She pulled out a soft toy penguin from her shopping bag. "I bought this for Jonas today on my lunch hour. Ever since we took him to the zoo and he saw real penguins, he's wanted one. Isn't it cute?" Several staff members smiled and nodded while others looked at her blankly, confused that she didn't know her son had left with Blue.

"Suzanne?" one of them called. "Jonas's mother is here." Naomi made small talk with the women, mentioning her shock about the news of Stewart's abduction.

"Isn't it terrible what happened?" she exclaimed to the staff. "It certainly wasn't *your* fault. Where was his mother, I wonder? I can't even *comprehend* what I'd do if that happened to my Jonas," she said, shaking her head.

Suzanne appeared, looking puzzled. "Jonas left with your daughter, Mrs. Matthews," she informed her. "You and your husband were to meet them for dinner tonight."

"My *daughter*? I don't *have* a daughter," Naomi said, her face contracting in fear. "What was her name?"

"Blue. She said her name was Blue," Suzanne replied, beginning to realize she'd been duped.

"Blue is *not* our daughter. She's Jonas's biological mother. We adopted him from her when he was three weeks old," Naomi said, her voice beginning to tremble.

"Oh dear, I didn't know," Suzanne said. "I just thought..."

"The trouble is," Naomi interrupted her, "you *didn't* think and you let someone you didn't even know walk out of here with our son!" Naomi was clearly angry, shaken that Jonas was out of her reach. "I need to call my husband right away."

"Here, use our phone – please," the director of the day care center offered. "We're so sorry, Naomi. It looks like one of our employees was *not* cautious when she should've been and we'll be taking immediate remedial action about this," she admitted. "Can we call the authorities for you?"

"I've got to talk to Robert," Naomi said, dialing the phone with a shaky hand. "I have no idea where this girl took Jonas... we've just got to find him," she said, her voice breaking. "Robert? Our Jonas is missing," her voice caught in a sob. "Blue Spencer has taken him somewhere." She paused while he spoke, listening. "This afternoon, before I came to pick him up I should've known something was up when you told me she was here with him the other day. I *trusted* her!" Naomi began to weep openly. "Please, call the police right away... and hurry over here before I fall apart," she begged her husband.

"I'm hungry," Jonas whined, as they drove. "Are we almost there?"

"Yes, goose," Blue said. "We're almost at your favorite place in all the world to eat."

"McDonald's?" he asked, eyes wide.

"Yep."

"I want a hamburger and French fries," he told her.

"You got it, Jonas," Blue said emphatically. She glanced in her rear view mirror, and then looked away. But something made her look again. Oh my god, she thought. It can't be. There's a car like George's behind me. She slowed down, to get a closer look. It *was* him. Don't panic, girl, she thought. Just use your wits and try to lose him.

Blue started to speed up, driving down side streets, turning Saffron first to the left and then to the right. Jonas pitched to one side, bumping his head on the door as the car angled sharply. He started to whimper, rubbing the spot that hurt. "Oh, Jonas. I'm sorry," she said. "Just hang on." He looked at her with big tears in his eyes.

The rear view mirror wasn't reflecting the convertible any longer. Blue breathed a sigh of relief. Pausing briefly at a four-way stop, she looked to her left and there was George. She floored the little car and raced down the mostly empty street. She found a major thoroughfare and turned onto it – heading east, and away from danger. She thought.

Out of the blue, there he was, right behind her at a stoplight. Her heart was in her throat. Trying not to panic, she pulled ahead on the green light and swerved in and out of lanes on the wide Ponca City street. "Come on, baby," she told Saffron. "Show us what you can do." George was several car lengths behind, which afforded her a little leeway. Zigging and zagging, she managed to pull ahead even further.

Jonas was scared and crying. Before Blue could stop him, he climbed into the back of the car and crouched on the floor. His crying reminded her of how he used to cry when he was a baby and it brought tears to her eyes. "You'll be okay," she told the little boy, trying to reach for him. "Just hold on, sweetheart."

Blue noticed bright neon lights ahead. A Ferris wheel came into view, illuminating the early evening sky as it circled. "An amusement park, Jonas!" she exclaimed. We can get lost in the crowd, she thought. She maneuvered the car into the right lane, slowed down and turned into the parking lot. An attendant took her dollar for parking and directed her to a spot. She barely let him finish his instruction before she drove off.

She wheeled into the parking space. "Okay, Jonas," she said. "Get ready to jump out – fast, like a bunny." She walked quickly around the car, opened the door and reached in, grabbing the duffel bag and Jonas. Slinging the heavy bag over her slight shoulders, she swooped him up in her arms and ran to the front gate of the park.

But this time, Blue wasn't laughing and Jonas wasn't giggling. Blue had never felt more terrified in her life. Not only was she in danger, but a defenseless child, the baby she had given up, was at risk as well.

What frightened her most was she now knew George was a deeply disturbed man… a man who had killed in his life without remorse. A man who had savagely raped her. And a man who would go to any length, even if it meant killing an innocent child, to get what he wanted.

Now what do I do, Blue thought, looking behind her for any sign of George. The park was jammed with people. Jonas had stopped crying and was pointing excitedly to a very tall clown walking toward them. Blue explained the clown was on stilts – long sticks – and that's what made him so tall. That gave her an idea.

"Can you tell me where the clown tent is?" she asked, approaching the towering pierrot. He leaned down, giving Jonas's finger a squeeze with his large, gloved hand. Jonas's eyes were wide with wonderment. The clown smiled and gave him one of the big, red balloons he was carrying.

"We hang out right over there, ma'am," he said politely. "See that big striped tent?" She nodded. "That's the one."

"Thank you, sir," she replied. As Blue hurried away, Jonas turned around to get a last look at the tallest man he had ever seen in his young life. Blue ducked into the tent, out of breath from carrying Jonas. He squirmed to get out of her arms. "Let's sit on this bench for a minute," she said, putting him down.

They both watched as clowns in groups of twos and threes rehearsed their acts. Jonas stared at them, transfixed. Blue gazed in awe at her son. How could I have given up such a precious one? she wondered. The image of handing Jonas over to Naomi and Robert filled her with heart-aching regret. But for this moment, it was just the two of them – mother and son, with shared ancestral blood in their veins and genes plucked from the same gene pool. Powerful thoughts like these left Blue feeling grateful... humbled – and distracted from the danger that lurked close by.

Suddenly she had a hunch telling her to be alert, to check outside the tent. She peered into the crowd from the safety of their hiding place. Out of a shifting sea of faces and bodies, her attention was drawn to two men talking. One was totally unfamiliar and the other unfortunately, too familiar. It was George, gesturing to one of the amusement park employees. It looked to Blue like he was describing two people to the stranger, one a child and the other a small woman.

She quickly pulled her head back into the tent. Jonas was still watching the clowns. "Come on," she said, taking him by the arm. "I've got to make sure we can't be recognized." All Jonas knew was that she was taking him away from something he was enjoying immensely. And he voiced his displeasure.

"No, Boo," he said, struggling to get out of her grasp. "I wanna see the clowns," he insisted, angry at her restricting him.

"Not right now," Blue said firmly, picking him up. She carried Jonas to the back of the tent, where she thought the clowns' dressing rooms might be located. He protested all the way, kicking his feet and reaching back for the disappearing clowns. "How would you like to *be* a clown, Jonas?" she asked, determined to gain control of the situation. "We can paint your face and dress you up in a clown suit. Then you'll look just like them."

Jonas abruptly stopped kicking and crying. "Good! *Now* I've got your attention," she exclaimed. She peeked cautiously into the dressing area. The clowns were out in the ring, getting ready for the next performance, so the room was empty. Everything she needed was there – face paint, clown outfits of all sizes, shoes, and wigs of every color.

Far out, she thought, examining costumes to find one that fit Jonas. This'll work, she surmised, holding up a small outfit. Probably belongs to one of the midget clowns I saw earlier. Blue found another that looked like one she could wear. Yanking it off the hanger, she quickly put it on over her jeans, having shed her pink dress hours ago. She stuffed her hair into a curly, red wig.

"Now for you, big boy," she told Jonas. "Let's get you outfitted." He was delighted with this game and cooperated willingly, excited about the prospect of being a clown. She helped him step into the one-piece costume and selected a green wig. Finally came the face painting. Easier said than done, she thought. Blue labored like a skillful artist to make their faces unrecognizable. "Weird looking, but good, Blue," she said, eyeing her work in the mirror.

"All we have to do now is pretend we're an act," she told Jonas, "and clown our way right out of this park." He nodded happily. She noticed a set of plastic bowling pins in the corner. "I'll take these. Try to juggle them. No, I can't do that and carry the bag too," she said. What *will* I do with this bag of money? she wondered. George'll recognize it right away.

She spied a brightly colored cloth bag hanging on a hook. She peered inside. It was filled with stuffed animals resembling ones used as game prizes. "Perfect!" she exclaimed. "I'll put the money in here, along with the animals. Then, on our way out of the park, I'll pass them out to kids. Doing that'll make us seem legit."

"Are you ready, my little buffoon?" He was busy tugging at his wig, trying to pull it off. "No, Jonas," Blue warned. "You mustn't take that off yet."

"It's hot," he whined. "I wanna take it off." He jerked at the synthetic green curls.

"Please, Jonas," she begged, taking him by the shoulders. "Just do this one thing for me now. As soon as we're out of the park, you can take it off," she said, kissing him on the forehead. With a preliminary look around, Blue took Jonas by the hand and began walking toward what she thought was the exit gate of the park. She handed the coveted stuffed animals to eager children as they walked along, all the while watching for any sign of George.

As she gave away the last of the stuffed animals, she felt Jonas tug on her arm. "What, Jonas?" she asked. Looking up, she realized they were only several feet from the huge Ferris wheel she had seen from the highway. She stared at it, openmouthed. The realization sickened her, sending shock waves through her belly. Oh my god, she thought. I'm turned around. I've taken us deeper *into* the park, rather than out of it.

Before she could stop him, Jonas had snatched the wig off his head in frustration. "It's too hot," he complained again. She knelt in front of him, attempting to put the wig and clown hat back on. "If you'll wear your wig," she bribed him; "I'll take us for a Ferris wheel ride." A promise like that to a little boy was too much to resist. He let her put the wig and hat back on.

A ticket booth was close by. Blue hurried to the window and tried to buy two tickets, but the ticket agent told her Jonas was too small for the ride. She bought them anyway. She turned around to take Jonas's hand. In one single, horrific moment, she saw George – like a doe that has just recognized a hunkered-down mountain lion ready to attack.

And from twenty yards away, George saw her – despite her

camouflage. Without hesitation, she picked up Jonas and began running toward the Ferris wheel. George pursued her, dodging between people, pushing others out of his way. She looked back through the crowd, but didn't see him.

A woman standing by the Ferris wheel was watching and waving to her husband and children, who were having a wonderful time being carried across the sky in the circle of lights. In desperation, Blue practically shoved Jonas at her. "Will you please hide my son for a few minutes?" she asked. "Don't let *anyone* take him," she told her. Blue's determination to protect her son must have moved the woman, for instinctively she reached out to Jonas and gathered him in her arms. "I'll be right back to get him," she explained as Jonas protested vigorously to being left behind.

Blue pressed her ticket into the hand of the ticket master, jumped the Ferris wheel line, ducked under the restraining bar and hopped into one of the seats. The ticket master gave her a hard-eyed look, but surprisingly did nothing to detain her. The Ferris wheel had slowed to a stop and people were starting to get out.

George, with his twenty/twenty eyesight, watched Blue, with her large cloth bag, board the circular ride. He sneaked around behind it and climbed onto the platform. Blue, searching the crowd for George, didn't see him carefully lift his six-foot frame into an empty seat directly behind her.

With a jerk, the wheel started its revolving journey again. Blue, afraid of heights, dared not look at the ground below. Her only prayer was that George was somewhere else in the park, away from her and from Jonas. As the giant wheel circled upward it came to a standstill, leaving Blue swinging at the very top. She kept her eyes closed and held tightly onto the rail in front of her. I'm up here and he's down there, she thought – and Jonas is protected. She opened her eyes, took a deep breath and settled back into the seat.

"Well, isn't this just *too cozy*," a voice said with deadly sarcasm, sending cold chills down her back. Blue whirled around. "We've gotta stop meeting like this, Spence." It was George, his eyes dark and wild, his lip curled into a cruel sneer.

"You just stay *right there* – or I'll scream," Blue said, using her most vitriolic tone.

He laughed. "No one's paying any attention to you, Miss Spencer," he told her. "Scream to your heart's content. Nobody will hear you. Now you either give me the money or you'll get cold steel in your back," he threatened, brandishing a shiny, silver knife.

"Okay, George," Blue said, feeling a rush of pure anger. "You wanna play kill or be killed with me, like in Vietnam? Well, I win – 'cause *this* is gonna kill you." She took the colorful, cloth bag of money in one hand and suspended it out, away from the Ferris wheel. Their eyes locked, and a surge of fear spread across George's face.

With a triumphant smile, Blue turned the bag upside down. Loose and packaged hundred-dollar bills fluttered and fell helplessly to the ground below.

Watching his $50,000 cascade to the ground, George let out a blood-curdling shriek. "You goddamm *bitch*! I'm gonna fuckin' *butcher* you!" Hanging onto the metal structure to anchor himself, he leaned across the space between the two seats, swiping at her with the knife. She managed to dodge the menacing blade by moving to one corner of the swaying seat.

He changed his position, swiping at her from another angle. Every cell in her body was on alert. Eyes focused on the tip of the knife, she dodged – but the edge of it caught her as she moved. She felt a sharp spasm of pain as the weapon cut through the costume, lacerating her chest just below the collarbone.

She gasped. "My god, what are you *doing*?" she screamed, instinctively covering the wound with her hand. This is it. He's gonna kill me, she thought, as adrenaline coursed through her body. Her instinct for survival peaking, she began to kick at George with her feet, trying to dislodge the knife from his grasp.

The wind had blown some of the money back into Blue's seat. At the precise moment that George noticed and made a perilous lunge to retrieve it, the Ferris wheel lurched into motion. The sudden movement made him lose his balance and he pitched forward into the night air.

He grabbed Blue's arm in a panic, almost taking her diminutive body with him as he dangled – powerless to pull himself up. "Help me," George pleaded, his eyes begging for delivery from certain death. Bracing herself against the side of the swinging car, Blue labored to hoist him back in, but his desperate grasp slipped, then released.

"George," she screamed, reaching for him and missing. It happened too fast – in one gruesome instant. Blue looked on in horror as the man she had once loved hurtled through space to the earth below. She felt her throat reflex in a gag and vomited clear spittle onto the seat.

A crowd gathered almost instantly. There was no shouting, no calling for an ambulance. People were strangely quiet. They seemed to know the man lying on the ground, his body twisted, neck obviously broken, was beyond saving. It was a grisly scene. Blood oozed from his mouth, nose and open eyes, his limbs askew. A body broken and a spirit's light no longer flickering – a soul was on its way to the unknown.

Blue felt the Ferris wheel gently transport her back to the platform. She felt sick as she stepped shakily off the ride. She ran to the woman who had taken Jonas for her. "Thank you so much for staying with him," she said, grabbing Jonas's hand.

"This little fella was fine. It was *you* I was worried about. Up there with that deranged man. When I saw that money floating down, I was afraid you were going to be next! Are you okay?" she asked.

"I'll be fine," Blue replied numbly. "Thanks again," she told her as the woman and her family left. She collapsed on the ground as her legs suddenly gave way.

"I want my mommy," Jonas cried.

"You're gonna be with your mommy as soon as we get out of here. I promise," she said, struggling to get up.

Jonas was inconsolable. "I want my mommy," he kept crying. His breathing became labored. Blue put him on her lap in an effort to comfort him – but he had reached the point of no return and didn't want to be held. It had all been too much for Jonas. It was almost too much for Blue. I have to stay strong for him, she thought. I can't fall apart now.

The police arrived with an ambulance. Several officers questioned individuals standing around the dead man. They collected the fallen money – minus what people had seized before they arrived. An employee of the park pointed the officers toward Blue. They came over to her. "Were you the woman on the Ferris wheel who was accosted by the man who was killed?" one of them asked.

"Yes I was," Blue replied grimly.

"Were you acquainted with the guy?" they inquired further. "And what do you know about the money? We've been told it was dropped from the top of the ride by somebody."

Blue wanted to tuck tail and run. Or lie. Dammit, she thought. You just saved your son and saved yourself. You can certainly talk to these cops. "Yes, I knew him... or I thought I did. He was trying to kill me," she said, looking them straight in the eye. "And I know about the money – it was money he'd stolen... and I was the one who dropped it. But before I answer any more of your questions, please, this child *has* to be taken home to his parents." Jonas was wheezing and whimpering. "He has asthma and needs his medication."

"Isn't he *yours*?" one of the officers asked.

I wish he was, Blue thought. "No, he's not mine," she said, with a bittersweet tone. "He belongs to his parents, the Matthews. I'm just a good friend," she told them, kissing Jonas on the cheek.

The officers looked at each other in recognition, then at her. "Young lady, looks like you've kidnapped the missing Matthews kid. We're gonna have to take you into custody for questioning. We'll drop the boy off at home. You're coming with us."

"Okay, but I'd like to say good-bye to the man who was killed before I leave," she said, as she watched two men in white uniforms lifting a gurney with George's body on it into the ambulance.

"Okay, but make it short," one of the officers instructed, holding her by the arm.

"Jonas, honey," Blue explained. "I'm going to walk over to that big truck with all the lights on it and you're gonna stay here with these nice men. Okay? I'll be back in a minute and then we'll take you home."

Jonas agreed; too weary to protest the delay. One of the officers knelt down and began talking to him. Blue and the officer approached the ambulance as the two men closed the doors. "I'm his girlfriend," she informed them. "And I need to see him before you take him away."

"No problem," they said. "Just don't be long."

One of them helped her up the steep stairs and into the vehicle. It was an eerie feeling being in the small, closed space with a dead body. The unmistakable smell of death sickened her. This can't be happening, she thought. Fearful that when she pulled the sheet back George would open his eyes and glower at her, she almost turned around and ran out of the ambulance. Wait a second, Blue. He's dead, remember? she reminded herself.

She walked over to his head, sitting down gingerly on the nearby seat. For a split second, she thought she saw the sheet move, like he had just breathed out. She kept watching, almost expecting it to happen again. But the sheet remained unmoved.

Blue reached out and delicately lifted off the covering. George's beautiful, dark hair was matted with blood. A sunken-in place on the side of his face was turning a dark purple and blue. His cheekbones were crushed – blood and exposed tissue was everywhere. His eyes were shut and his mouth slack.

She glanced at his body – so familiar to her, but now disfigured and broken. Seeing him this way reminded Blue of the time George told her how his father would hit him and he'd "fly across the room like a piece of paper." I wonder how his father would feel *now*, seeing his son like this, she wondered.

"Oh George, what happened to you? You let that stolen money end your life," Blue said, stroking him lightly. "I loved you, but your wounded places finally got the best of me... and you," she faltered, starting to cry. "I do *forgive* you for the things you did to me, but I will never *forget*. She wiped her tears on her sleeve.

"You altered my life forever, you miserable bastard... the morning you raped me. But, you know what, George," she said thoughtfully, "it wasn't the rape that hurt me so. Or even when you killed Muss. It was the fact that you never really loved me..."

She paused to reflect. "Maybe we were in a previous life together G.G., and I hurt you really bad. Maybe getting raped by you was karma I had to pay..." I guess I'll never know, she thought, as a knock on the ambulance door signaled it was time to leave.

"Good-bye, George," she whispered in his ear. "Have a good trip. Say hello to Denny for me," she told him, kissing the dead man lightly. She opened the doors of the vehicle and stepped down. "Thanks," she mumbled to the medics. Strangely, nothing was real. She didn't even feel the ground under her feet.

Blue was grateful to be whisked away from the park, even in custody. At least I'm out of danger, she thought, and thank God, so is Jonas. She stroked the little boy's dark hair as he slumbered. He had fallen into a sound sleep, exhausted by his ordeal. Blue put her cheek against his forehead, her tears making a silent exit.

"I'll miss you, goose," she said softly. "I'm sure your parents will never allow me to see you again... after what I've done." She was quiet, thinking about the gravity of the choices she had made in the last two days. "I love you, my angel," she whispered to him. "You're the greatest gift God ever gave me."

"This the place?" one of the officers asked.

"Yes sir. This is it." Blue replied. "Can I go in and talk to his parents?" she asked hesitantly.

The officers consulted each other. "Go ahead. You can have fifteen minutes."

"Thank-you. Come on, Jonas. It's time to wake up, sweetie. You're home," she said, nudging him gently. She got out of the police car with Jonas still in her arms.

"Mommy," Jonas cried, now awake. He wriggled away from Blue. She put him down and he ran, unsteadily, to the front door of the house. It was locked. Blue rapped on the door. Robert opened it immediately, like he'd been right there, waiting for someone to bring his boy home. When he saw Jonas he let out a yell and scooped him up.

"Sweetheart, guess who I'm holding?" he called to his wife, crying and covering Jonas with kisses.

Naomi ran to her son with open arms. "My baby! Oh Jonas, my sweet baby! You're alive! Thank you, Lord. You've brought him back to us!" She held onto Jonas like she would never let him go. "Thank you, God. Thank you, Lord. Oh, thank you, thank you, thank you," she repeated.

Blue had never witnessed such love. The scene brought tears to her eyes... tears that come from being touched by something as simple and profound as a parent's love for their child. *"Now do you see that you did the right thing?"* an inner voice said. *"It's love that makes families strong. And you gave Jonas a chance for that love, by giving him up for adoption."*

"I'm putting this child to bed. He's worn out," Naomi announced. "Then we have to talk, Blue." She lovingly carried the small boy up the stairs, still kissing him and thanking God. Robert followed, carrying Jonas's shoes and his asthma medication.

Blue sat very still, as if not moving a muscle would prevent the inevitable consequence. After a few minutes, Naomi and Robert came down the stairs together and sat on the couch directly across from her. A shadow of fear and expectancy clouded their faces as they waited for Blue to speak. She took a breath. "Okay. I know this is gonna sound strange, but I kidnapped Jonas in order to save him."

"You *what*?" Naomi asked.

"Save him – from *what*?" Robert asked, his voice unbelieving.

"From being hurt by my boyfriend," Blue replied. "You see, George, my boyfriend, stole a lot of money. When I threatened to go to the local police, he told me he would hurt Jonas, even kill him, if I did." Naomi gasped, reacting with horror to the unfolding story. Robert's face was chalky. "I got real scared and decided I couldn't tell the police anything. So I left for Ponca City and took the money with me.

I wanted to get here before George did, to give the police a description and turn the money over to them... so they could arrest him as soon as he got into town. Then I thought – no, I've gotta do this without the police. George might find out they are after him and stay one step ahead of them and get Jonas. It's just too dangerous."

They both were looking at her, shocked and disbelieving. "That afternoon,' she continued, "George left a note at my motel, demanding that I meet him later with the money. So I decided I had to cooperate," she told them. "But I had a flat tire, so I was late and missed him. He thought I didn't show up on purpose. It was then I *knew* he would go after Jonas for sure... to make certain he got his money. That's when I went back to the day care center the next day and took your son," she concluded ashamedly.

Naomi interrupted her. "You mean, you put our son's life *at risk* by taking the money, knowing that homicidal maniac would hurt our baby?" she asked angrily. "Why on earth didn't you call us right away when he threatened Jonas's life... so *we* could go to the police?"

"I was scared if I told you, you *would* call the police and that'd make George even madder – and one way or another, he would get to Jonas." Blue's chin began to quiver. Telling them the awful truth was bringing on tears and she was sobbing by the time the doorbell rang. When Robert answered, Blue could hear the three of them talking.

"They asked me if we wanted to press kidnapping charges," he informed Blue.

"Oh," Blue replied, tears smarting her cheeks.

"Blue," Naomi said firmly, "you *must* know you have seriously breached your relationship with the three of us. We just simply cannot have Jonas subjected to this kind of danger – *ever* again. I'm convinced he was traumatized by what happened tonight, so I'm sure his asthma kicked up. It does that when he gets upset or is overly tired."

"I know," Blue said sadly. "He *was* having problems breathing. I'm so sorry. I just couldn't bring myself to get you two or the police involved. I guess I felt it was *my* responsibility to protect him from George." A stillness filled the room. "Are you saying that I can't visit him anymore?" she asked hesitantly, dreading the answer.

"I don't know *what* I'm saying, Blue. I'm still in shock," Naomi told her. "Robert and I will have to talk about it. But the way I feel right now is that, no, I don't think you should visit him – not until you've grown up and straightened out your life."

Blue looked at Naomi, hoping by some miracle she would take back everything she just said and allow her to continue seeing Jonas. She glanced at Robert, who was looking at the floor, his head in his hands. "Well, I guess I'd better go," she mumbled, realizing a change of heart wasn't forthcoming. "Are you going to press charges against me?" she asked them.

Robert looked at Naomi. "We certainly have that right. You *did* kidnap our son, Blue," she said. "But we already decided we're not going to."

"Thank-you, Naomi," Blue said, her eyes downcast. "I'm sure not knowing where Jonas was scared you to death. But I was just so afraid that George might hurt him. I'm very sorry I scared you," she said, remorseful. She walked to the front door with a heavy step. The sadness in her heart felt overwhelming. "Please say good-bye to Jonas for me, will you?" she asked. "I love the little guy." Naomi nodded to her, smiling wanly.

As she got into the police car, Blue looked up at Jonas's darkened bedroom window. It reminded her of the night she sat, watching him sleep, and then crawled into bed with him. Goodnight, Jonas, she thought. I just wanted to save you, goose. I love you. She shut the car door and the cruiser pulled away slowly. She rode to the station; thinking about what happened and wishing it had all just been a bad dream.

The officer interrupted her thoughts. "Mr. Matthews told us they wouldn't be pressing charges, but we still need to ask you some questions, miss." He pulled the car into the parking lot of the police station. "Right this way, ma'am," they said, shepherding her into the building. "Just have a seat," he said, motioning for her to sit down.

There were people everywhere, in every condition and color – blacks, whites, Mexicans, Native Americans, hippies, drunks, blue collar workers, prostitutes, women with children, teen-agers. Some looked unhappy, others tired, a few were angry.

One woman looked like she'd been beaten, probably by her husband, Blue surmised. Her small children huddled around her... sleepy and clinging to whatever part of their mothers' body they could grasp. Everyone stayed in their own groups, refusing to connect with anyone who wasn't like they were. The precinct staff seemed disgusted by the motley menagerie. They looked haggard, overwhelmed, underpaid... and like they'd had one too many cups of rot gut, precinct coffee.

The officers finally called Blue into a small office, apologizing for the delay. They pulled up a couple of chairs, turned them around and straddled them to face her. "Now," the older one suggested. "Why don't you tell us who this guy was to you and what you know about all that money?"

Blue looked first at one, then the other. All that's missing is one of those horrible bright lights I've seen in the movies, she thought... the ones they use on suspects when they want to make them talk. Being questioned by the police was upsetting for this naive minister's daughter... never having been in trouble with the law before. "Well, uh," she stammered nervously. "I guess you could say he was my old man, you know, my boyfriend."

"Uh-huh. Can you tell us exactly what was happening between the two of you at the top of that Ferris wheel?" one of the officers asked.

"He was trying to stab me – with a knife," she answered.

"Yeah, looks like he almost made it," one of them said, pointing to the slit in her costume.

Blue looked down, realizing only then that she was still wearing the clown outfit.

"You'd better take a look at that cut," he suggested.

"I will. It's just a superficial wound," she replied offhandedly.

"So why was he trying to stab you?" the other officer inquired.

"He was angry because I had the stolen money," she answered.

"The *stolen* money?" they both asked simultaneously.

"Yeah. I thought you knew it was stolen," she said.

"We suspected, but didn't have any confirmation. So, let's get this straight. Your boyfriend George committed a robbery?" they asked.

"Right," Blue answered. "He stole $100,000 from a company in Wichita Kansas, where he worked. He wanted to go to Nashville and get famous... be a singer. He hid the money in our bedroom closet. I found it, but I didn't let him know."

"Why not?" they asked in unison.

"Because if I did, I was afraid he would get really pissed at me and go ballistic. But one day, we were fighting and I got mad at him. So I blurted out that I had discovered the money and was going to report it to the police. That's when he threatened to hurt Jonas, the little boy I had with me at the park."

"So this kid," one of the officers said, "must mean something to you for you to come all the way from Wichita to Ponca City to protect him. What's the connection?"

Blue hesitated. "He's my biological son that I gave up for adoption," she answered. "To Naomi and Robert Matthews."

"The plot thickens," the officers said, looking at each other. "So, what were you going to do with the money?"

"I was gonna turn it over to the police," Blue told them. "But on the Ferris wheel, when I realized that George might kill me, I decided to dump the money. I wanted to make sure, in case I died, he couldn't have it."

"Do you realize that keeping the money your boyfriend stole and not reporting it is possession of stolen property and that knowing about it and not reporting it is obstruction of justice?" the officer asked Blue.

"No," she said, eyes widening in surprise. "Am I going to get arrested for that?"

"Under ordinary circumstances – yes. But since what's left of the money is going to be returned to its rightful owner, we're not going to charge you for either one. But consider this a warning," the older officer told her. "You should've told the police in Wichita immediately when you found the money or turned it in to us."

"I understand that now," Blue replied. "I was just so afraid of what he would do to Jonas and me if I went to the police."

"We understand you were scared, but you shouldn't try to take on a maniac like that by yourself," the officers told her.

"I know. You're right," Blue replied, slightly embarrassed.

"Well, you're a lucky young lady. We've let you off the hook and so did they. My advice to you is to stay away from crazies like this guy from now on. Men like that are trouble and the first thing you know, you're right in the soup with 'em." The officer reached out and squeezed her shoulder. "Now, go back to Wichita and get yourself a life – a good one."

"Thank you, officers," Blue said gratefully. "You've been very kind to me. I think I've learned an important lesson."

"And what's that?" one of them asked, curious.

"Don't make a man your whole life, that's what," Blue said. "Because when you do, you lose yourself. Being under someone else's thumb isn't love, it's ownership," she continued. "George controlled me because I let him. I guess it took kidnapping my own son for me to take back my... my..."

"Power?" the officer finished her sentence.

Blue was startled to hear a man say that. She looked at him and nodded. "Yeah," she replied. "My power."

"Just remember the next time, young lady, that kidnapping is a criminal offense," the older officer told her. The three were silent for a moment.

"You know, we endured the sixties – being called pigs, among other names, but there have always been some of us who *do* have a sensitive side," one of the officers quipped.

"Yeah," the other one interrupted. "He even tried to kiss me the other day. That's a little too sensitive for my taste," he said, winking at Blue. They all laughed.

"What's gonna happen to George?" she asked, suddenly serious. "What are they going to do with his... his body?"

"We'll be contacting next of kin to make the necessary arrangements," was the answer.

"His mother is the only one left in the family," Blue revealed. "His dad's dead and so is his brother. I can give you her phone number, if that would help," she offered. She wrote it on a piece of paper and gave it to the officer. "Am I free to go now?" she asked. "I'd like to go home."

"You're free to go," both officers replied.

"Thanks – for everything. Peace and love," she said, flashing the two-fingered sign. "I can't help it," she said apologetically, referring to her gesture. "I'll always be a flower-child." The two officers just smiled and shook their heads.

The police station was on a major street in Ponca City, so Blue had little trouble flagging a cab. Even at 2:30 in the morning. "Where to, miss?" the cabby asked, a cigarette hanging from his mouth. She panicked for a split second. With his slight mustache and dark hair, the cabby's profile looked strikingly like George. And there was something about his voice...

"Uh... uh..." Blue mumbled, feeling jarred and shaken.

"Cat got your tongue?" he asked, turning around. She stared at a man who looked so much like George, it took her breath away.

"No sir," she replied, her voice trembling. "It's just that you resemble somebody I used to live with who just died. He was killed a few hours ago. I thought I'd seen a ghost," she told him, her voice still shaky.

"Hey, I love being compared to a dead man, lady," he joked. The cabby paused. "I'm sorry," he said, realizing the crassness of his remark. You gonna be okay?"

"Yeah. I'll be fine," she replied. "My car's at that amusement park on Superior Avenue. I hope I can get it out of there."

"Hey, don't worry 'bout a thing," he told her. "I have connections at the park. I'll take care of you if there's a problem."

Blue didn't feel like talking as the cab wove its way to her destination. The last ten hours had been a nightmare. Part of her wanted to curl up in a little ball, like Muss, and never come out. And yet, another part of her wanted to render the most god-awful scream Ponca City had ever heard.

The yellow Volkswagen was the only car left in the parking lot. "Just shine your headlights on my car so I can see – okay?" she asked.

"Sure, no problem," the cabby replied as Blue stepped out of his vehicle. "Sorry you lost your friend. Take 'er easy."

She got into the car and rested her head on the steering wheel for a minute. "Thank god you were still here, Saffron," she told the ever-reliable car. "And thank god *I'm* still here." The amusement park was dark. The Ferris wheel sat silent and unlit, like a giant starfish at rest. Blue felt a sudden chill seeing it again. The memory of George falling to his death was so fresh.

"I can't believe you're dead, George," she said. I keep expecting to hear his voice calling me Spence, she thought. The man who fell from that Ferris wheel was a man I didn't know anymore. "What happened to you, George?" she queried. "I loved your sense of humor, the way you cared about the underdog, how you loved music, the good times we had... what made it all disappear?"

Blue started the car, her thoughts full of her former lover. She drove out of the parking lot and onto Superior Avenue. Distracted, she turned in front of an oncoming car. The driver angrily blasted her horn, swerving dangerously to avoid an accident. Gee zooey, she thought. I may not make it out of Ponca City alive yet.

The tension in Blue's shoulders subsided as the motel sign came into view. I'm almost home – and I'm safe, she thought, taking a deep breath. She locked the car and trudged wearily up the stairs to her room. As soon as she switched on the light, George's angry, scribbled message became visible. Crudely scrawled in her lipstick, again his acrimonious words assailed her.

"Dammit, George!" she said. "You could be so bad-mannered and mean. I *won't* miss that! Applying make-up remover to the mirror, Blue erased the message. The remover's oily residue left the mirror cloudy and streaked. Like my life, she thought, dim and unclear.

Peering into the glass, she recalled a verse from the Bible her father had quoted often. *"For now we see through a glass darkly; but then face to face"* ...or something like that, she thought. She looked at her blurred image. This streaky mirror is me, she mused. George was right. I don't know who I am so I depend on other people to create my reflection for me. Now that he's gone, she thought, who will I be?

"That's a sobering thought, Blue," she said reflectively. She felt a sharp pain in her chest. "Oh geez, that hurts," she said, inspecting the superficial knife-wound. The swipe George made with his knife had left a small cut.

She dabbed alcohol on the dried blood around it. It stung. She found a Band-Aid in the bottom of her purse and covered the cut. "A few beers should help numb the pain," she said. She remembered a small, all-night grocery several blocks away. I'll get a six-pack and some cigarettes, she thought.

The night air was temperate. A breeze blew the hair away from her face as she headed back to the motel with her purchases. Walking felt good, with the wind caressing her face. She tried not to think of George, but it was difficult. Barely escaping her own demise, witnessing someone else's death, and then talking to a dead body, were not events easily brushed aside.

Propped up in bed, an open bottle of beer at her side, Blue took periodic swallows, anticipating the numbness to follow. Wait a minute, she thought. What am I doing? Is drinking until I pass out going to change things? Is *this* the way I want to handle problems in my life – like George did? Her awareness sharp and swift, she took the bottle of beer and poured it down the sink.

Blue began reviewing her life – the injuries from her childhood, her wounds as an adult, the losses she'd suffered. Without alcohol to deaden her feelings, Blue spiraled into the dark night of the soul. Thoughts of killing herself came back. She felt waves of guilt about endangering Jonas's life. Death couldn't have felt lonelier than right now.

It was a sleepless night in hell for Blue. And she was alone in her hell. But somehow, she knew she would be all right because she could at least recognize the courage it took to risk her life for her son... and the choice to stay sober now no matter how bad she felt. At 5:00 a.m., she slid under the clean, cool sheets and closed her eyes. Blue, who had aged five years in a single day, finally fell asleep.

Blue slept restlessly, her sleep filled with disturbing dreams. Waking up, she stumbled in the dark over something, on the way to use the bathroom. Probably a shoe, she thought as she recalled the clothes she'd left in a pile at the end of the harrowing day. Squinting at the motel clock radio, as far as she could tell, the hands read 6:45 a.m. Crawling back into the oversized bed, she clutched a pillow to her chest and curled up in a fetal position.

But sleep remained an elusive luxury. Her neighbors in adjacent rooms were getting up, taking showers, talking, starting their cars. "Meet 'cha over at the Big Boy for breakfast," a male voice announced just outside her door.

"Okay. You buyin'?" another male voice answered. Then laughter. Noises dimmed as sleep took over.

A hand on the back of her head pushed her roughly. She fell through the blackness, down and down – silently screaming before she hit the ground. Blue awoke with a jerk and a gasp, her clothes soaked with sweat. "Oh, god," she said, her heart pounding. "Somebody just pushed me off a Ferris wheel." I had a nightmare, she thought, wide-awake. It was 9:50 a.m.

Blue showered, trying to wake up. She changed her clothes and packed. The sooner I get out of here, the better I'll feel, she thought. She bought a black coffee to go, skipping breakfast. A cigarette was the first thing in her mouth, a habit growing increasingly determined to take hold. "How do I get out of this godforsaken town?" she said, studying the map. She found route thirty-five, the one that would take her back to Kansas.

The car filled with gasoline, Saffron purred along – the only one with breakfast in her belly. Blue was feeling relieved the further away she got from Ponca City. Soon, she had the windows open and the radio turned up full volume. *"Can't buy me love... can't buy me love...",* the classic Beatles song blasted.

She became aware of scenery whizzing by. Glancing at the rich, azure sky, a large bird came into view – wind surfing. A soaring hawk, she thought, reminding Blue of her bus companion. He just appeared at my seat that day, she remembered – out of the blue. And ever since, his words have gotten me through the worst of times. I guess he navigated me through this one too. He was a messenger, sent to me from Great Spirit...

There was lots of time to think during the long stretch of road. Characters in her life drama appeared on the stage in her mind – Jonas, Naomi and Robert, Carlos, George, Ruby, her father, Soaring Hawk, Love Mae, Olivette, Muss. They were all there... all a part of her journey.

Driving down that Oklahoma highway, Blue was experiencing an epiphany. Saving Jonas had been transforming... it had awakened something inside her. Placing his life before her own for a brief twenty-four hours, she was able to protectively mother the son she'd given away. It felt like a reprieve... a second chance, she thought.

If George hadn't stolen the company's money, she thought... if I hadn't warned him I would go to the police... if he hadn't threatened Jonas's life... if I hadn't taken the money with me to Ponca City... I would've never had the chance to defend the son I abandoned as an infant.

Her mind continued to jump back and forth between Jonas and George as she drove Saffron toward home. A roadside sign indicated she was approaching the border between Oklahoma and Kansas. She thought about Harriet and Bodey... and Sam. Remembering them gave her comfort, like an oasis in the middle of a desert.

Her heart was feeling lighter. Besides the priest and Soaring Hawk, the only other man who made her smile when she thought of him was Sam. She began looking for his gas station. Where was it? she wondered. Suddenly, she remembered that Sam had given her his phone number. I'll call him, she thought. She drove by a cafe so obscure, she almost missed it. The sign read – Border Cafe. Making a quick U-turn, she went back.

The cafe looked a hundred years old. Its wooden sign was cracked and faded, swinging gently with the dry, dusty wind. In fact, the entire front of the cafe was covered with reddish-brown dust. Stepping up on the wooden porch, Blue couldn't resist writing her name on one of the dirty windows – letting the world know she'd been there. The door's bell jingled as she opened it. The cafe's only customers were cowboys, looking as dusty as the world around them. Almost in unison, they turned in their seats to eyeball her.

She felt three pairs of eyes assessing shapely legs that extended from her jean shorts and three pairs of eyes admiring young, full breasts that filled out her peasant blouse. Uncomfortable with such close scrutiny, she looked away, toward the pony-tailed, aging waitress behind the counter. "Do you have a phone I could borrow?" she asked.

"Nope," the woman answered, "Don't have one you can borrow, but I got one I'll let ya use," she quipped, getting a laugh from the men at the counter. "But you'll have ta keep it under three minutes." She motioned Blue to follow her behind the counter to the kitchen. She could feel the cowboys' eyes on her. The cafe floor was slippery – greasy from decades of fried hamburgers.

The smell of chili soup filled her nostrils as she walked by a large pot of the bubbling, reddish-brown mixture. The cafe's walls were covered with yellowing calendar pictures – semi-nude vixens, fish-hooked trout flying through the air, and close-up photos of famous country western singers – some autographed.

The woman noticed Blue staring. "Take a look at this one over here," she motioned, pointing to a black and white glossy photograph taped to the wall above the cash register. It was Gene Autry, dressed in cowboy gear, with a scrawled signature – *"With love to Tootsie and Bill – Gene."*

"He gave us that when Bill was still alive. Sat right over there, where Tom's sittin' now. As pretty as you please," she recalled, her eyes taking on the faraway look of someone whose best times are past.

"That's the day I fell in love. Not that I didn't love my husband, mind you," she assured her audience of four. "But that Mr. Autry. He was somethin' to see. When he shook my hand and called me Tootsie, I thought I'd faint," she concluded with reverence in her voice. Having concluded her recollection, Tootsie noticed Blue. "Oh, you wanted the phone, didn't ya," she remembered. "It's back there on the wall, next to the employee restroom."

Blue walked carefully across the worn, greasy floor to the black phone that hung on the wall. Feeling a sudden nervousness, she took the scrap of paper with Sam's number on it and dialed. "Sam's Petrol," a man's voice answered. He sounded busy and not in the mood for a chat.

"Sam?" Blue asked.

"You got him."

"Sam, it's Blue," she said, not knowing if he'd remember her.

There was a silence on the other end of the line. "You mean the incredibly pretty little Blueflower woman with the out-of-gas, yellow Volkswagen bug?" he finally said.

Blue laughed – the first in a long while. "The very one," she confirmed.

"Where *are* you?" he asked.

" I'm at the Border Cafe. Is it close to your station?"

"Sure is. I'm up the highway about a mile. You're so close, you can smell my gas fumes!" he joked.

"I thought maybe you could check Saffron over for me. She's been running kind of rough." Blue told him.

"Sure, no problem," he replied. "Bring her on in."

"Okay, thanks. Be there in a few," Blue replied, hanging the receiver back on its grimy cradle. "Thanks, ma'am," she said, walking in front of the cowboys who still swilled coffee and puffed on their hand-rolled cigarettes. One of them smiled at her through spaces where teeth were missing, an unlit cigarette protruding from his mouth. It reminded her of how cigarettes would dangle from George's lower lip. Everything reminded her of him.

"You come back now," Tootsie called out. "Who knows? Maybe next time, I'll have Johnny Cash up there next to Gene," she boasted. "You just never know who's gonna walk in this place!"

"We don't rate," one of the cowboys said. "Tootsie likes them singers, especially the ones with deep pockets. She's lookin' for a new husband – one that's got money."

"Aw, get outt'a here," the woman chided him. They laughed the good-natured way that people do who know each other well.

The bell jangled loudly as Blue let the cafe's screen door bang shut behind her. Within a half mile, as she came up over a rise, Blue saw a tall figure standing in the road, waving his arms. Oh geez, someone's in trouble, she thought. "Wait a minute," she said, realizing who it was.

It was Sam. He put his finger out, hitchhiker style, as she zoomed up beside him and squealed to a stop. "Are you so hard up for customers that you're flagging them down?" she kidded him, trying to act light-hearted.

"Nope," he replied. "Only the pretty ones who just come out of the blue." She pulled into the station and parked. It felt good to see someone she knew. "Well, howdy," he said, offering her a hug. Blue welcomed it. His arms felt like the shelter of a warm woolen blanket in a snowstorm. "I was *hoping* you might stop by on your way to wherever," he said.

Blue was tongue-tied. No words, not even a hello, would come. All she knew was that his warm embrace began to release a trembling inside her. It was like the subtle tremors that come from deep in the earth, before an earthquake. "I'm sorry," she whispered. With the utterance of her words came a slow, but uncontrollable shaking.

Everything that had been holding her together undid itself. Her muscles became weak and quivery. Her knees buckled. "I'm sorry. I'm sorry. I'm sorry," was all she could say, as sobs convulsed her body. She was... literally, falling apart.

"Hey, hey, hey... Blueflower, there's nothing to be sorry about," Sam said. With his strong arm around her waist, he walked her to a chair in his office. Blue collapsed into the hard, vinyl seat. Sam pulled a clean bandanna out of his back pocket and put it on her lap.

She picked up the purple square and covered her face with it, crying like she would never stop. Sam tried to comfort her, patting her on the back and telling her to just go ahead and "let it out." The truth was, she had no choice. The tears soaked the bandanna with a definite will of their own.

Oblivious to Sam's presence, Blue continued weeping until there were no more tears. She felt exhausted and emptied. This is the first time I've cried about George, she thought. She blew her nose and looked up at Sam through reddened, swollen eyes.

"You're a sight to behold," he said teasingly. "What a beautiful woman you are Blueflower, especially now. But you've been through something. I know it... something that's seared your soul."

Blue felt the tears coming again, but pushed them back. "You're right," she said, looking down, "but I can't talk about it right now."

"That's okay," Sam told her. "I understand." He paused. "Well, in spite of whatever you've gone through, you are *lovely*, Blue. You'd sure be welcome 'round these parts," he mimicked an Oakie accent. Embarrassed and a little put off by his compliments, she said nothing.

"Why don't I take a look at your car," he said, breaking the silence. "You just sit here and rest. There's a pot full of coffee and a water cooler in the back room. Help yourself."

"Thanks. Here's the keys," she said, pulling a set of car keys out of her jeans shorts pocket. She walked, unsteadily, to the back room and filled a cup with water. Her mouth was dry and her legs were like jelly. She looked at her watch. The hands read 1:30. I could be home before dark, she thought. It's just that I can't seem to get my body to move.

Blue walked back to the chair and sat down heavily. She surveyed Sam's office. Several framed photos graced one corner of the desk. One was of a young Sam in cap and gown, posing with his arms around two proud-looking adults, probably his parents, Blue guessed. Another was of the Grand Canyon, with Sam and two other men smiling broadly, geared up for some serious backpacking.

She spied a tired-looking, hardback book on the floor beside the chair. Blue reached down and turned it over. It was *War and Peace*. Heavy reading, she thought. By the phone, a half-eaten cheese sandwich in plastic wrap was attracting flies.

The station was getting busy and Sam had to stop what he was doing to wait on customers. He stuck his head in the door. "Hey, wanna help me pump gas?" he inquired.

225

Blue's first impulse was to be polite and say yes, but nothing in her being cooperated. "I'm sorry, Sam. Sounds like fun, but I really don't think I can," she replied.

"No problem," he responded with a smile. "I just thought a little distraction might help. Work is good therapy for me sometimes."

The word jarred her. Therapy. Love Mae. She yelled out the door to Sam. "You mind if I use your phone – for a long distance call?"

"Go right ahead. It's on my desk," he told her.

Blue dug in her purse for her book of phone numbers. Pulling it out, she thumbed down the M's. "Montgomery... Montgomery. Here it is," she said. She dialed the operator and gave her the number.

An unfamiliar voice came on the other end of the line. "Dr. Montgomery's office. May I help you?"

Blue was surprised. "Is this Beatrice?" she asked.

"No, ma'am. This is Dr. Montgomery's answering service," the voice monotoned.

"Well, I don't want to talk to her answering service. How can I reach the doctor?" Blue said with irritation.

"I can take your name and number Miss..." the voice continued.

"Miss Spencer." Blue couldn't conceal her disappointment.

"Dr. Montgomery is out of the office for several weeks, so all I can do is take your name and number and have her return your call when she gets her messages."

"Never mind," she said, resignation in her voice. "Is she...I mean, all right?"

"We're not allowed to divulge personal information," the operator droned on. "This is just an answering service. I can take your number and have her call..."

Blue hung up. "Robot." she said disgustedly. She pulled the last cigarette out of its crumpled pack and lit up. Staring at the floor, she watched as a large black bug patiently traversed its way from one side of the room to the other. Seeing it reminded her of the countless hours she spent as a little girl in her backyard playing with every crawling creature she could find.

Suddenly, the shadow of a man's work boot loomed over the unsuspecting insect, ready to obliterate it.

"No! Don't kill it!" Blue screamed, an out-of-nowhere anger

erupting. "That bug isn't hurting you! You men think you have the right to annihilate anything that gets in your way!" she shouted, red-faced with rage. "What *is* it with you?" She glared at Sam. "We women were doing *fine* until you came along and tried to *possess* us!" Impulsively, Blue picked up a nearby coffee mug and threw it toward Sam's astonished face. He ducked and it hit the wall, sending splinters of cheap ceramic everywhere.

A country song coming from Sam's radio was the only sound. Blue leaned against a wall; hand on her hip, staring at her shoes. Sam sat in the vinyl chair, an unmistakably puzzled look on his face. As the disc jockey told his listeners the name of the twangy tune, Blue spoke up. "I had no right to do *any* of that to you. I just lost it... completely. I'm really sorry, Sam," she said quietly. "You hit a raw nerve in me and it had nothing to do with you."

"That was my best coffee cup," Sam finally said solemnly.

"What?" Blue couldn't believe what she was hearing.

"That was my best coffee cup," he repeated, this time with a grin.

"I lost it, almost hit you in the head over a bug... and that's all you can say?" she asked incredulously.

"Blue. I was kidding," Sam told her.

"Oh," she mumbled. "Can I ask you something?" she said after a few minutes.

"Shoot," Sam replied.

"Do you believe I was just having a childish temper tantrum?" she asked. "Is that what you think?"

"No... not at all," Sam replied. "I think you're pretty goddamn angry about *something*... but I'm not one to pry. I just hope that whoever it was... or is... that you're so angry with is either in jail or dead – because, if you ever got a hold of him, I think you'd kill him. He must've really fucked you over."

The truth of Sam's comment made Blue avert her eyes from his gaze. She stared out the window. "Let me put it this way. What I've been through has been enough to convince me never to want to be with a man again," she said. "With everything that's happened in my life, I feel forty-five instead of twenty-five. Life's been a real intense ride so far," she remarked, looking back at Sam.

"I believe you," he said sincerely. They were silent. "Listen, *chicquita*, you look beat. Why don't you crash at my place tonight instead of driving back to Wichita?" he offered. "You can have my bed and I'll sleep on the couch."

"Oh... I don't know," she said tiredly. "That's a generous offer, but..."

"Your car needs an oil change and a tune-up," Sam interrupted her. "I can take care of that, then we'll get a bite. After you've eaten something, you'll be chilled out and ready to hit the sack. Tomorrow morning, you can leave feeling like a real human being," he said with a persuasive tone.

Blue considered his invitation for a moment. "Okay," she replied. "I *am* pretty exhausted."

"Cool," Sam said with a smile. A customer blew his horn for service. "I'll take care of this guy, then work on your car. Hey, if you feel like breaking any more mugs, I've got some I want to get rid of in the back room," he teased.

"Very funny," Blue retorted. Why is this guy doing all this for me? she wondered as she watched him pumping gas. If he thinks I'm going to sleep with him, he's in for a big surprise. Blue's trust in men, since the rape and George's attempt on her life, had plummeted to its lowest point.

"No matter how things look around you, trust Great Spirit." There they were again, those words. Why are you speaking to me now, Hawk? she wondered. And why in the *hell* should I trust a voice I can't even see?

In that moment, Blue realized she was outraged... at her father for dying... at Carlos for abusing her... at George for raping her... then for trying to kill her... finally for dying needlessly himself... and at a male God her father told her to "let Him have His way with her." Every one of them, including the God of her childhood, had disappointed, betrayed and abandoned her.

"You hungry?" Sam's inquiry interrupted her thoughts. "Your car's ready to go. She's like new."

"Oh... huh... thank-you Sam," she stammered. "What do I owe you for the tune-up?"

"It's on the house, my friend," he replied. Blue smiled gratefully. "Hop in my vehicle and we'll ride down to Border's. Catch some of

Tootsie's fresh chili."

An image of the greasy, brown mixture she'd seen earlier, bubbling on the cafe stove, made her stomach turn. "I think I'll pass on the chili," she told him. "Do they have any other specialty items?" she asked, climbing into the front seat of Sam's truck.

"Their shredded pork sandwich isn't bad. Tootsie's favorite, though, is Rocky Mountain Oysters," he told her. "Mouth-waterin' delicacy around these wheat fields," he said with a deliberate twang.

"I like oysters," Blue said innocently. "Shrimp too."

Sam guffawed so loud; she almost jumped out of her seat. "I'm afraid these oysters aren't the ones with the shell on them."

"They're not?"

"No, Blueflower. *These* oysters are actually the testicles of a bull," he told her.

"You eat – bulls' balls?" Blue asked in disbelief.

"If that's short for testicles, yes, I do. We'll order a big mess of 'em," he teased. The truck had come to a stop in front of the cafe. Blue couldn't get out fast enough. She felt like gagging.

"I think I'll order something safe, like a tuna salad sandwich, if you don't mind. Just the thought of eating that part of an animal's anatomy makes me queasy," Blue remarked.

"Well, look who's back," Tootsie exclaimed as the two of them walked in the cafe door. "And she's got that retired big-shot lawyer with her."

"Hey, that's supposed to be our little secret," Sam joked.

Tootsie grinned with delight. "Ain't no secrets 'round here. You oughta know that by now, Sam." She came out from behind the counter, motioning for them to take a seat. "Best seat in the place, right here," she said, swiping at several stray crumbs that lingered on the tabletop. "Sit yerselves down," she invited, as she pulled out a chair for Blue.

"Thanks," Blue murmured.

The cafe owner rambled on, resting her hand on Blue's shoulder. "This girl got the Gene Autry story last time she was here," she reported. "Real polite, she was. Listened to the whole thing." She gave Blue a heavy-handed pat on the back, one that practically knocked the wind out of her.

Sam suppressed a grin. "Tootsie, what's on special today?" he asked, changing the subject.

She turned around, squinting at the blackboard menu that hung on the wall behind the counter. "Well, lemme see. All we got left is... uh, the meat loaf plate, the breaded codfish sandwich, Hungarian goulash and of course, my *famous* chili." She paused, waiting for them to decide. "Sorry, but we're out of Rocky Mountain oysters," she added. "Had a whole truckload of wheat fielders came in for lunch and every last one of 'em ordered the dang things."

"Thank god," Blue murmured under her breath. "I'll have the meat loaf plate, please," she said, looking up at Tootsie. "And milk."

"You, Sam?"

"I'll take a big bowl of your mouth-waterin' chili. And give me some cornbread, too," he told her.

"Drink?" Tootsie inquired.

"Water's fine," he answered.

"Okay, you two. It'll be comin' right up," she said, springing into action, her spindly legs supporting a blossoming middle-aged backside.

"Sorry, Blue," Sam apologized, reaching over to squeeze her arm. "The woman doesn't know her own strength. She means well, though."

"That's okay," she told him. "It just startled me."

Their food arrived, steaming hot and smelling amazingly good. Blue's meat loaf plate was enough food for two and Sam's chili was bowl-rim high. The cornbread was the size of a small cake, with real kernels of corn imbedded in the yellow-colored square. And an oversized glob of melting butter threatened to slide over the side of the plate – which Sam immediately rescued with a swipe of his finger.

"Will that do ya?" Tootsie asked, lingering at their table for a compliment.

"This'll more than do me, Tootsie," Sam told her. "Looks great."

"How 'bout you, young lady?"

"I think I'm gonna need some help with all this. But it looks delicious," Blue acknowledged.

"Just give Sam what ya can't eat. Man's got the biggest appetite this side of the Oklahoma line," she remarked, as she cleared a nearby table. Three people walked in and sat at the counter. "Howdy, folks," she said, carrying dirty dishes to the kitchen. "Make yerselves to home. Be with you quicker'n a rattlesnake bite."

Blue all but finished her meat loaf plate. It had been tasty and the first hot meal she'd had in awhile. She listened as Sam told her about his college days at Harvard. She was minimally interested in what he was saying, but tried to appear attentive. *I like this guy*, she thought as he talked. *But I think I'd rather be home by myself, with my own thoughts.*

"And then, right before I graduated, I lost my mind, went on a rampage and murdered the President of the school – in cold blood," Sam told her, leaning forward to make sure she heard.

Blue was jerked back to the present. "You *what?*" she asked.

"Just wanted to see if you were listening," he said.

"Oh, I'm sorry," she apologized. "I guess my mind was wandering. You know, Sam; I'm startin' to crash. Would you mind if we left?"

"Hey Tootsie, how about a black coffee to go?" Sam yelled. "Don't worry about it, Blueflower. Let's head out," he said, standing up and reaching in his jean pocket to pay the bill. "Dinner's on me."

"Thanks," Blue said appreciatively, "but I'd like to pay for my own meal."

"Knock yourself out," he said, sounding miffed. Blue paid for her meal and left a generous tip.

"Okay, you kids stay out of trouble now," Tootsie called after them. "And come back when you're hungry." Sam gave her a wave as they left.

"You're a real independent woman, Blue," Sam commented, starting up the truck. "You have a hard time lettin' a guy be a gentleman."

"Truth is, I've let myself be *too* dependent on men in my life – but they haven't been the right kind," she countered. "And I've allowed them to treat me just about however they wanted," she continued, "Because I thought I needed them... and their brand of love. So I probably wouldn't recognize *real* love if it bit me in the ass," she said sardonically.

Sam was quiet. When he finally spoke, his voice was full of compassion. "Blue, can I tell you something?"

"Sure," she replied.

"I learned a bit of wisdom from a great teacher – in India. He was talking about love. He said that there's great joy in getting acquainted with ourselves and learning to love ourselves and others. Whatever's happened to you in your life, Blue, remember that love is the most powerful force there is – and you deserve it just as much as the next person. But you gotta start with yourself."

Blue thought about what Sam was saying. They had pulled into the gas station and were sitting in the truck. "Do you love yourself?" she asked.

"Most of the time," he replied. "I think it helped to have parents who accepted me and showered me with a lot of love."

"Well, I don't love myself – yet," she admitted. "And I didn't have parents like yours. But I've decided it's gonna be the next chapter in my life – to learn how," Blue said, climbing out of the truck.

"Good woman," Sam replied, as he unlocked the office door.

Blue walked over to Saffron, who was waiting patiently for her driver. "What do you think, girl? Should the two of us just head for home?" she said, feeling better with some food in her stomach.

232

She walked into the office. Sam was counting the money in the cash drawer. "I'll just be a minute," he said, without looking up. "Gotta put this in the safe before I close up." Blue sat down in the burgundy, vinyl chair and watched him. It'd be real easy to go home with Sam so he could lick my wounds – but I don't think I will, she thought. I need to go back to Wichita now and start my life over. Maybe another time...

He glanced up at that moment, surveying her expression. "You've decided to leave, haven't you," he said.

"How'd you guess?" Blue was surprised.

"Didn't have to," he replied. "It's all over your face. You've made a decision and it looks damn good on you."

Blue laughed. "You should've been a shrink instead of a lawyer," she told him. "You read people like it's second nature."

"I *like* people, Blue. So it's easy for me to pick up on what their body language is saying. It's this way," he explained. "When you come to know yourself, well, then you know others – because we're all essentially the same. We're one."

Blue felt an unexpected surge of emotion. "Is that why you don't seem miserable and lonely in your life?" she said, tears moistening her eyes.

"You got it," he said. "It's because I have lots of good company in the world." Placing the money in the safe, he shut the metal door and checked the handle. "It's locked," he said with satisfaction. "I had a break-in here once, so I got myself a safe... one anybody would have trouble carrying out of here." He noticed Blue's perplexed look. "I said I liked people, but I'm not going to wear a sign that says 'fuck me – I'm a victim.'"

"Yeah, I'm learning that the hard way," she confessed. "I've always been naive about people, believing what they tell me and excusing their bad behavior. No more, though. Blue's becoming a different woman," she said decisively. "I'll introduce her to you someday."

"I think the one I met is just fine," Sam quipped. "She has great legs and an indomitable spirit." He got serious. "Are you sure you can make it home okay?" he asked, extending his hand and pulling her out of the chair. It seemed natural to melt into an embrace. The two of them stood quietly, holding each other.

"I know I can," she murmured against his flannel shirt. "I've got some healing to do and a new life to create – and I'm anxious to start." Sam kissed her gently on top of her head and they broke apart.

"I'll always remember you, Blueflower," he said tenderly. "You must know by now that I'd like to start something with you, but you're not ready."

"You're right, Sam," she agreed. "I'm not. But maybe someday."

"Will you call me sometime, just to let me know how you're doing?" he asked, walking her out to the car.

"I won't promise, but I *will* keep your number," Blue said sweetly. She got behind the wheel. It felt good to know she and Saffron would be on the road once more. "Thanks again for tuning up my car," she told him. She started the engine and soon, Saffron was idling contentedly.

"So long, Sam," she said, flashing one of her finest million-dollar smiles. He gave her a wave. The yellow Volkswagen took off, seeming to know its destination and impatient to get there. Sam watched until the car became a tiny yellow dot on the road.

They say the color blue is defined as "darkness made visible... the color of rarefied atmosphere." That's the opportunity life gives us – to make our darkness visible, allowing us to be re-born and emerge... as the cerulean blue of ethereal air.

It was a fine moment, a new day. And it came, not surprisingly – out of the blue.

* * *